STAR TREK

THE NEXT GENERATION®

HIVE

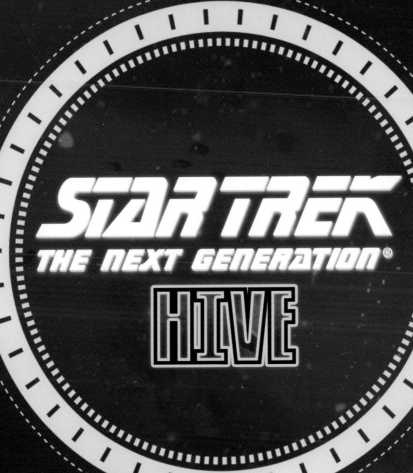

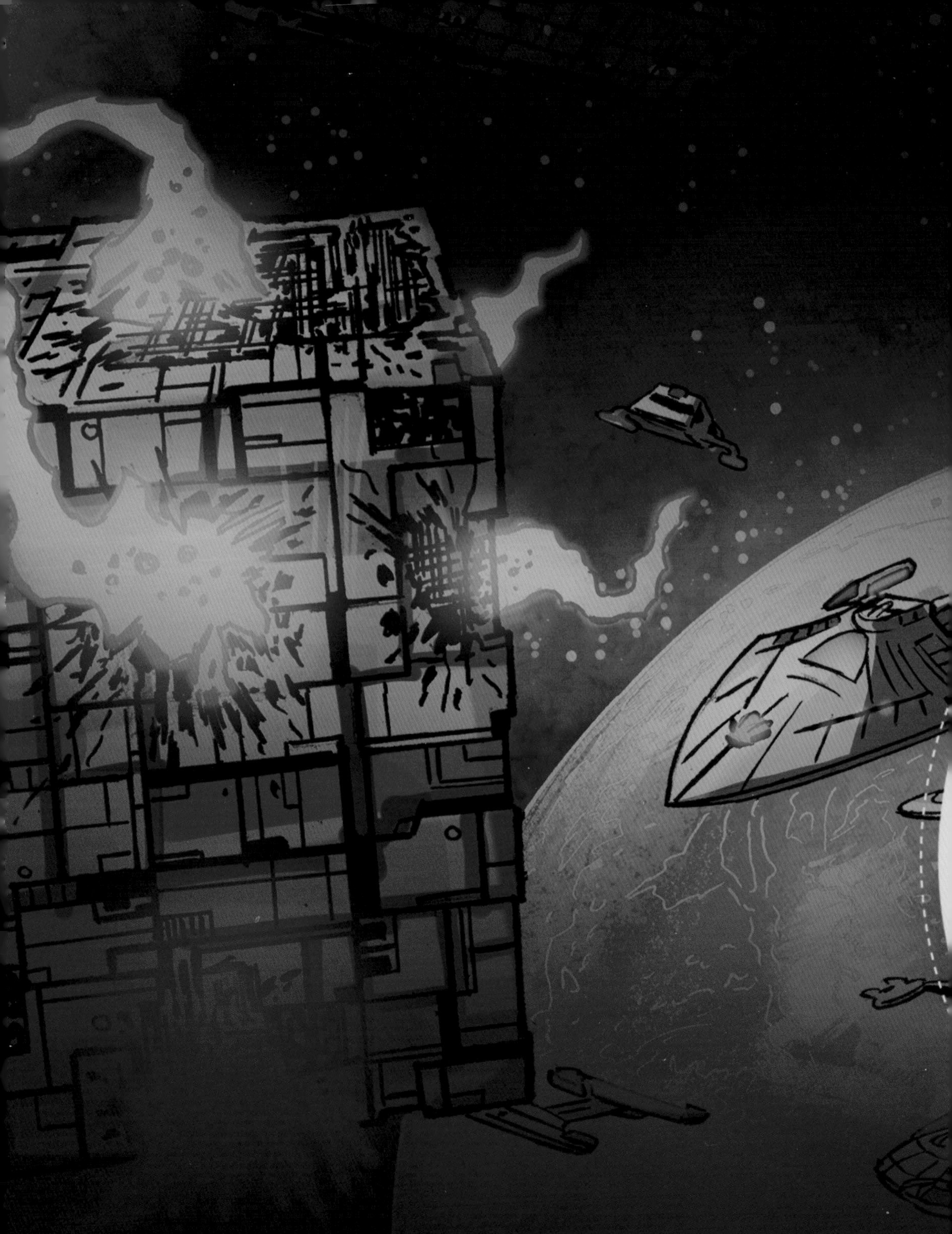

Grateful acknowledgement to Mark Rademaker for Merian-Class Starship design.
Special thanks to Risa Kessler and John Van Citters of CBS Consumer Products for their invaluable assistance.

IDW founded by Ted Adams, Alex Garner, Kris Oprisko, and Robbie Robbins

ISBN: 978-1-61377-566-0

16 15 14 13 2 3 4 5

IDW®

Ted Adams, CEO & Publisher
Greg Goldstein, President & COO
Robbie Robbins, EVP/Sr. Graphic Artist
Chris Ryall, Chief Creative Officer/Editor-in-Chief
Matthew Ruzicka, CPA, Chief Financial Officer
Alan Payne, VP of Sales
Dirk Wood, VP of Marketing
Lorelei Bunjes, VP of Digital Services

Become our fan on Facebook **facebook.com/idwpublishing**
Follow us on Twitter **@idwpublishing**
Check us out on YouTube **youtube.com/idwpublishing**
www.IDWPUBLISHING.com

Originally published as STAR TREK TNG: HIVE Issues #1–4.

BRANNON BRAGA
STORY

TERRY MATALAS
TRAVIS FICKETT
SCRIPT

JOE CORRONEY
ART

MATT FILLBACH
SHAWN FILLBACH
INK ASSIST

HI-FI
COLORS

SHAWN LEE
LETTERING

SCOTT DUNBIER
ORIGINAL SERIES EDITS

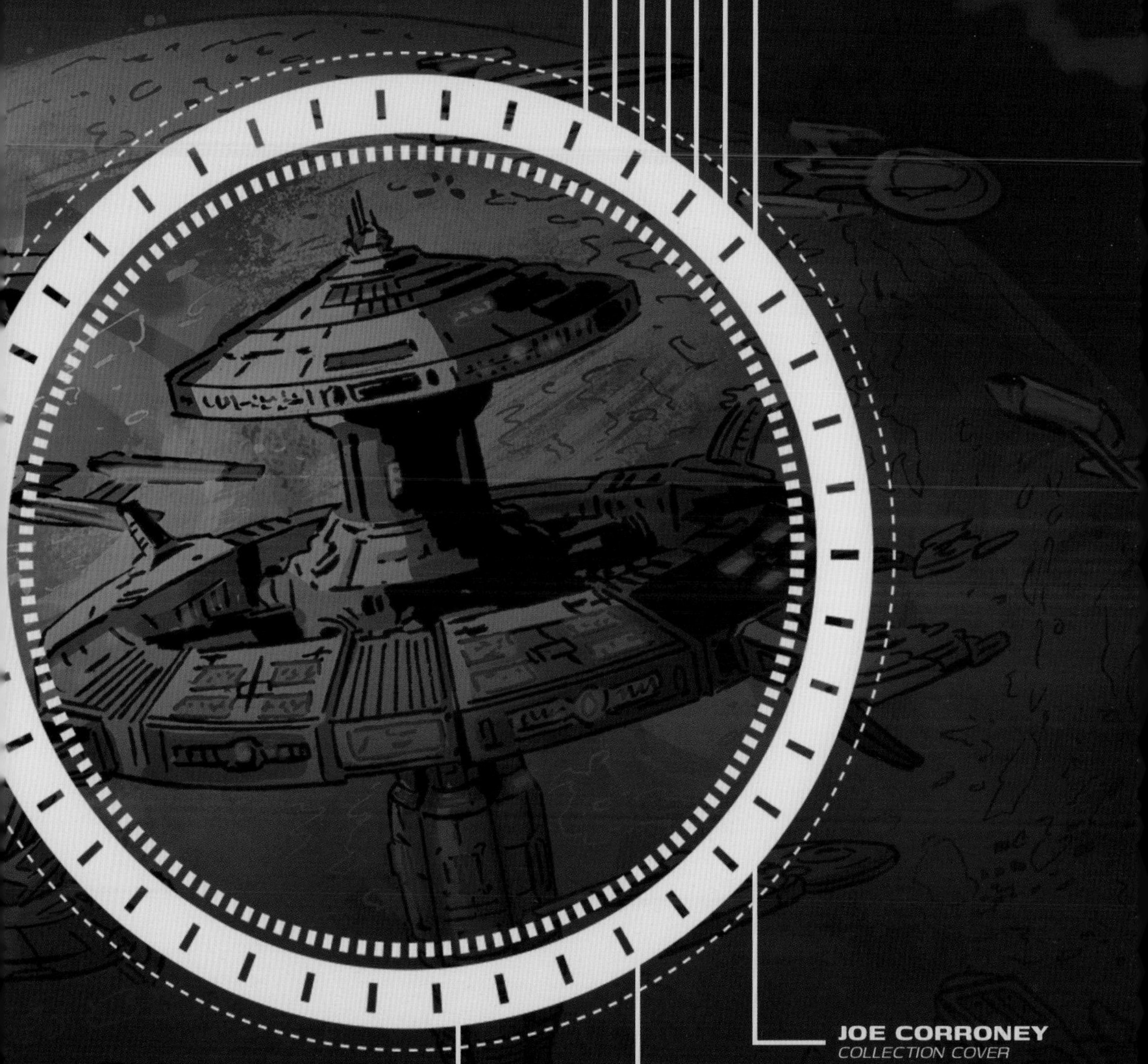

JOE CORRONEY
COLLECTION COVER

JUSTIN EISINGER
ALONZO SIMON
COLLECTION EDITS

SHAWN LEE
COLLECTION DESIGN

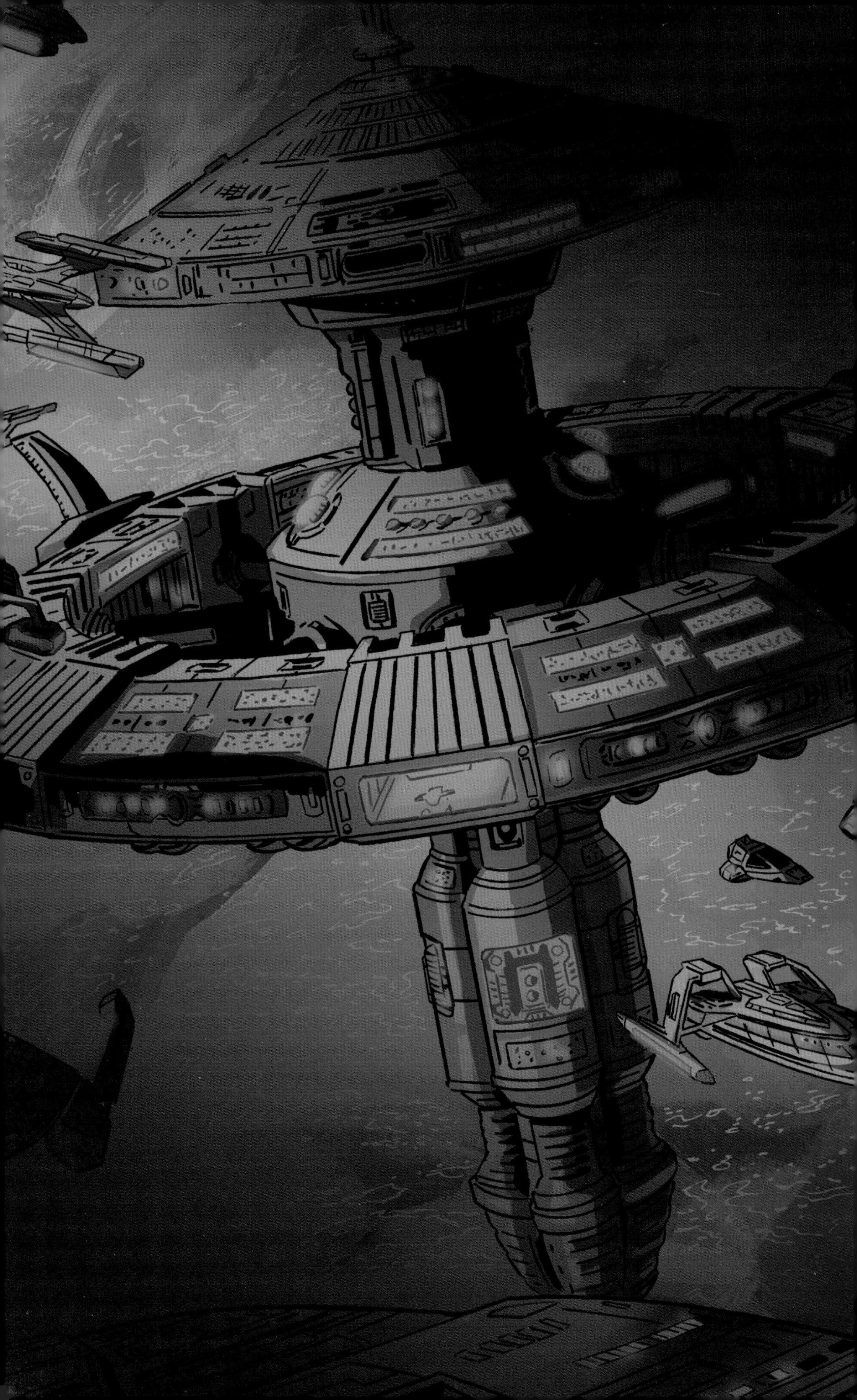

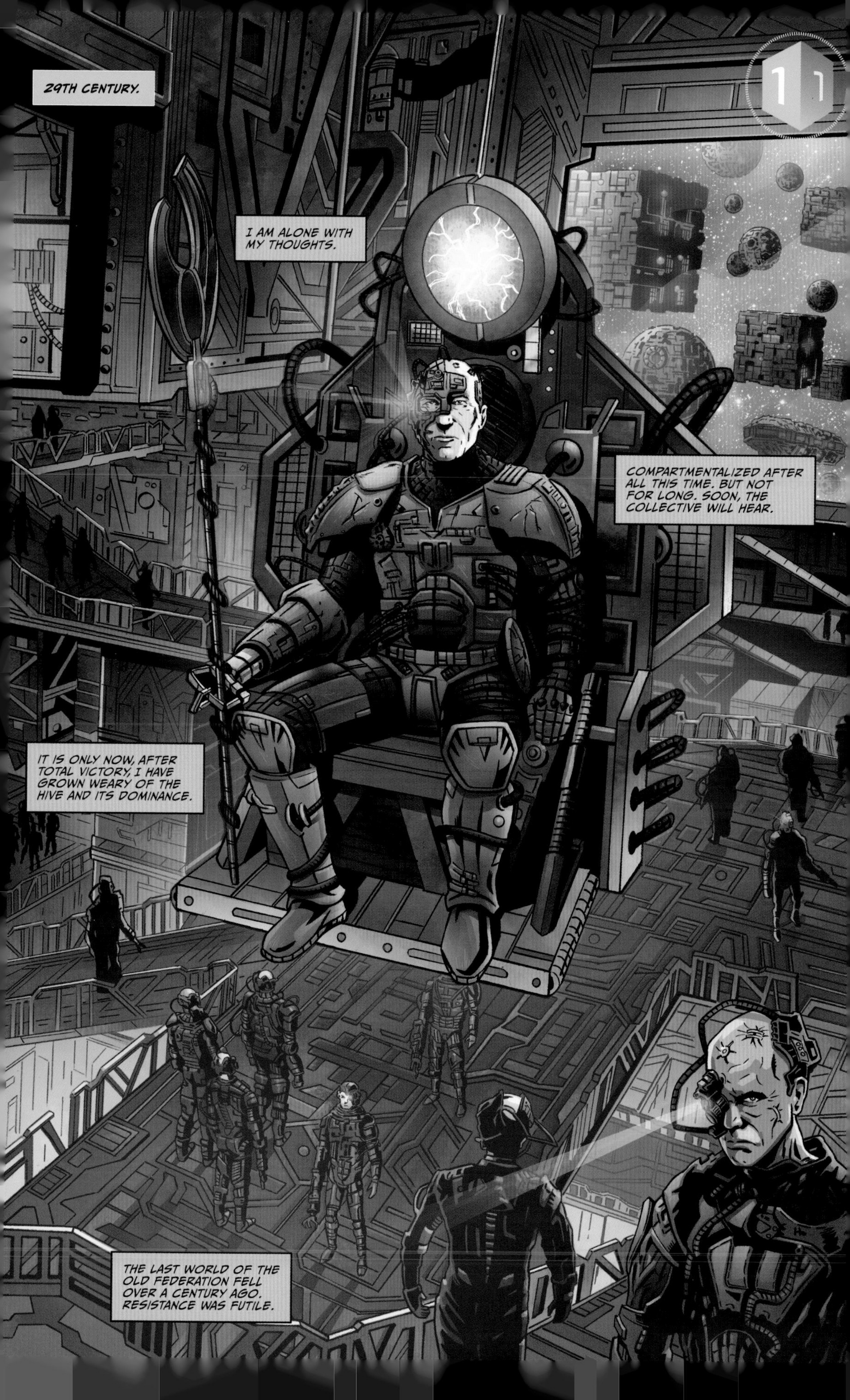
29TH CENTURY.
I AM ALONE WITH MY THOUGHTS.
COMPARTMENTALIZED AFTER ALL THIS TIME. BUT NOT FOR LONG. SOON, THE COLLECTIVE WILL HEAR.
IT IS ONLY NOW, AFTER TOTAL VICTORY, I HAVE GROWN WEARY OF THE HIVE AND ITS DOMINANCE.
THE LAST WORLD OF THE OLD FEDERATION FELL OVER A CENTURY AGO. RESISTANCE WAS FUTILE.

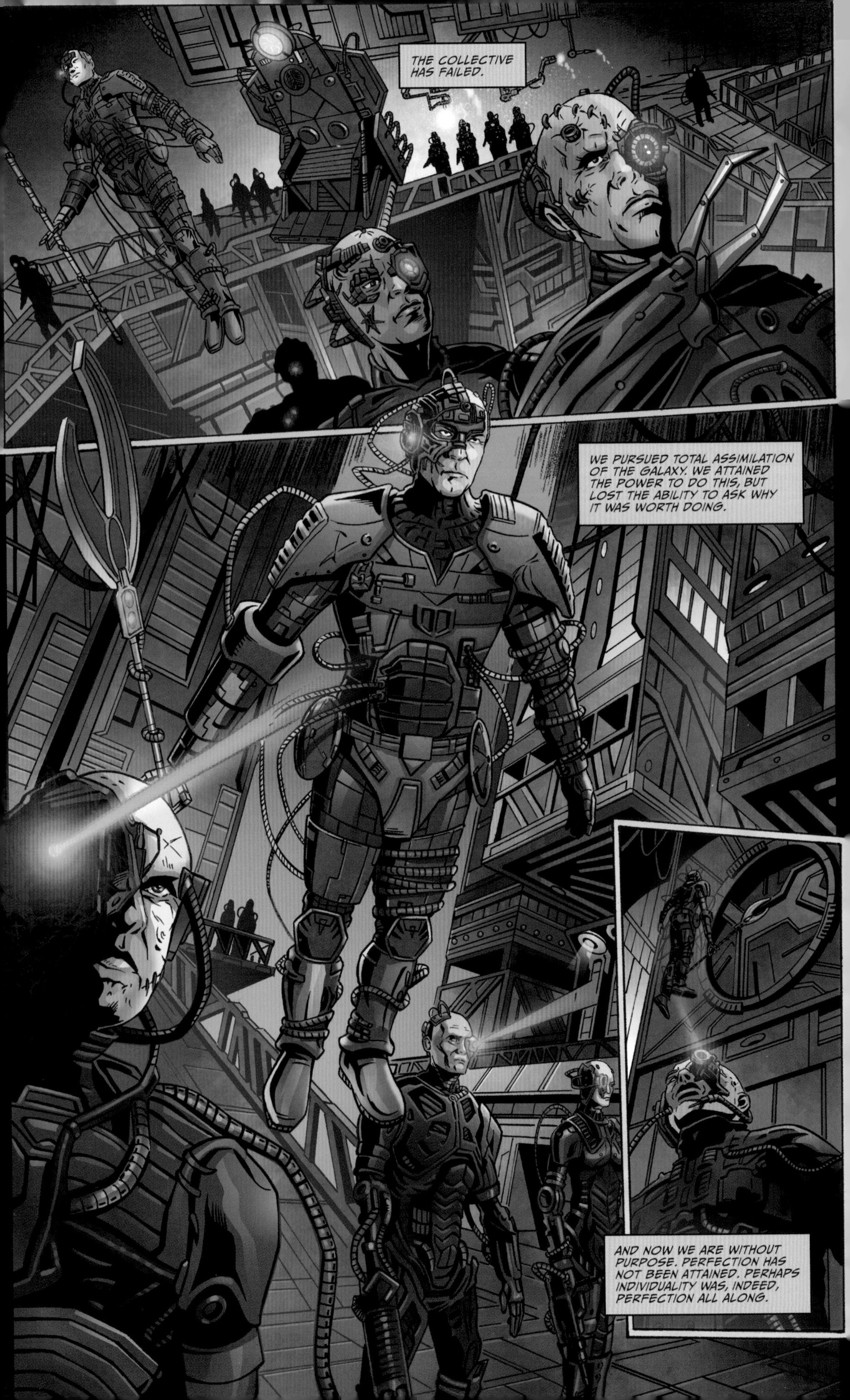
THE COLLECTIVE HAS FAILED.
WE PURSUED TOTAL ASSIMILATION OF THE GALAXY. WE ATTAINED THE POWER TO DO THIS, BUT LOST THE ABILITY TO ASK WHY IT WAS WORTH DOING.
AND NOW WE ARE WITHOUT PURPOSE. PERFECTION HAS NOT BEEN ATTAINED. PERHAPS INDIVIDUALITY WAS, INDEED, PERFECTION ALL ALONG.

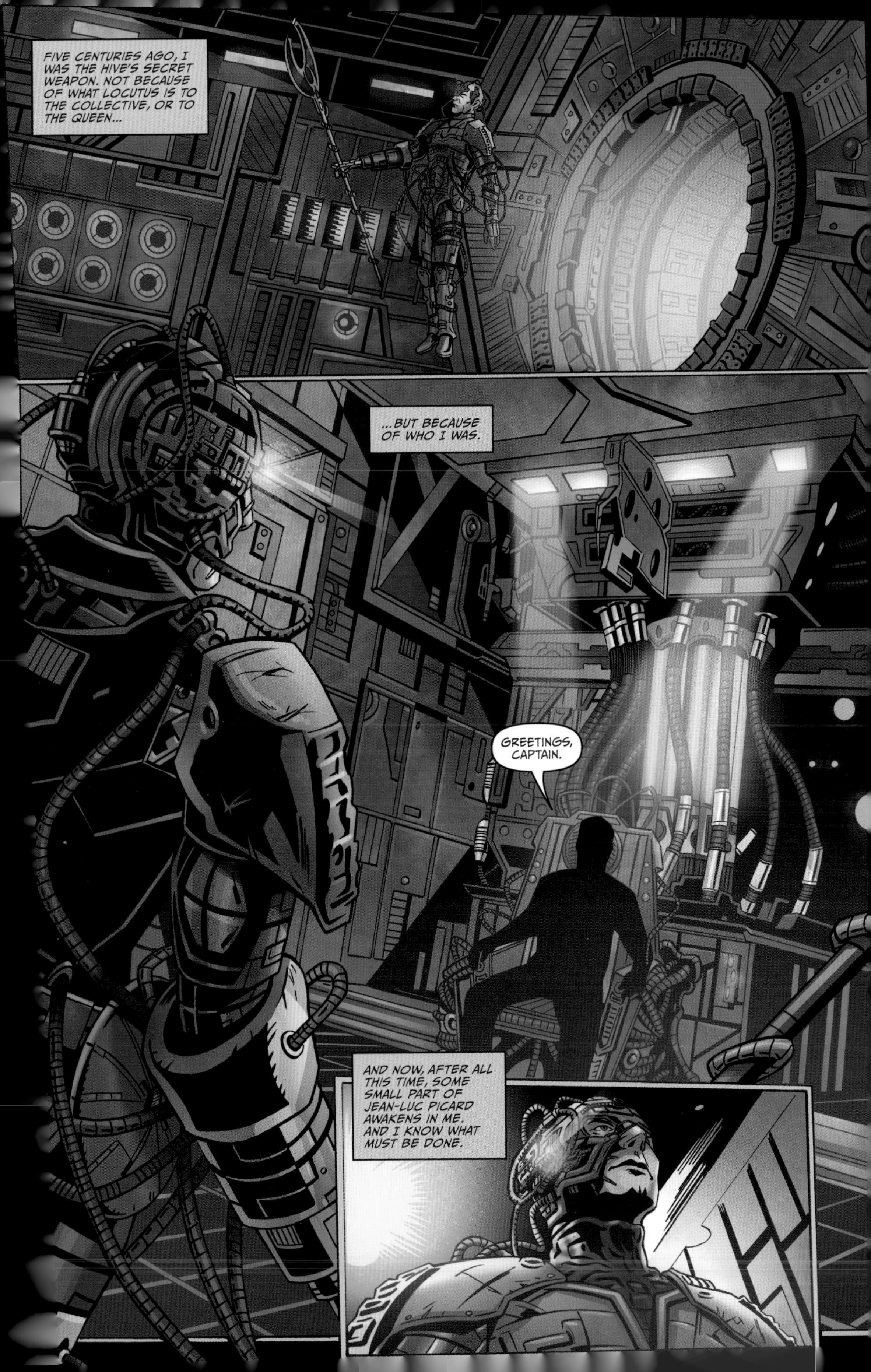
FIVE CENTURIES AGO, I WAS THE HIVE'S SECRET WEAPON. NOT BECAUSE OF WHAT LOCUTUS IS TO THE COLLECTIVE, OR TO THE QUEEN...
...BUT BECAUSE OF WHO I WAS.
GREETINGS, CAPTAIN.
AND NOW, AFTER ALL THIS TIME, SOME SMALL PART OF JEAN-LUC PICARD AWAKENS IN ME. AND I KNOW WHAT MUST BE DONE.

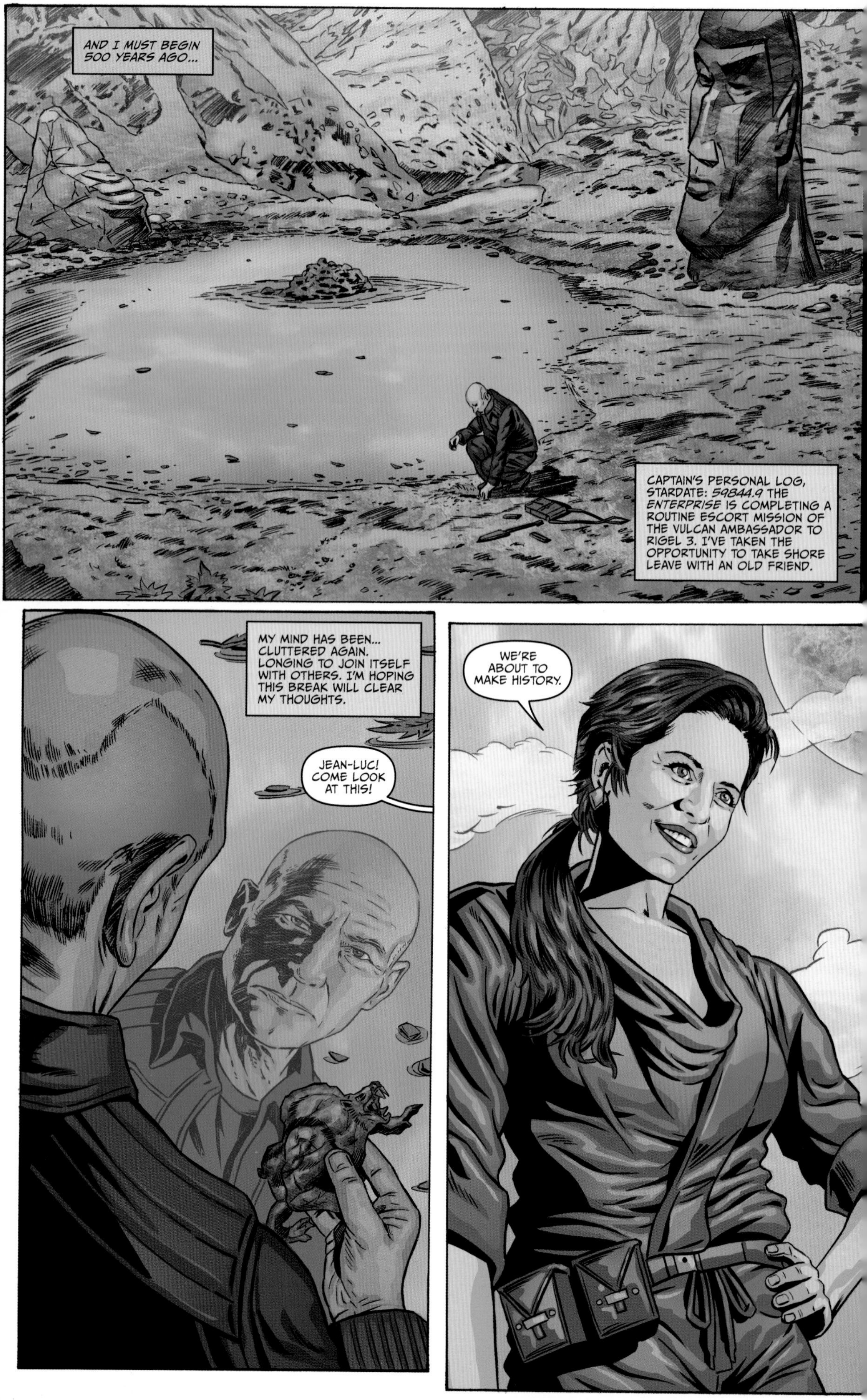
AND I MUST BEGIN 500 YEARS AGO...
CAPTAIN'S PERSONAL LOG, STARDATE: 59844.9 THE ENTERPRISE IS COMPLETING A ROUTINE ESCORT MISSION OF THE VULCAN AMBASSADOR TO RIGEL 3. I'VE TAKEN THE OPPORTUNITY TO TAKE SHORE LEAVE WITH AN OLD FRIEND.
MY MIND HAS BEEN... CLUTTERED AGAIN. LONGING TO JOIN ITSELF WITH OTHERS. I'M HOPING THIS BREAK WILL CLEAR MY THOUGHTS.
JEAN-LUC! COME LOOK AT THIS!
WE'RE ABOUT TO MAKE HISTORY.

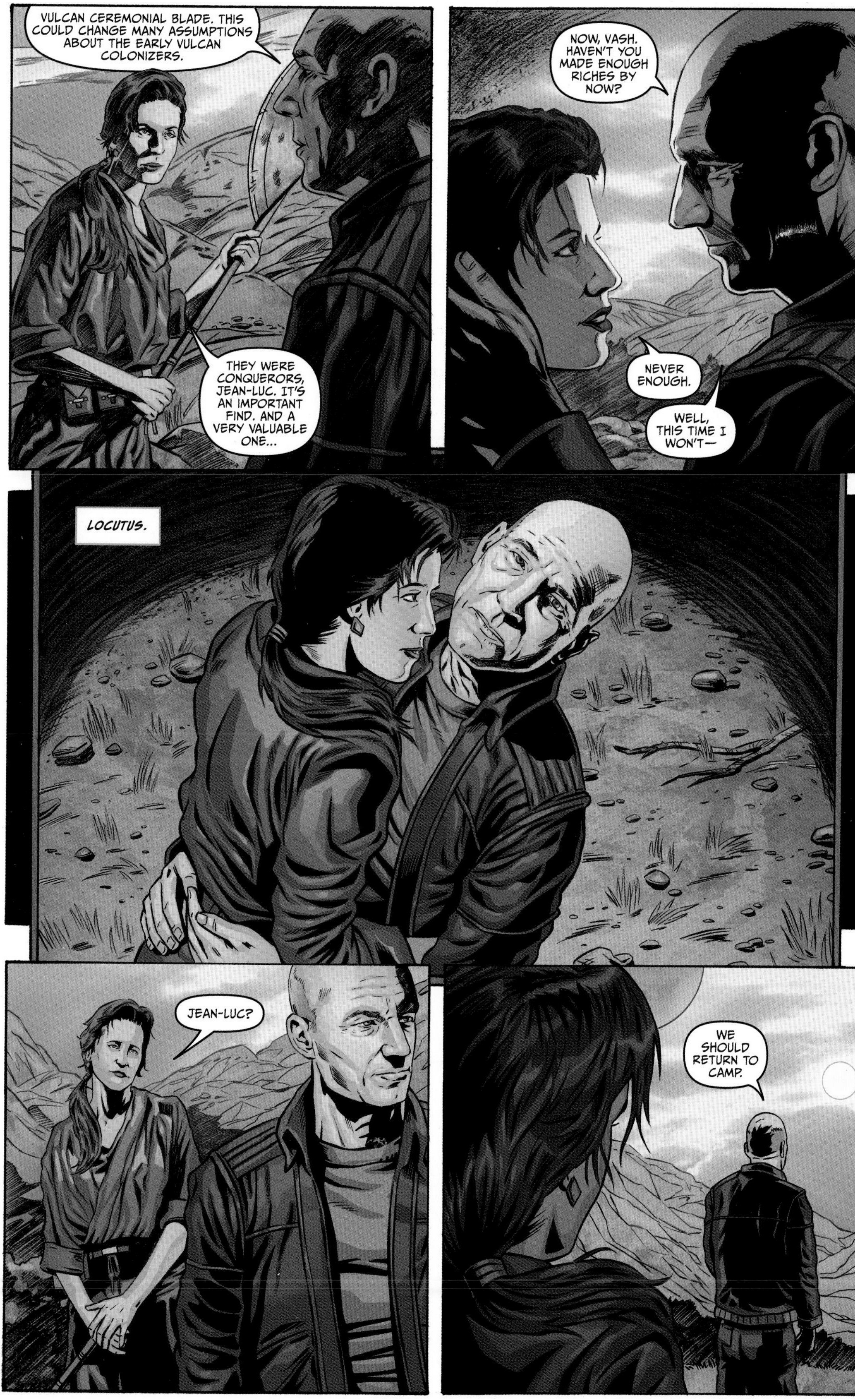

VULCAN CEREMONIAL BLADE. THIS COULD CHANGE MANY ASSUMPTIONS ABOUT THE EARLY VULCAN COLONIZERS.
THEY WERE CONQUERORS, JEAN-LUC. IT'S AN IMPORTANT FIND. AND A VERY VALUABLE ONE...
NOW, VASH. HAVEN'T YOU MADE ENOUGH RICHES BY NOW?
NEVER ENOUGH.
WELL, THIS TIME I WON'T—
LOCUTUS.
JEAN-LUC?
WE SHOULD RETURN TO CAMP.

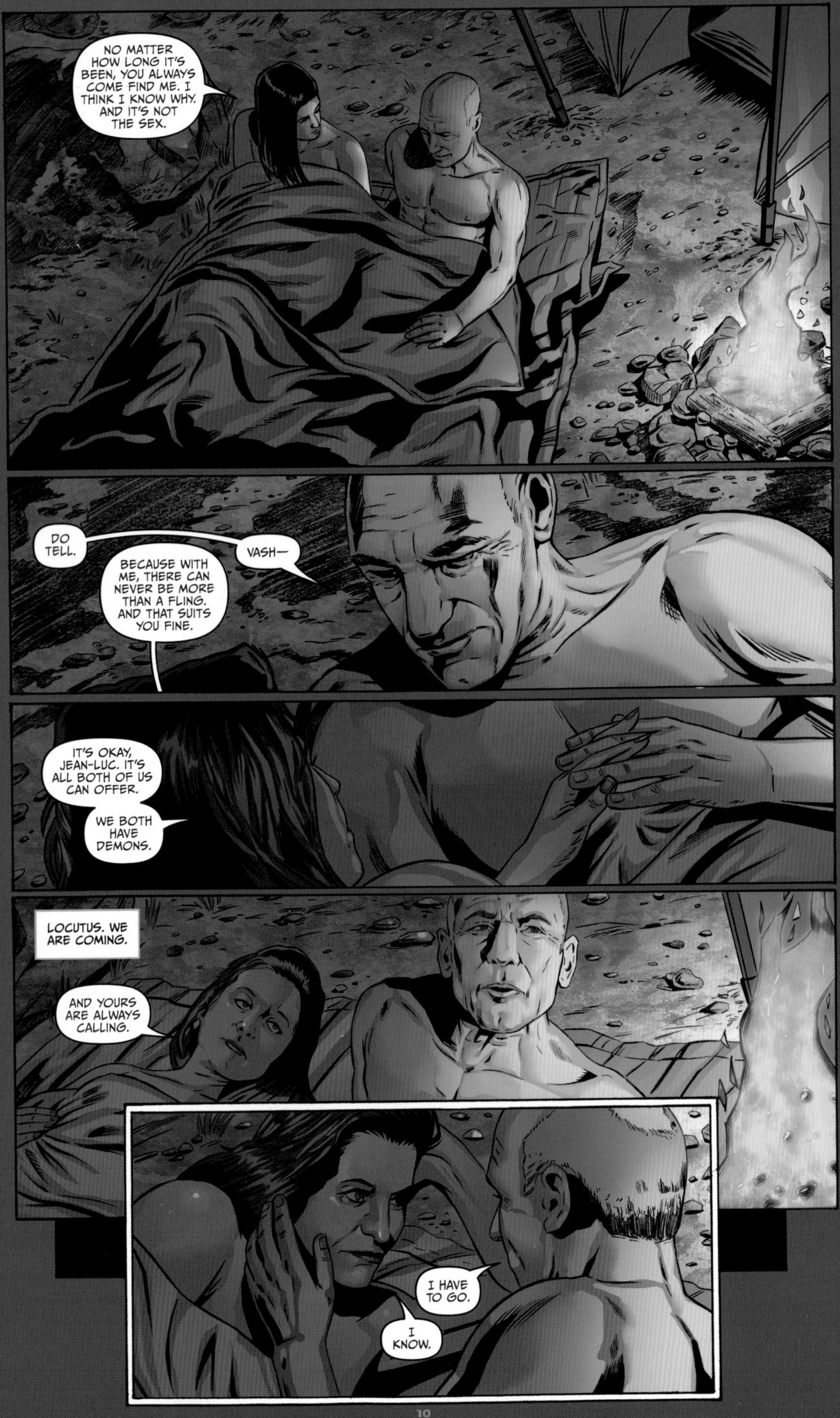
NO MATTER HOW LONG IT'S BEEN, YOU ALWAYS COME FIND ME. I THINK I KNOW WHY. AND IT'S NOT THE SEX.
DO TELL.
VASH—
BECAUSE WITH ME, THERE CAN NEVER BE MORE THAN A FLING. AND THAT SUITS YOU FINE.
IT'S OKAY, JEAN-LUC. IT'S ALL BOTH OF US CAN OFFER.
WE BOTH HAVE DEMONS.
LOCUTUS. WE ARE COMING.
AND YOURS ARE ALWAYS CALLING.
I HAVE TO GO.
I KNOW.

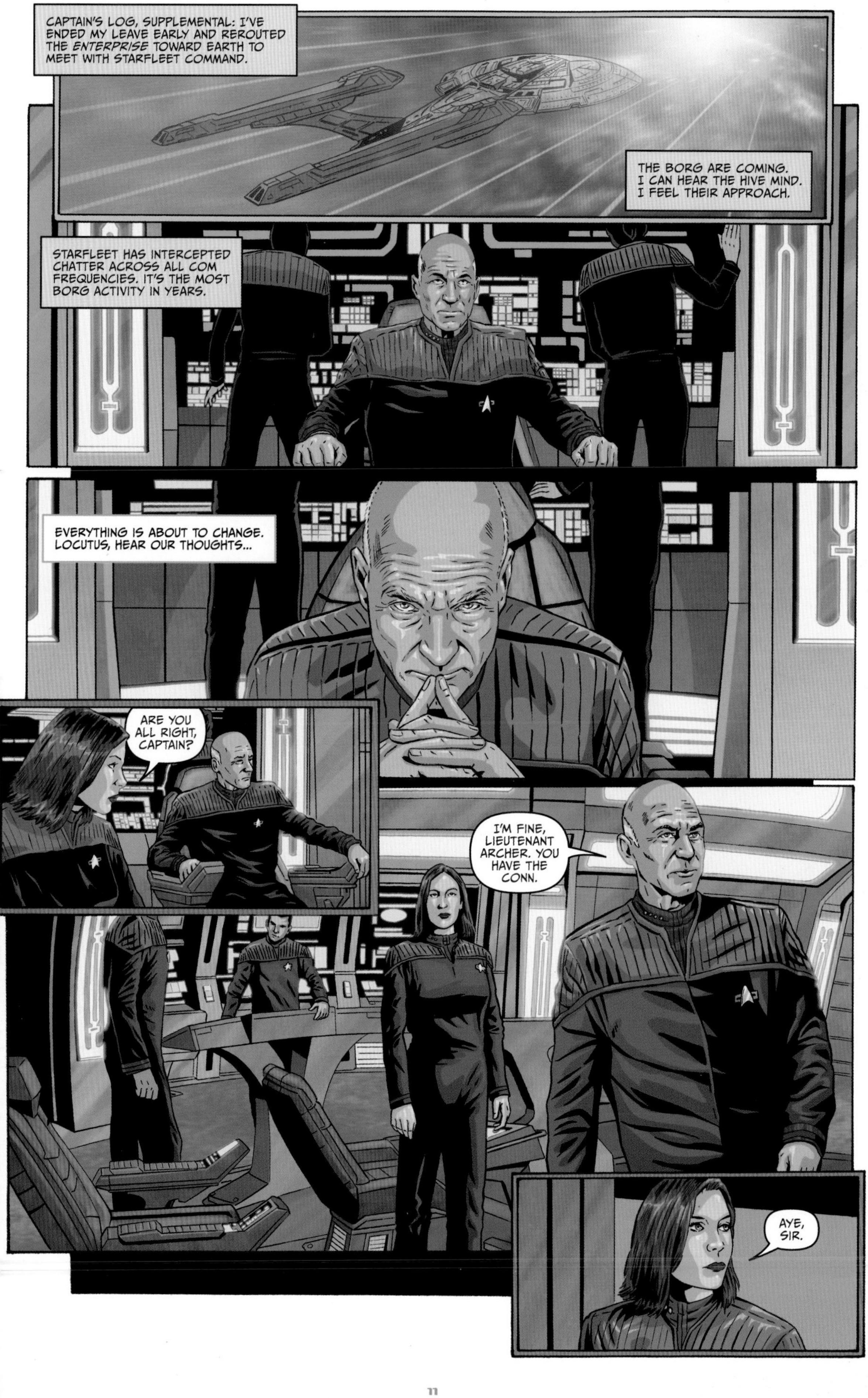
CAPTAIN'S LOG, SUPPLEMENTAL: I'VE ENDED MY LEAVE EARLY AND REROUTED THE *ENTERPRISE* TOWARD EARTH TO MEET WITH STARFLEET COMMAND.
THE BORG ARE COMING. I CAN HEAR THE HIVE MIND. I FEEL THEIR APPROACH.
STARFLEET HAS INTERCEPTED CHATTER ACROSS ALL COM FREQUENCIES. IT'S THE MOST BORG ACTIVITY IN YEARS.
EVERYTHING IS ABOUT TO CHANGE. LOCUTUS, HEAR OUR THOUGHTS...
ARE YOU ALL RIGHT, CAPTAIN?
I'M FINE, LIEUTENANT ARCHER. YOU HAVE THE CONN.
AYE, SIR.

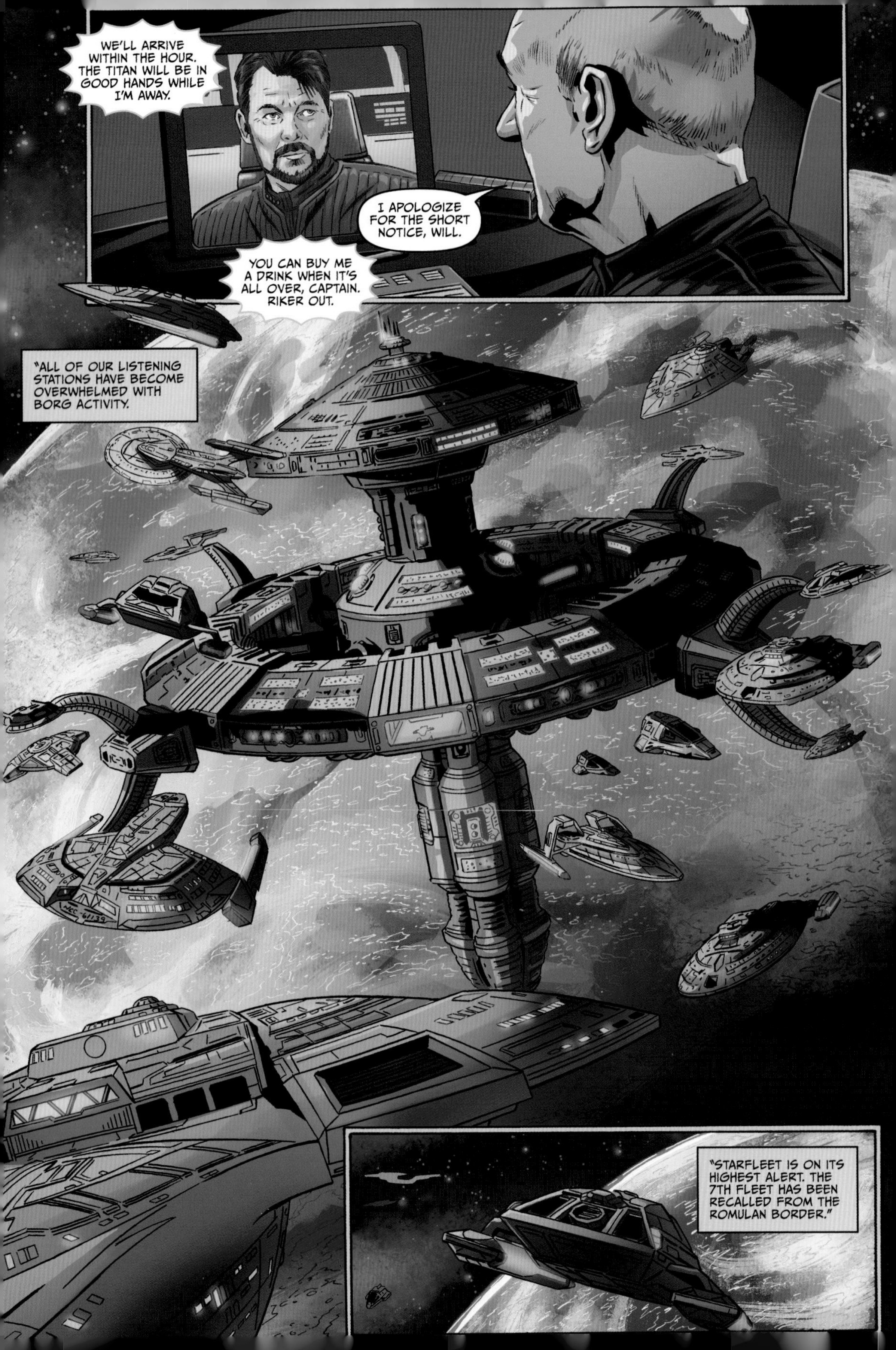
WE'LL ARRIVE WITHIN THE HOUR. THE TITAN WILL BE IN GOOD HANDS WHILE I'M AWAY.
I APOLOGIZE FOR THE SHORT NOTICE, WILL.
YOU CAN BUY ME A DRINK WHEN IT'S ALL OVER, CAPTAIN. RIKER OUT.
"ALL OF OUR LISTENING STATIONS HAVE BECOME OVERWHELMED WITH BORG ACTIVITY.
"STARFLEET IS ON ITS HIGHEST ALERT. THE 7TH FLEET HAS BEEN RECALLED FROM THE ROMULAN BORDER."

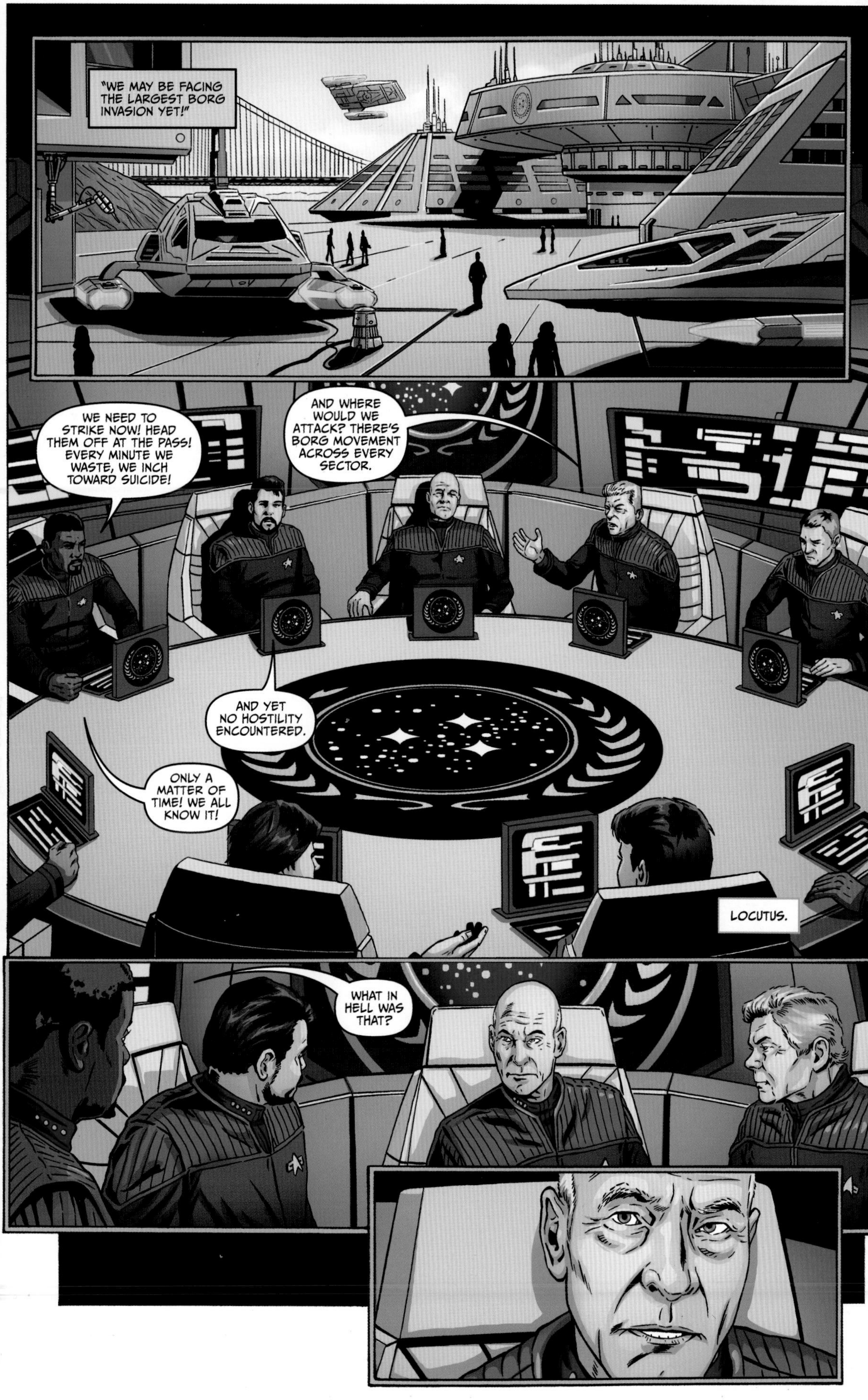
"WE MAY BE FACING THE LARGEST BORG INVASION YET!"
WE NEED TO STRIKE NOW! HEAD THEM OFF AT THE PASS! EVERY MINUTE WE WASTE, WE INCH TOWARD SUICIDE!
AND WHERE WOULD WE ATTACK? THERE'S BORG MOVEMENT ACROSS EVERY SECTOR.
AND YET NO HOSTILITY ENCOUNTERED.
ONLY A MATTER OF TIME! WE ALL KNOW IT!
LOCUTUS.
WHAT IN HELL WAS THAT?

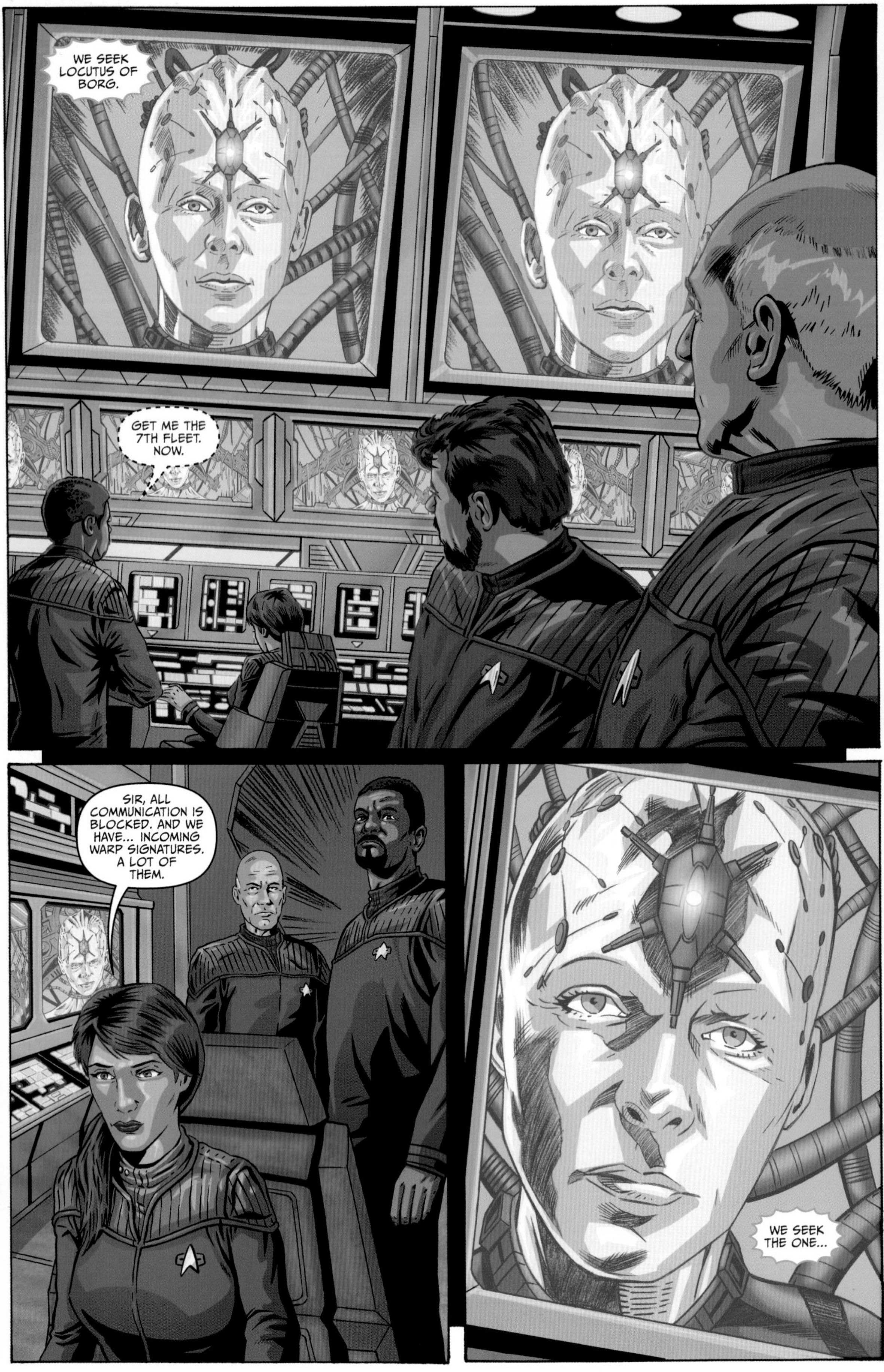
WE SEEK LOCUTUS OF BORG.
GET ME THE 7TH FLEET. NOW.
SIR, ALL COMMUNICATION IS BLOCKED. AND WE HAVE... INCOMING WARP SIGNATURES. A LOT OF THEM.
WE SEEK THE ONE...

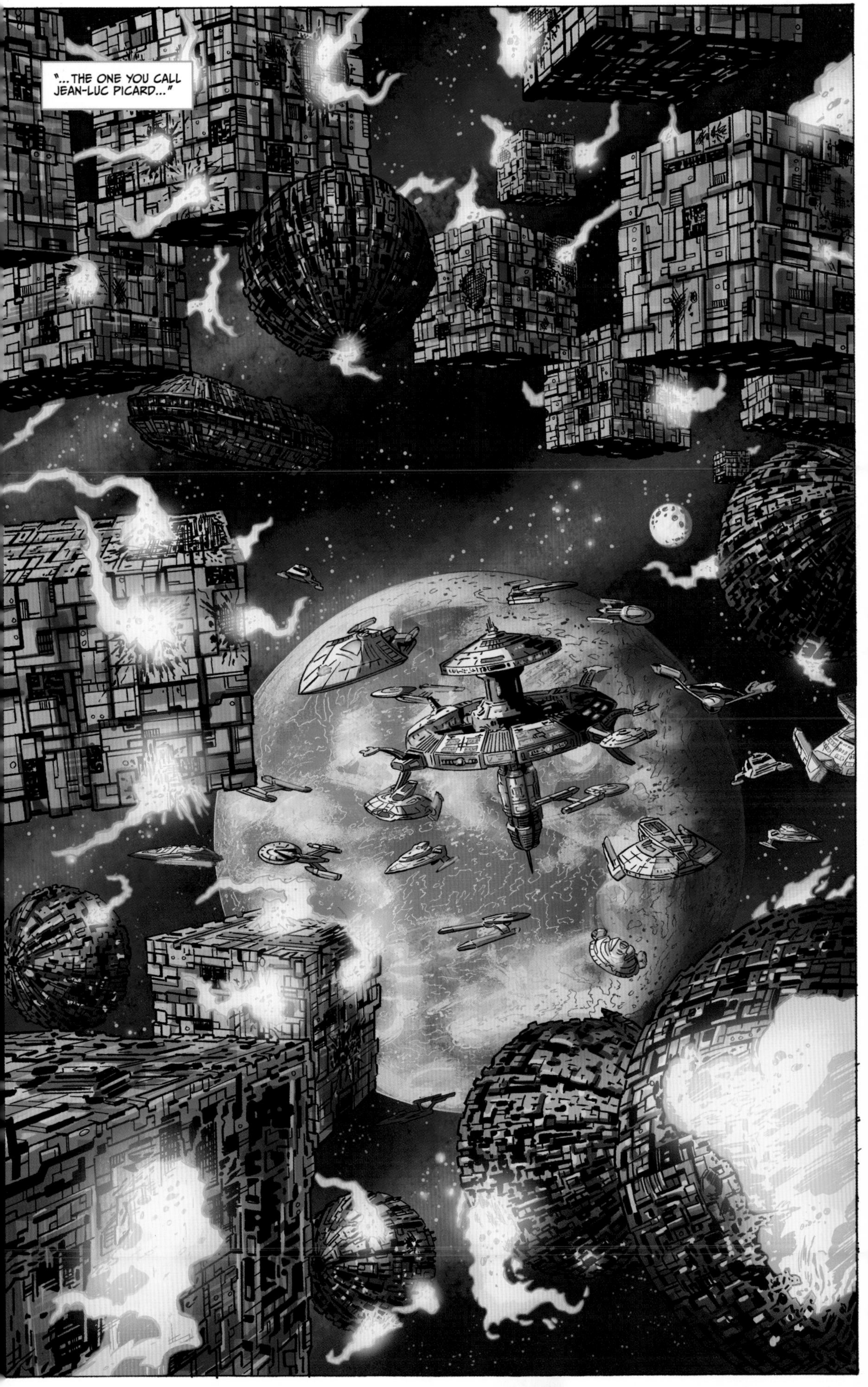
"...THE ONE YOU CALL JEAN-LUC PICARD..."

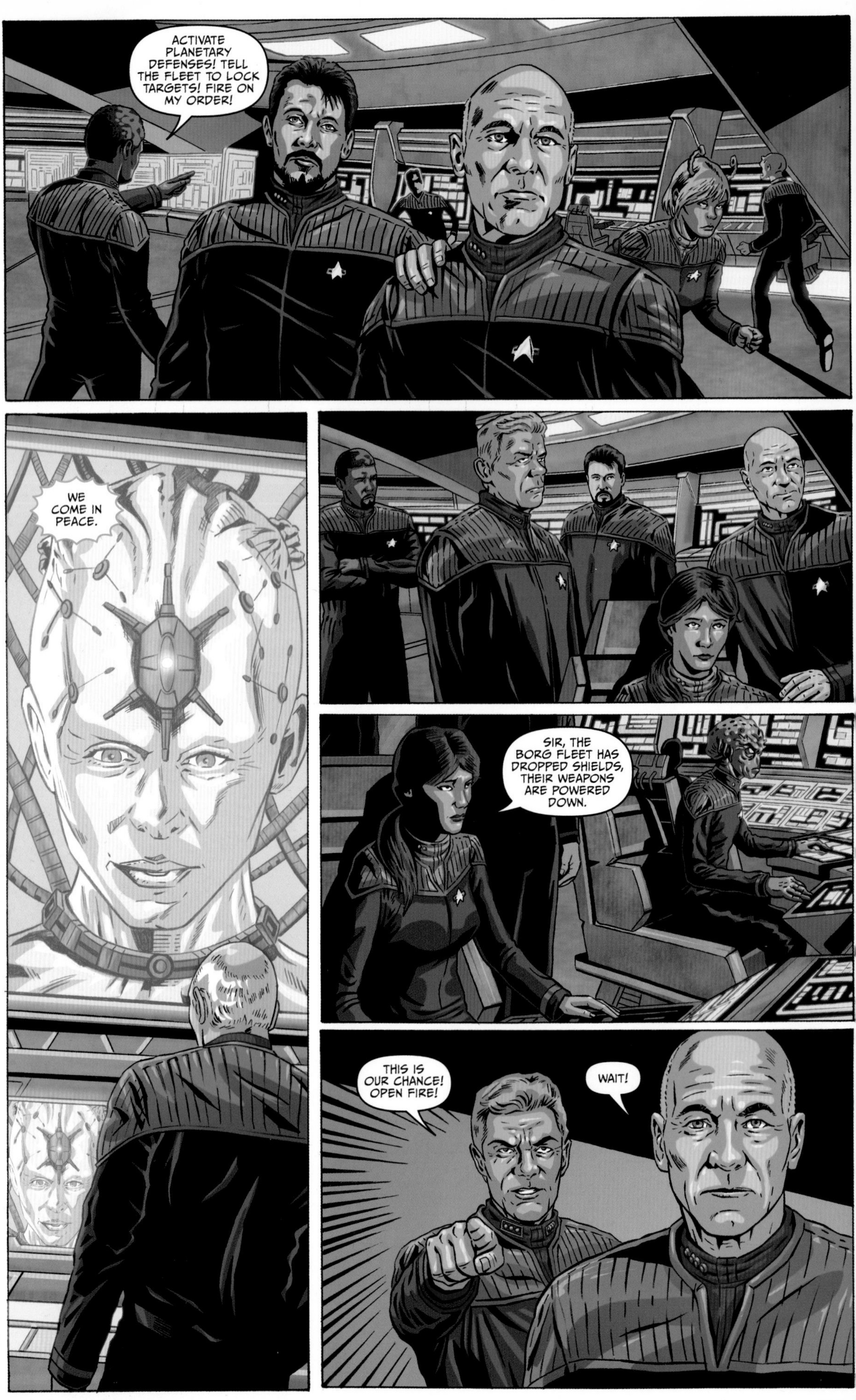
ACTIVATE PLANETARY DEFENSES! TELL THE FLEET TO LOCK TARGETS! FIRE ON MY ORDER!
WE COME IN PEACE.
SIR, THE BORG FLEET HAS DROPPED SHIELDS, THEIR WEAPONS ARE POWERED DOWN.
THIS IS OUR CHANCE! OPEN FIRE!
WAIT!

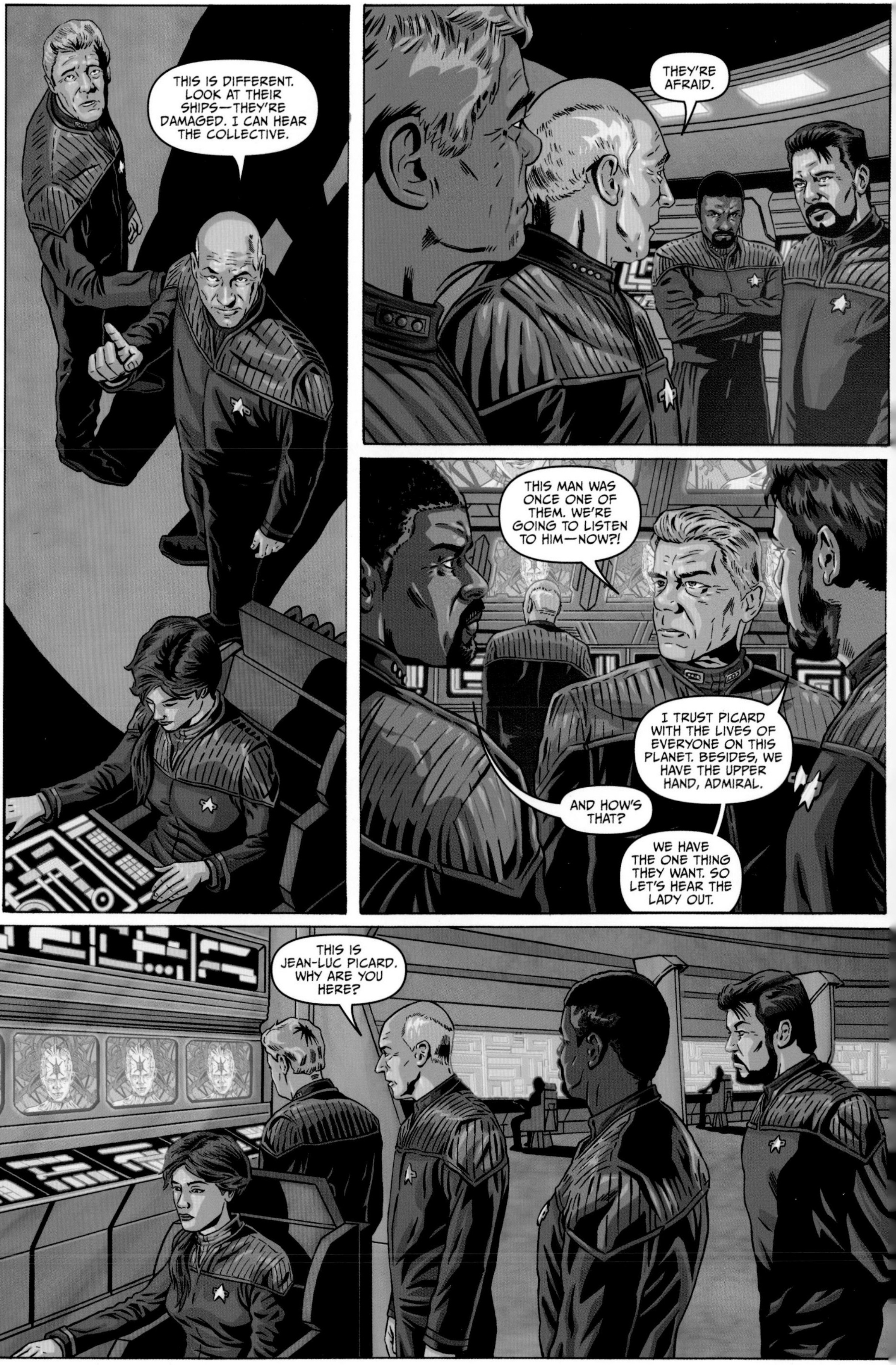
THIS IS DIFFERENT. LOOK AT THEIR SHIPS—THEY'RE DAMAGED. I CAN HEAR THE COLLECTIVE.
THEY'RE AFRAID.
THIS MAN WAS ONCE ONE OF THEM. WE'RE GOING TO LISTEN TO HIM—NOW?!
I TRUST PICARD WITH THE LIVES OF EVERYONE ON THIS PLANET. BESIDES, WE HAVE THE UPPER HAND, ADMIRAL.
AND HOW'S THAT?
WE HAVE THE ONE THING THEY WANT. SO LET'S HEAR THE LADY OUT.
THIS IS JEAN-LUC PICARD. WHY ARE YOU HERE?

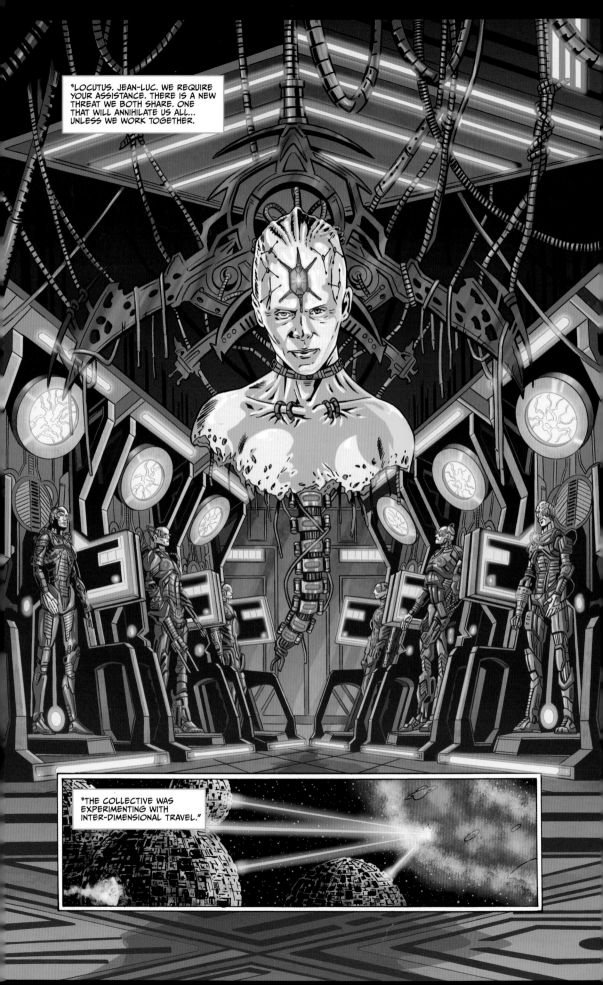

"LOCUTUS. JEAN-LUC. WE REQUIRE YOUR ASSISTANCE. THERE IS A NEW THREAT WE BOTH SHARE. ONE THAT WILL ANNIHILATE US ALL... UNLESS WE WORK TOGETHER.

"THE COLLECTIVE WAS EXPERIMENTING WITH INTER-DIMENSIONAL TRAVEL."

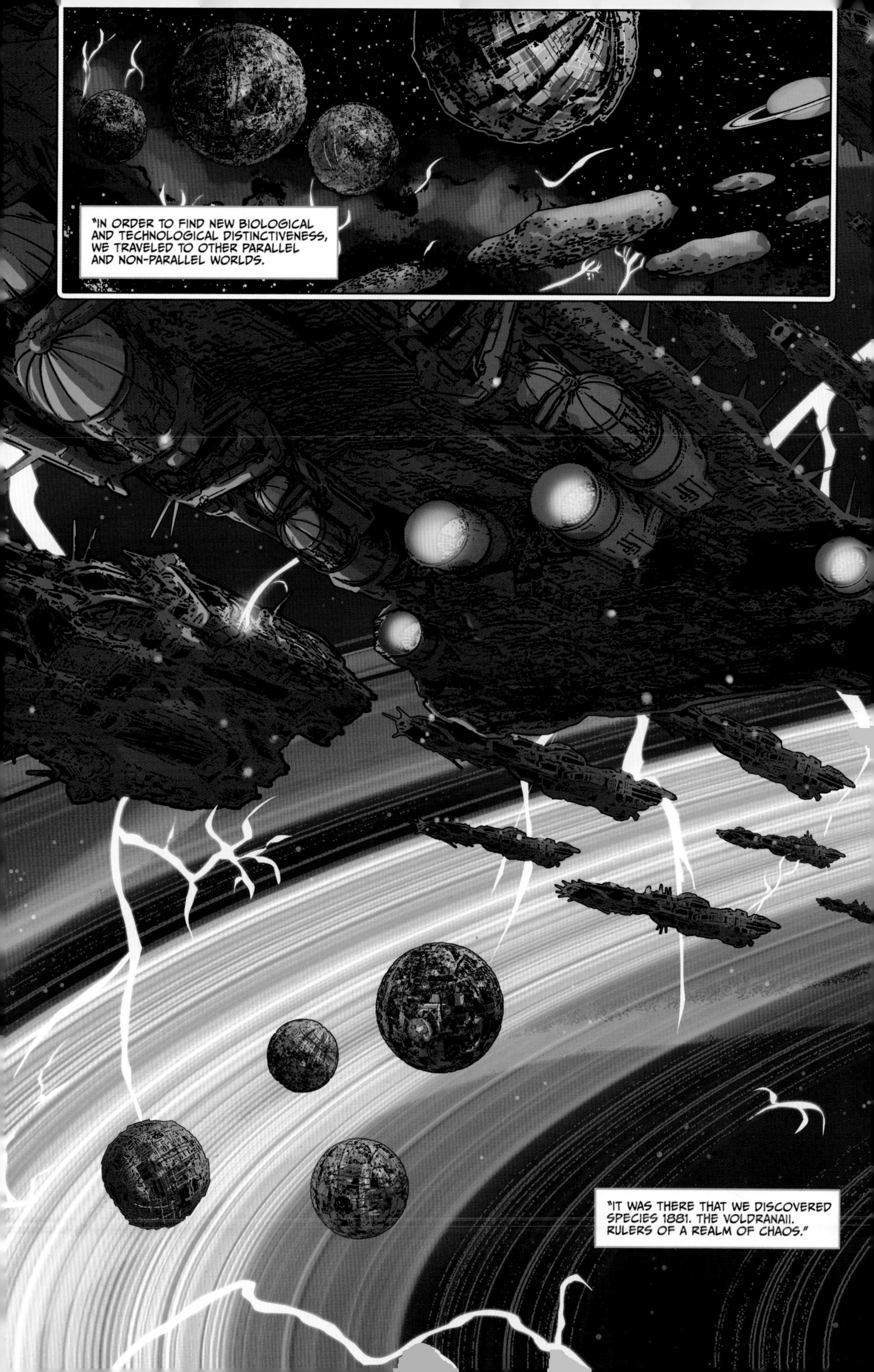
"IN ORDER TO FIND NEW BIOLOGICAL AND TECHNOLOGICAL DISTINCTIVENESS, WE TRAVELED TO OTHER PARALLEL AND NON-PARALLEL WORLDS.
"IT WAS THERE THAT WE DISCOVERED SPECIES 1881. THE VOLDRANAII. RULERS OF A REALM OF CHAOS."

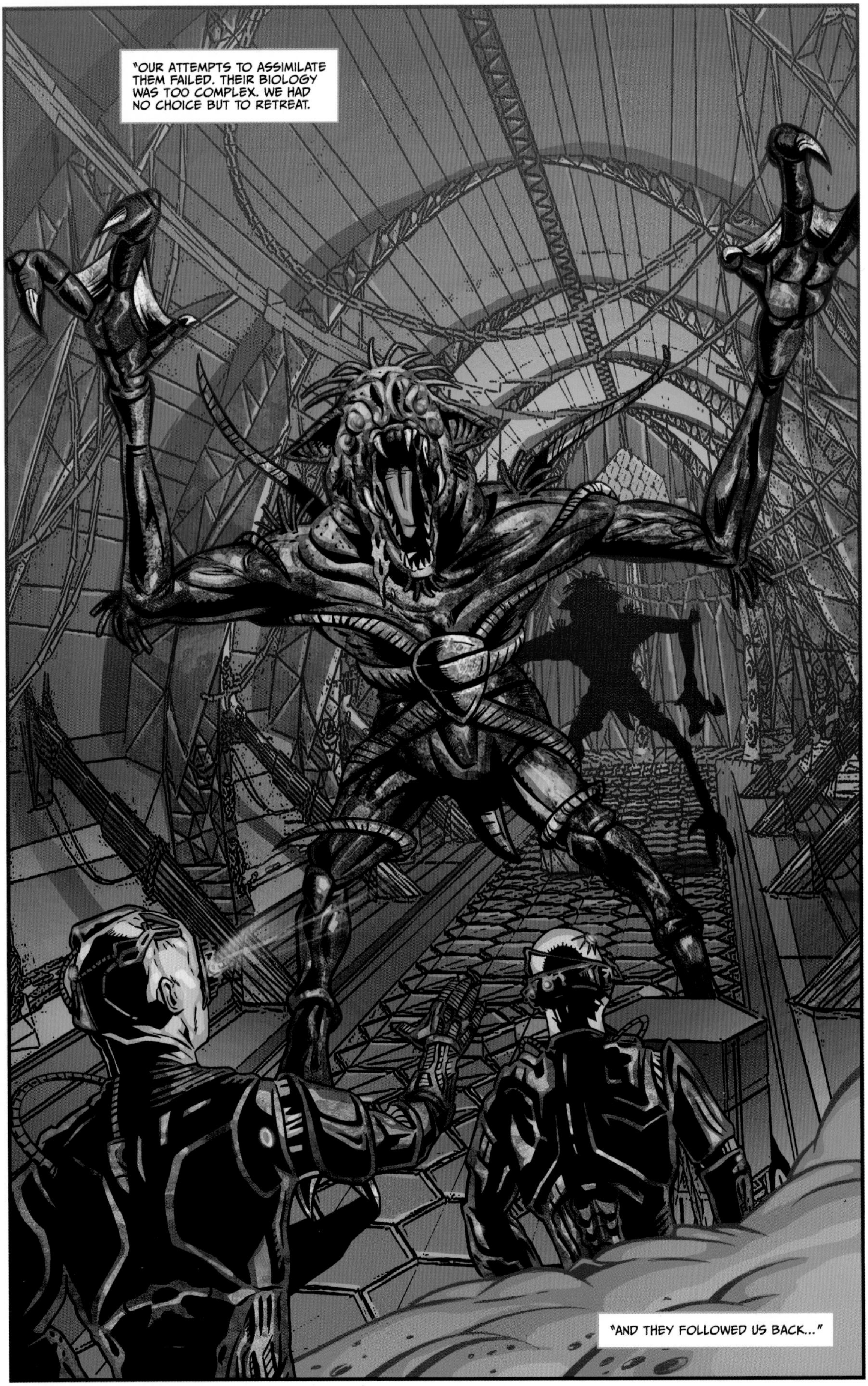
"OUR ATTEMPTS TO ASSIMILATE THEM FAILED. THEIR BIOLOGY WAS TOO COMPLEX. WE HAD NO CHOICE BUT TO RETREAT.
"AND THEY FOLLOWED US BACK..."

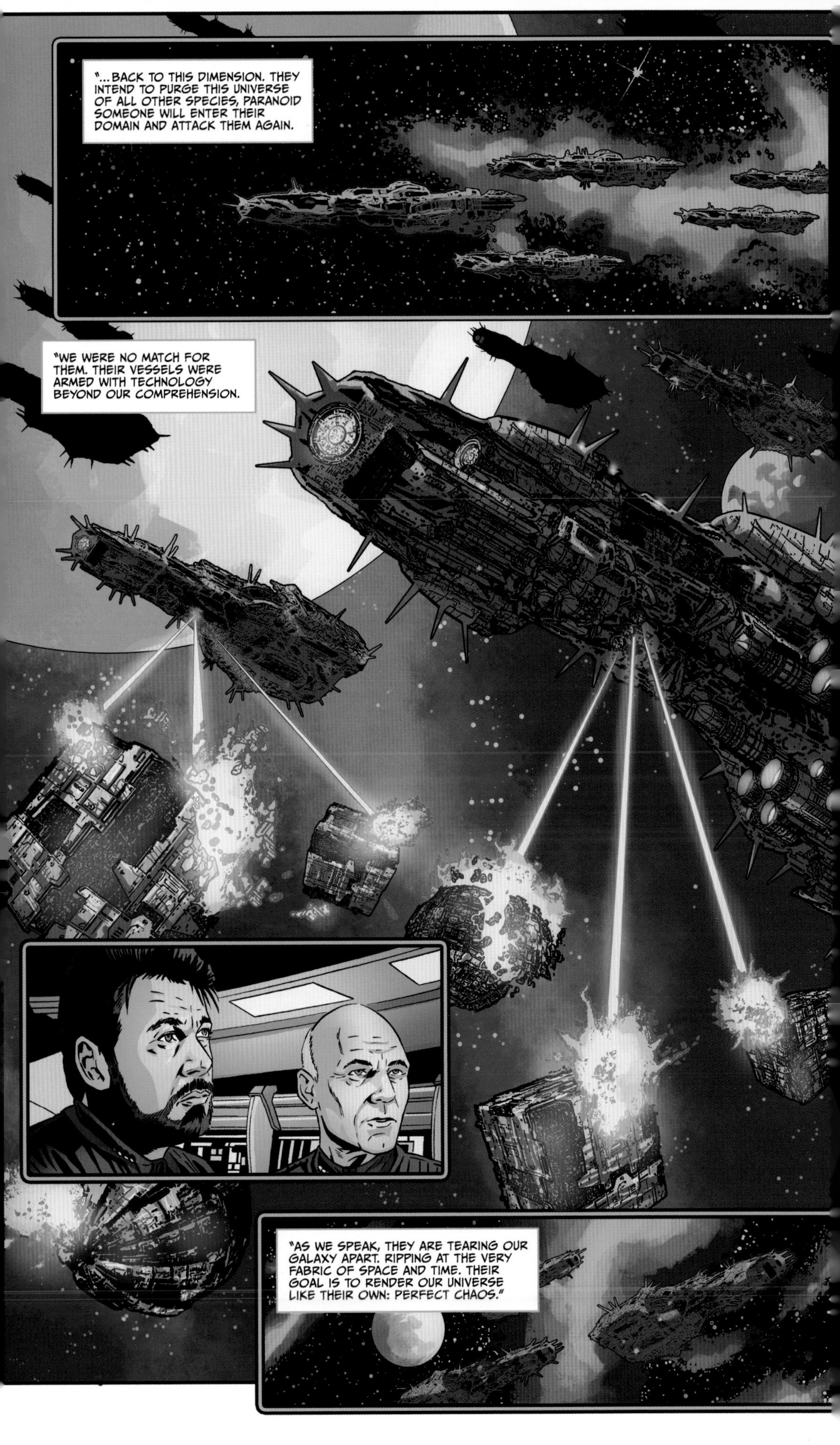
"...BACK TO THIS DIMENSION. THEY INTEND TO PURGE THIS UNIVERSE OF ALL OTHER SPECIES, PARANOID SOMEONE WILL ENTER THEIR DOMAIN AND ATTACK THEM AGAIN.
"WE WERE NO MATCH FOR THEM. THEIR VESSELS WERE ARMED WITH TECHNOLOGY BEYOND OUR COMPREHENSION.
"AS WE SPEAK, THEY ARE TEARING OUR GALAXY APART. RIPPING AT THE VERY FABRIC OF SPACE AND TIME. THEIR GOAL IS TO RENDER OUR UNIVERSE LIKE THEIR OWN: PERFECT CHAOS."

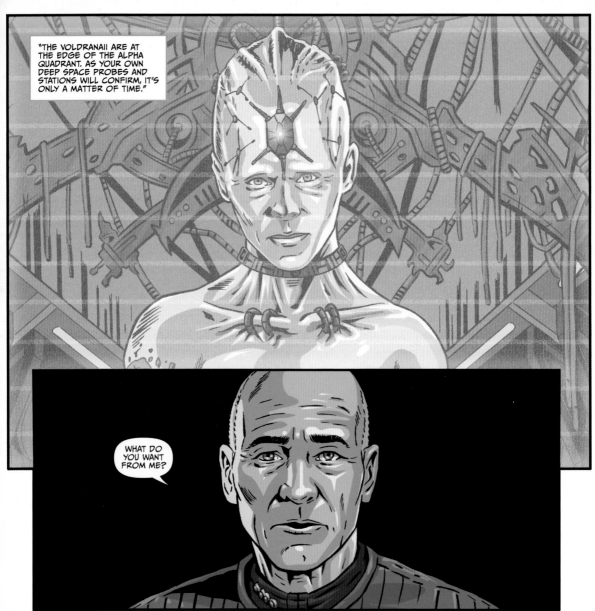

"THE VOLDRANAII ARE AT THE EDGE OF THE ALPHA QUADRANT. AS YOUR OWN DEEP SPACE PROBES AND STATIONS WILL CONFIRM, IT'S ONLY A MATTER OF TIME."

WHAT DO YOU WANT FROM ME?

'WE KNOW OF NO MORE FORMIDABLE OPPONENT THAN YOU, JEAN-LUC PICARD... LOCUTUS OF BORG. YOU AND YOUR SPECIES.

"ONLY BY JOINING FORCES CAN BOTH THE COLLECTIVE AND THE FEDERATION SURVIVE."

AND IF WE AGREE TO THIS TRUCE, TELL ME HOW YOU INTEND TO WORK TOGETHER. HIVE MIND AND HUMANS.

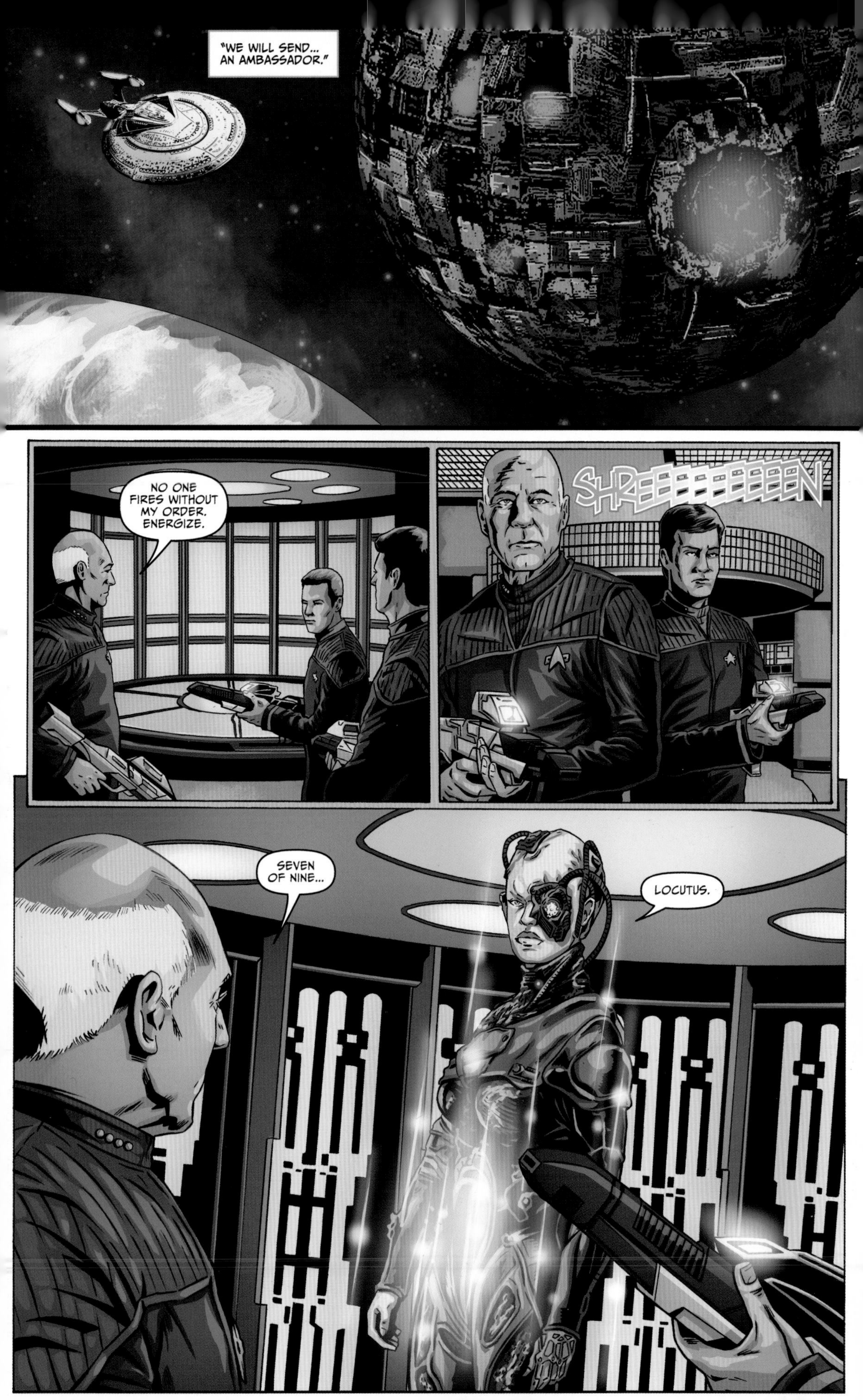
"WE WILL SEND... AN AMBASSADOR."
NCC-1701-E
NO ONE FIRES WITHOUT MY ORDER. ENERGIZE.
SHREEEEEEEEEN
SEVEN OF NINE...
LOCUTUS.

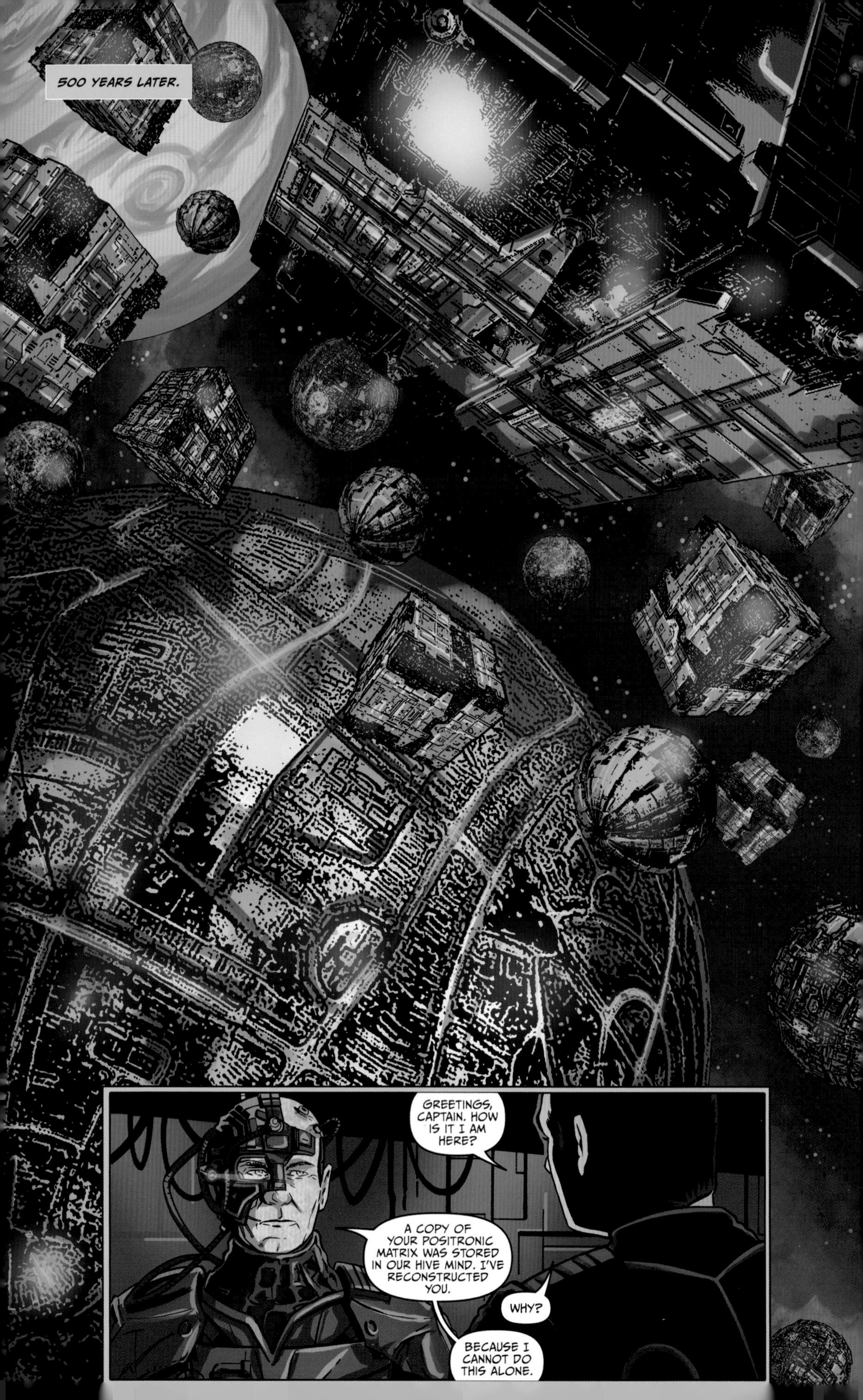
500 YEARS LATER.
GREETINGS, CAPTAIN. HOW IS IT I AM HERE?
A COPY OF YOUR POSITRONIC MATRIX WAS STORED IN OUR HIVE MIND. I'VE RECONSTRUCTED YOU.
WHY?
BECAUSE I CANNOT DO THIS ALONE.

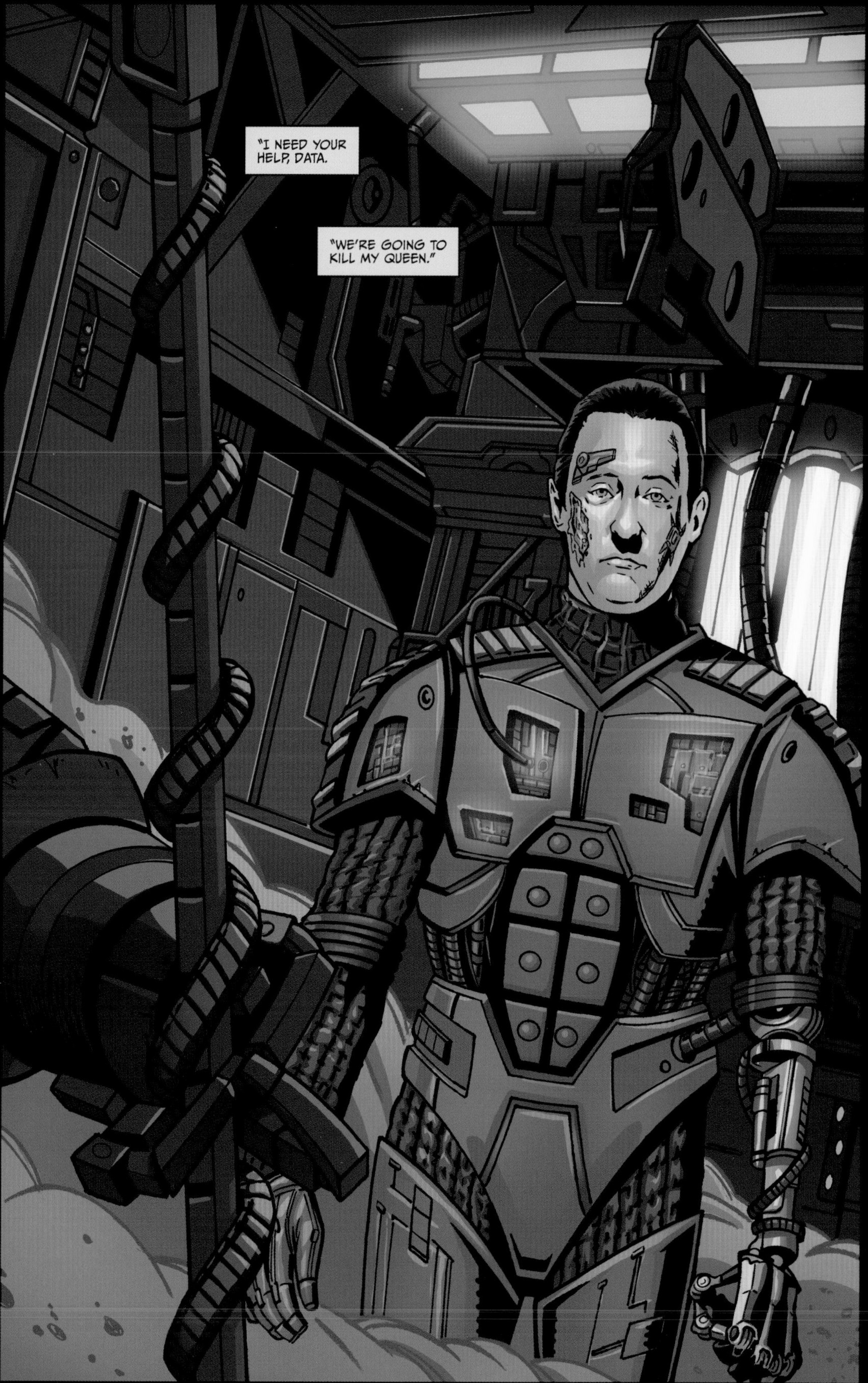
"I NEED YOUR HELP, DATA.
"WE'RE GOING TO KILL MY QUEEN."

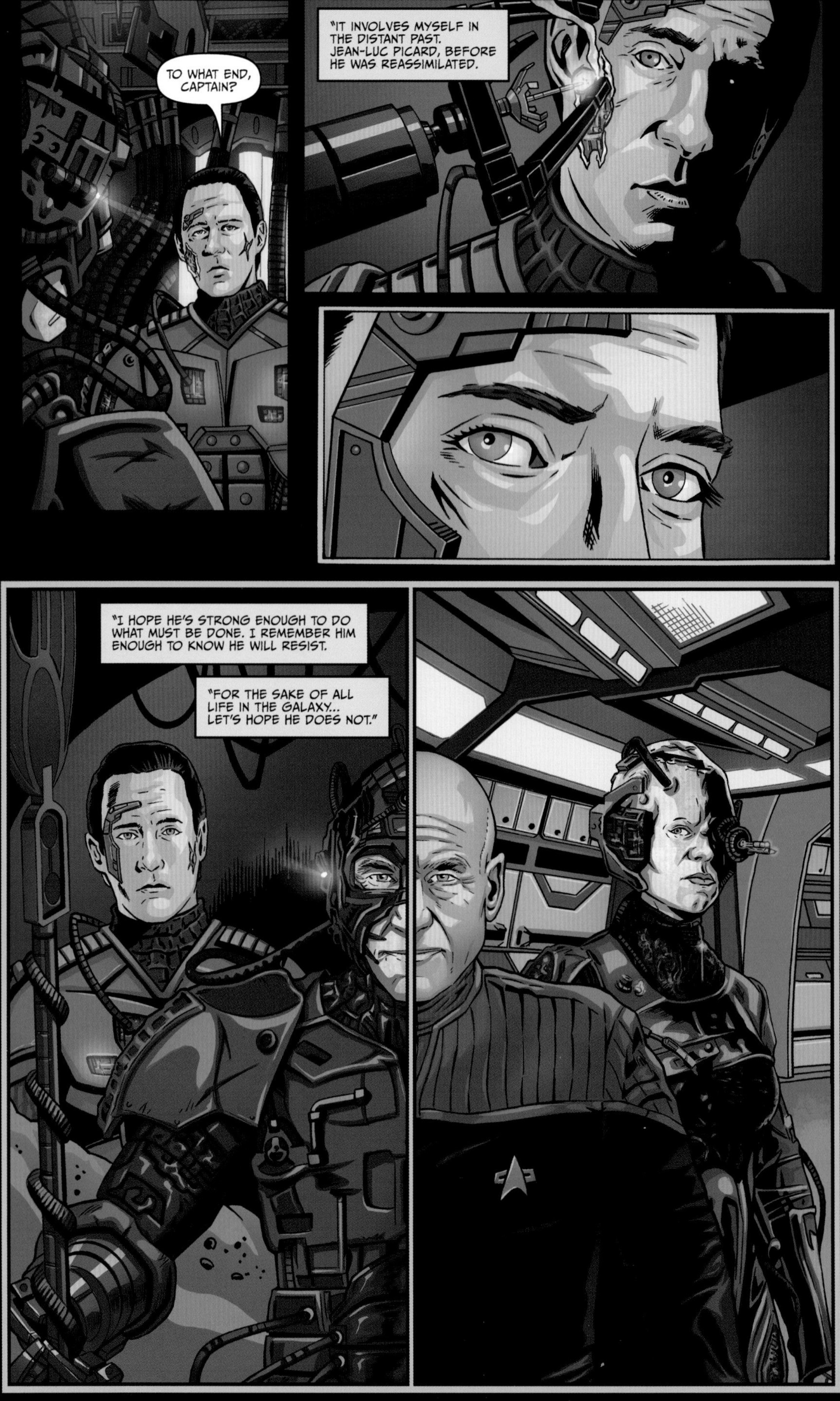
TO WHAT END, CAPTAIN?
"IT INVOLVES MYSELF IN THE DISTANT PAST. JEAN-LUC PICARD, BEFORE HE WAS REASSIMILATED.
"I HOPE HE'S STRONG ENOUGH TO DO WHAT MUST BE DONE. I REMEMBER HIM ENOUGH TO KNOW HE WILL RESIST.
"FOR THE SAKE OF ALL LIFE IN THE GALAXY... LET'S HOPE HE DOES NOT."

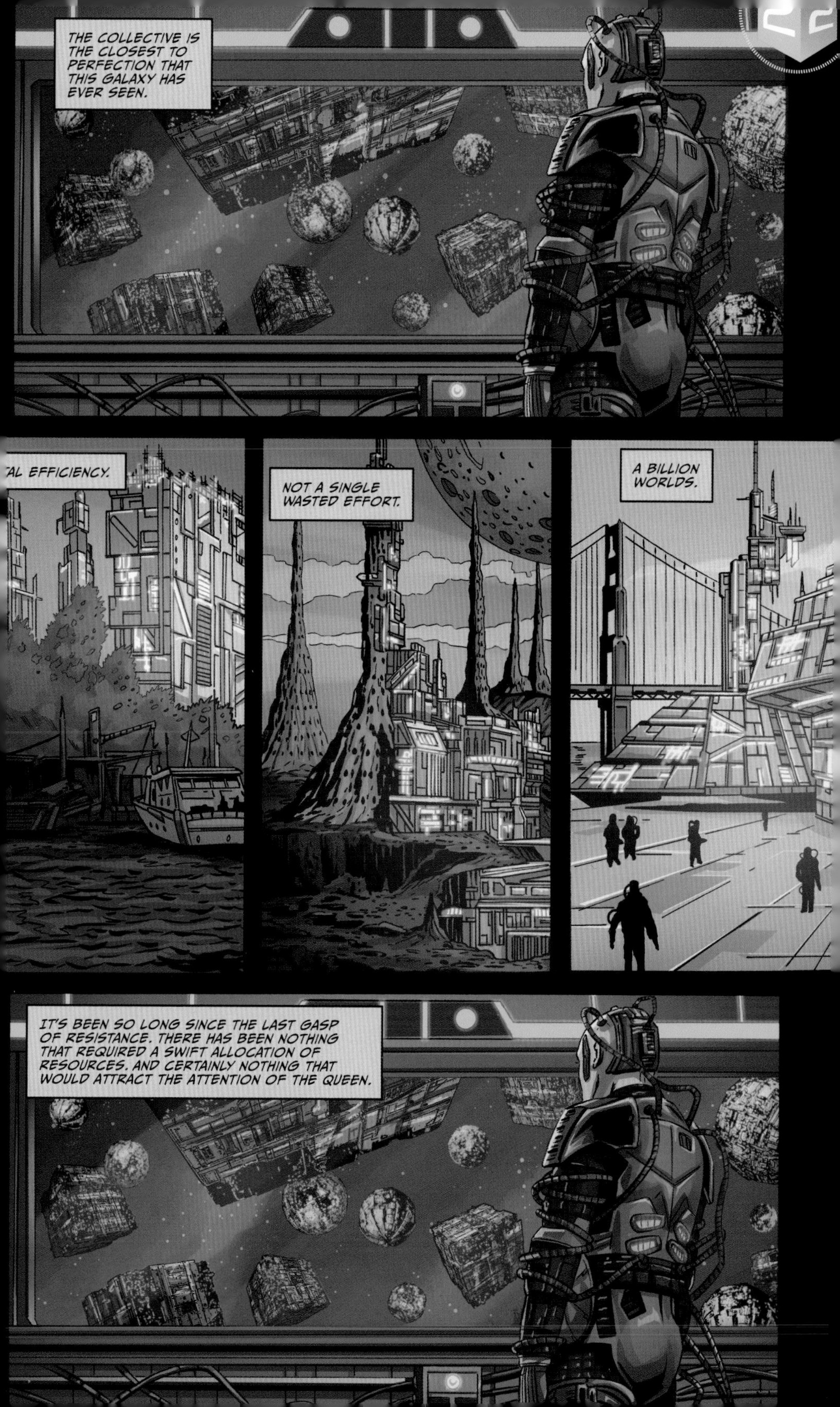
THE COLLECTIVE IS THE CLOSEST TO PERFECTION THAT THIS GALAXY HAS EVER SEEN.
TAL EFFICIENCY.
NOT A SINGLE WASTED EFFORT.
A BILLION WORLDS.
IT'S BEEN SO LONG SINCE THE LAST GASP OF RESISTANCE. THERE HAS BEEN NOTHING THAT REQUIRED A SWIFT ALLOCATION OF RESOURCES. AND CERTAINLY NOTHING THAT WOULD ATTRACT THE ATTENTION OF THE QUEEN.

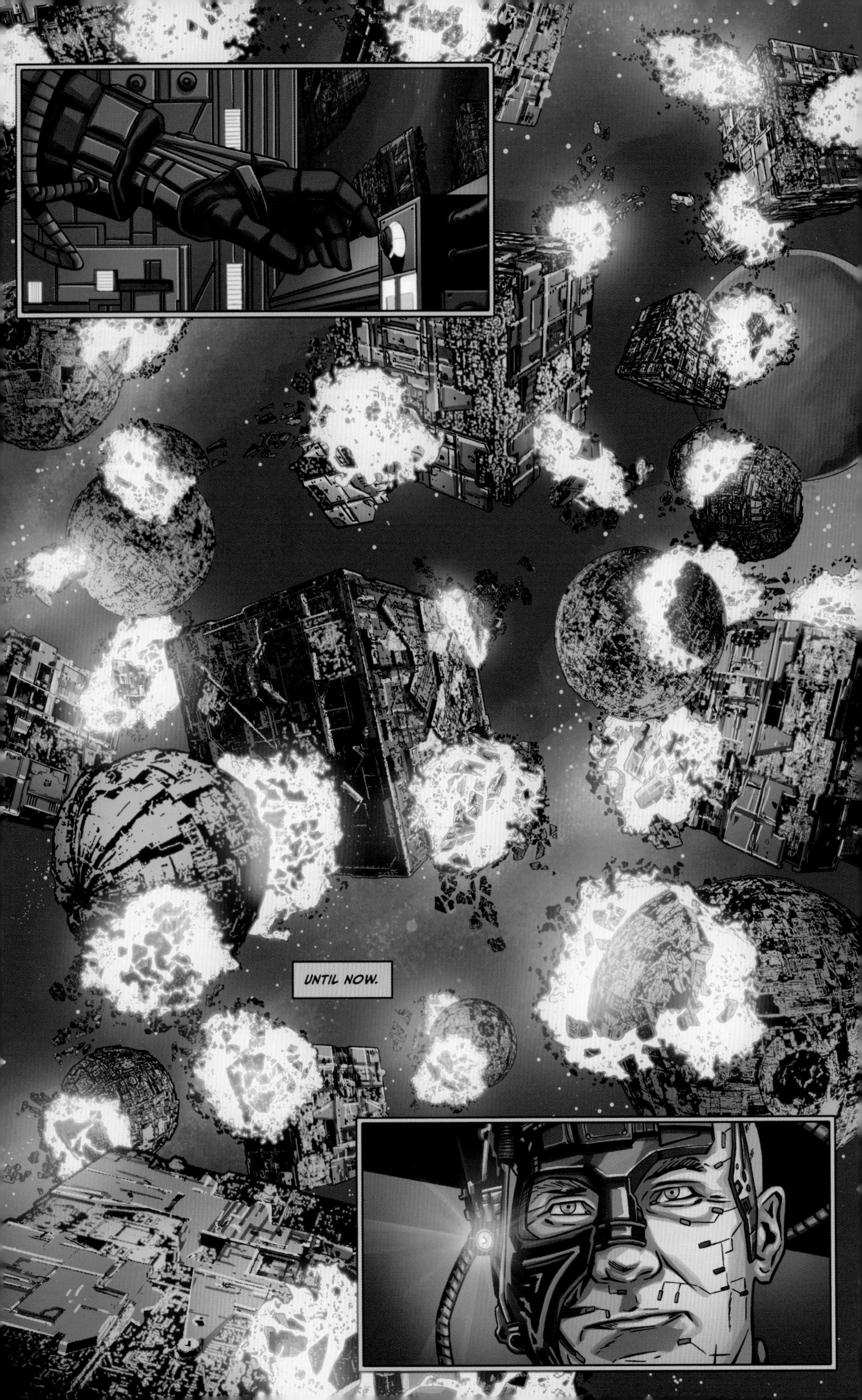
UNTIL NOW.

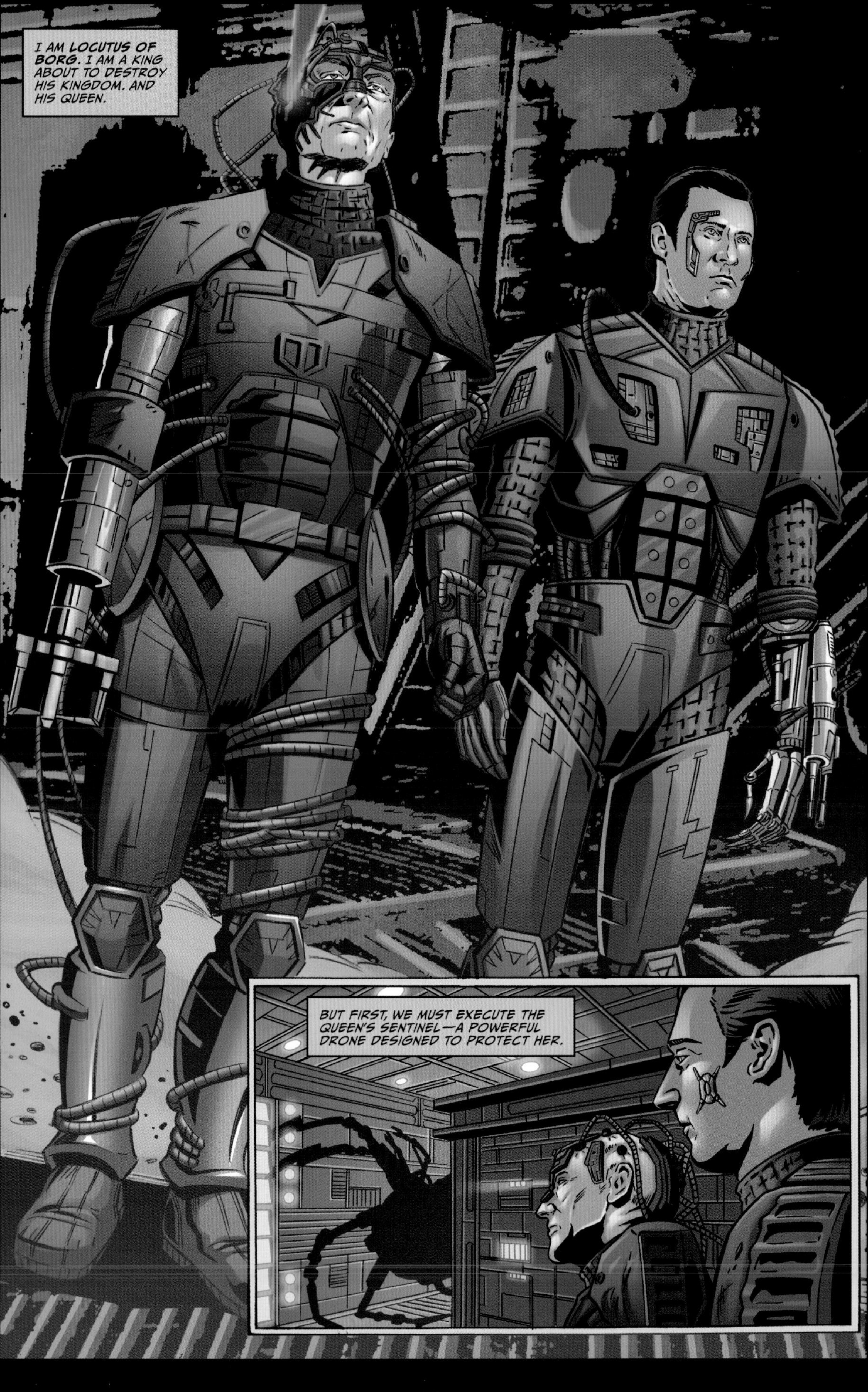
I AM LOCUTUS OF BORG. I AM A KING ABOUT TO DESTROY HIS KINGDOM. AND HIS QUEEN.
BUT FIRST, WE MUST EXECUTE THE QUEEN'S SENTINEL—A POWERFUL DRONE DESIGNED TO PROTECT HER.

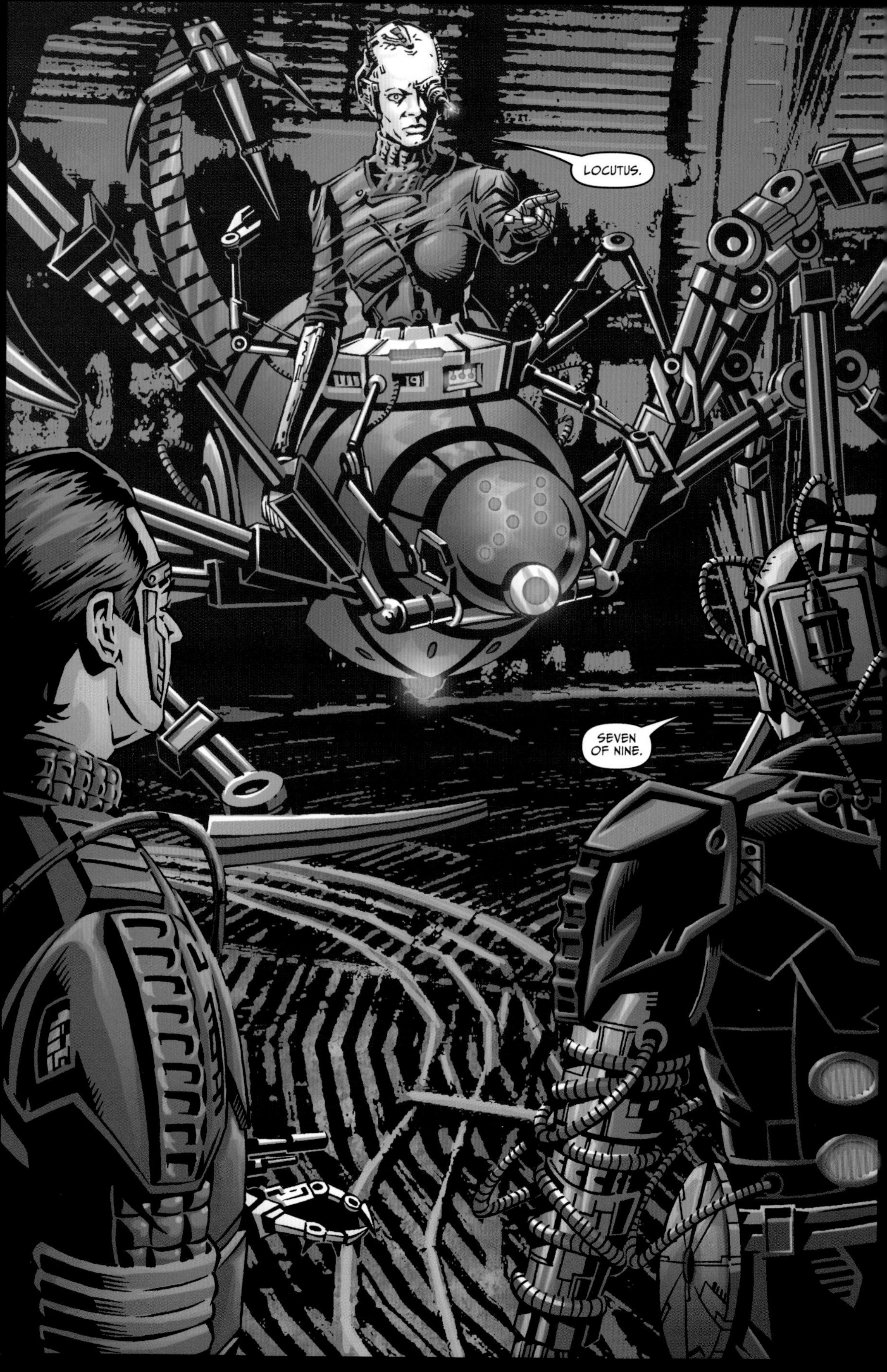
LOCUTUS.
SEVEN OF NINE.

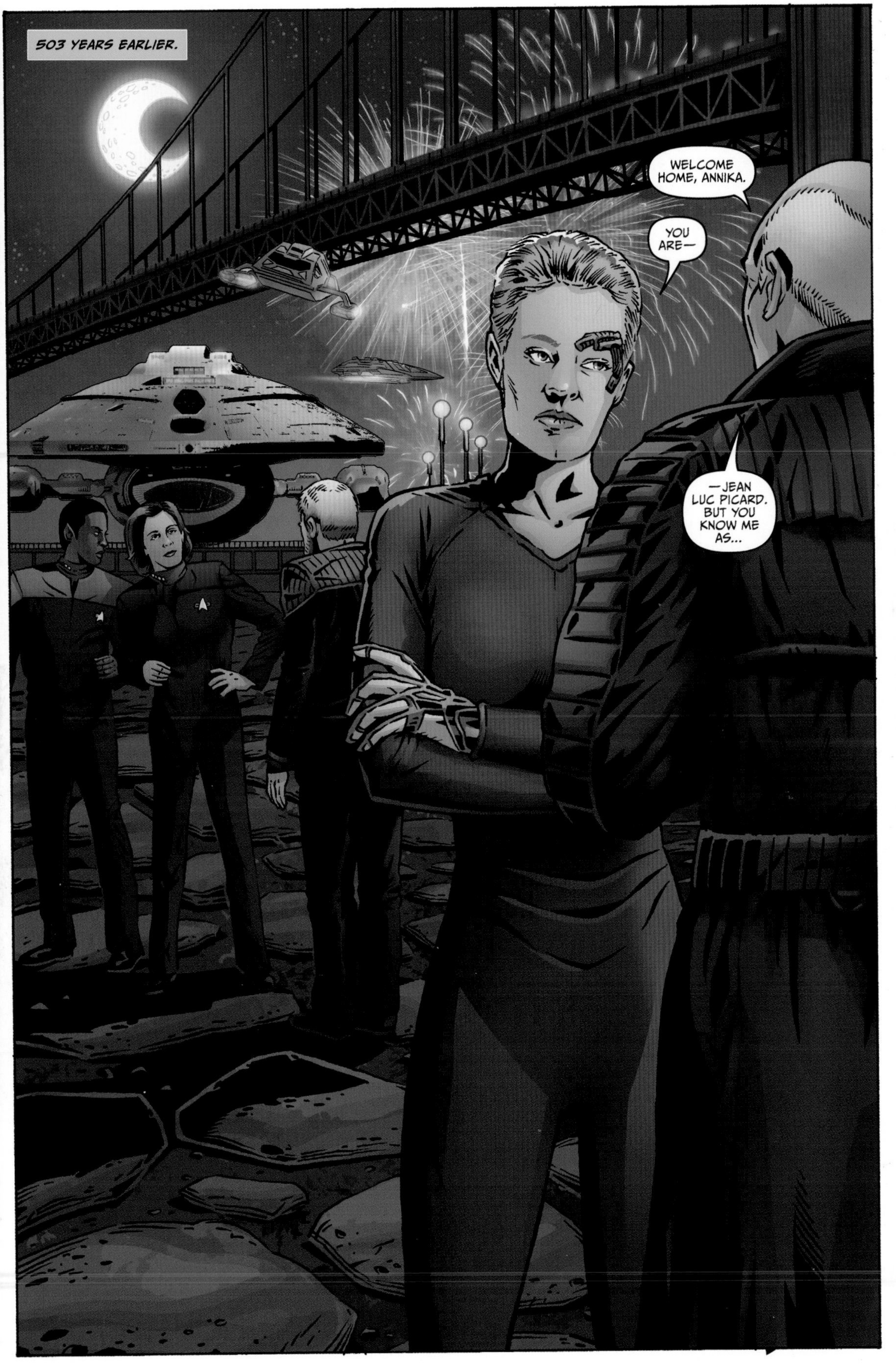
503 YEARS EARLIER.
WELCOME HOME, ANNIKA.
YOU ARE—
—JEAN LUC PICARD. BUT YOU KNOW ME AS...

...LOCUTUS OF BORG.

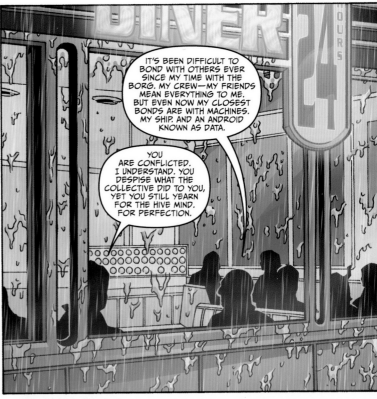

IT'S BEEN DIFFICULT TO BOND WITH OTHERS EVER SINCE MY TIME WITH THE BORG. MY CREW—MY FRIENDS MEAN EVERYTHING TO ME. BUT EVEN NOW MY CLOSEST BONDS ARE WITH MACHINES. MY SHIP. AND AN ANDROID KNOWN AS DATA.

YOU ARE CONFLICTED. I UNDERSTAND. YOU DESPISE WHAT THE COLLECTIVE DID TO YOU, YET YOU STILL YEARN FOR THE HIVE MIND. FOR PERFECTION.

THEY MUST BE DESTROYED, JEAN-LUC.

I KNOW.

I'D LIKE YOU TO HELP ME SPEARHEAD AN OPERATION TO DO JUST THAT. A COVERT MISSION TO INFILTRATE THE BORG. FIND A WEAKNESS. SOMETHING THE QUEEN HASN'T REALIZED. EXPLOIT IT.

AND TEAR THEM APART FROM THE INSIDE OUT.

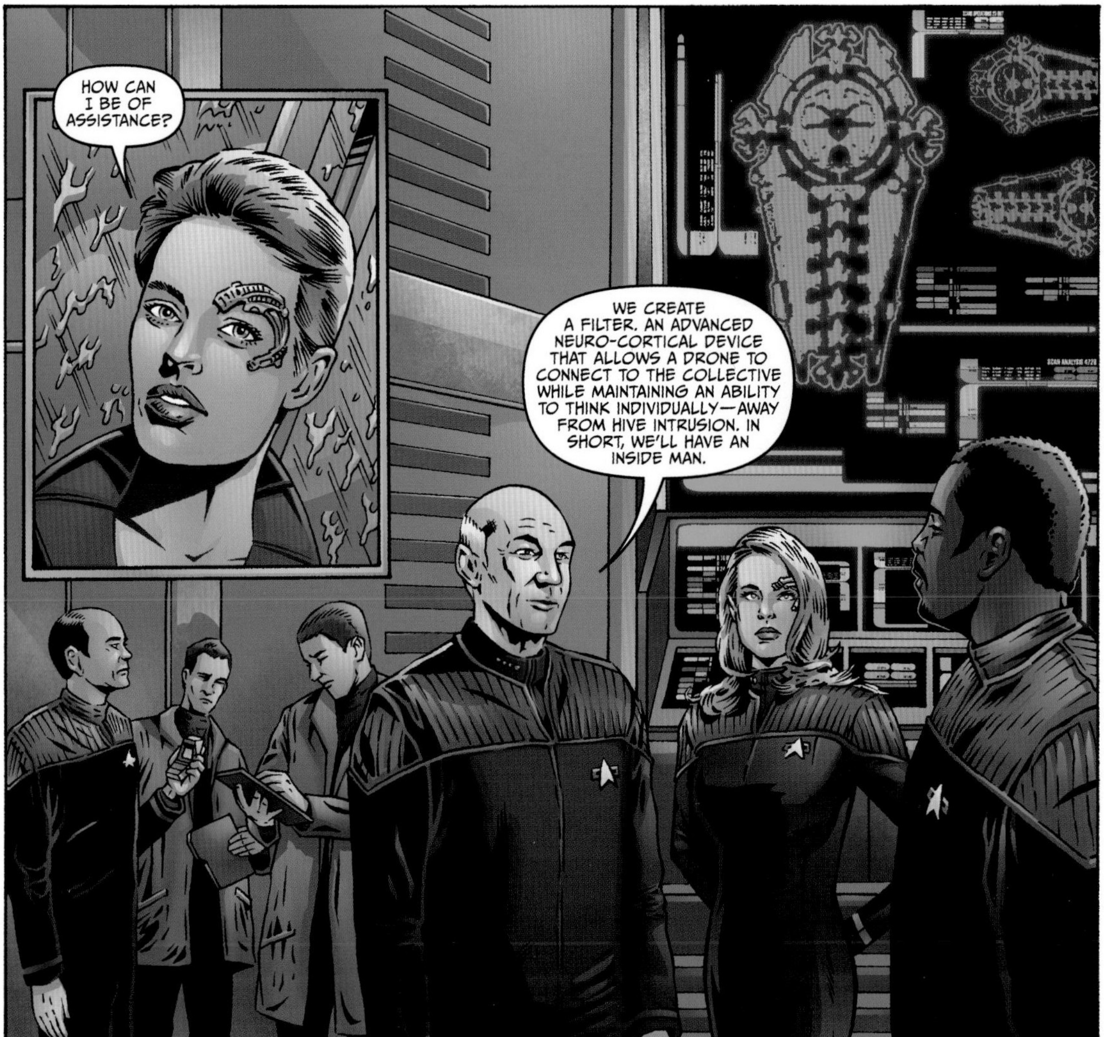
HOW CAN I BE OF ASSISTANCE?
WE CREATE A FILTER. AN ADVANCED NEURO-CORTICAL DEVICE THAT ALLOWS A DRONE TO CONNECT TO THE COLLECTIVE WHILE MAINTAINING AN ABILITY TO THINK INDIVIDUALLY—AWAY FROM HIVE INTRUSION. IN SHORT, WE'LL HAVE AN INSIDE MAN.

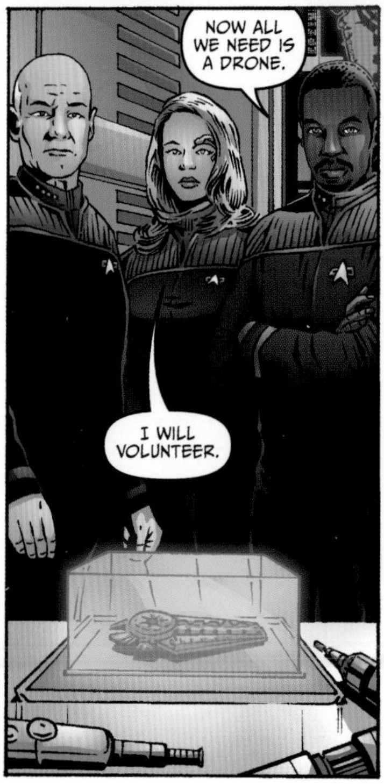
NOW ALL WE NEED IS A DRONE.
I WILL VOLUNTEER.

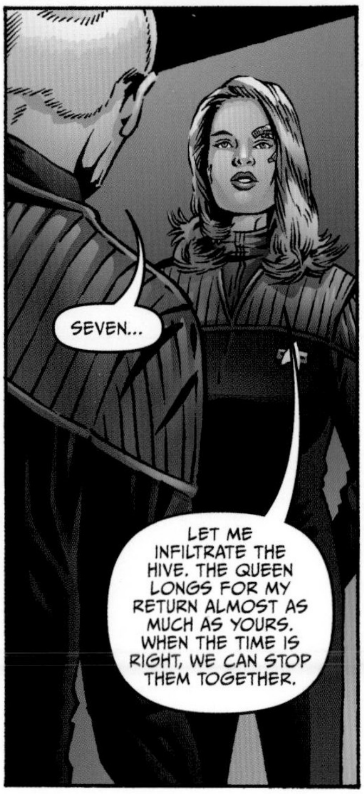
SEVEN...
LET ME INFILTRATE THE HIVE. THE QUEEN LONGS FOR MY RETURN ALMOST AS MUCH AS YOURS. WHEN THE TIME IS RIGHT, WE CAN STOP THEM TOGETHER.

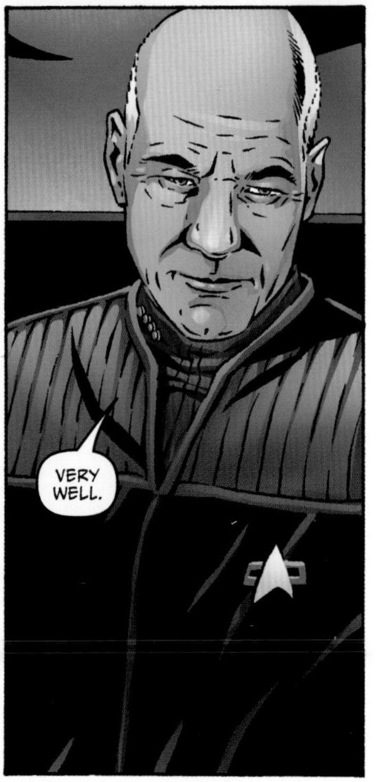
VERY WELL.

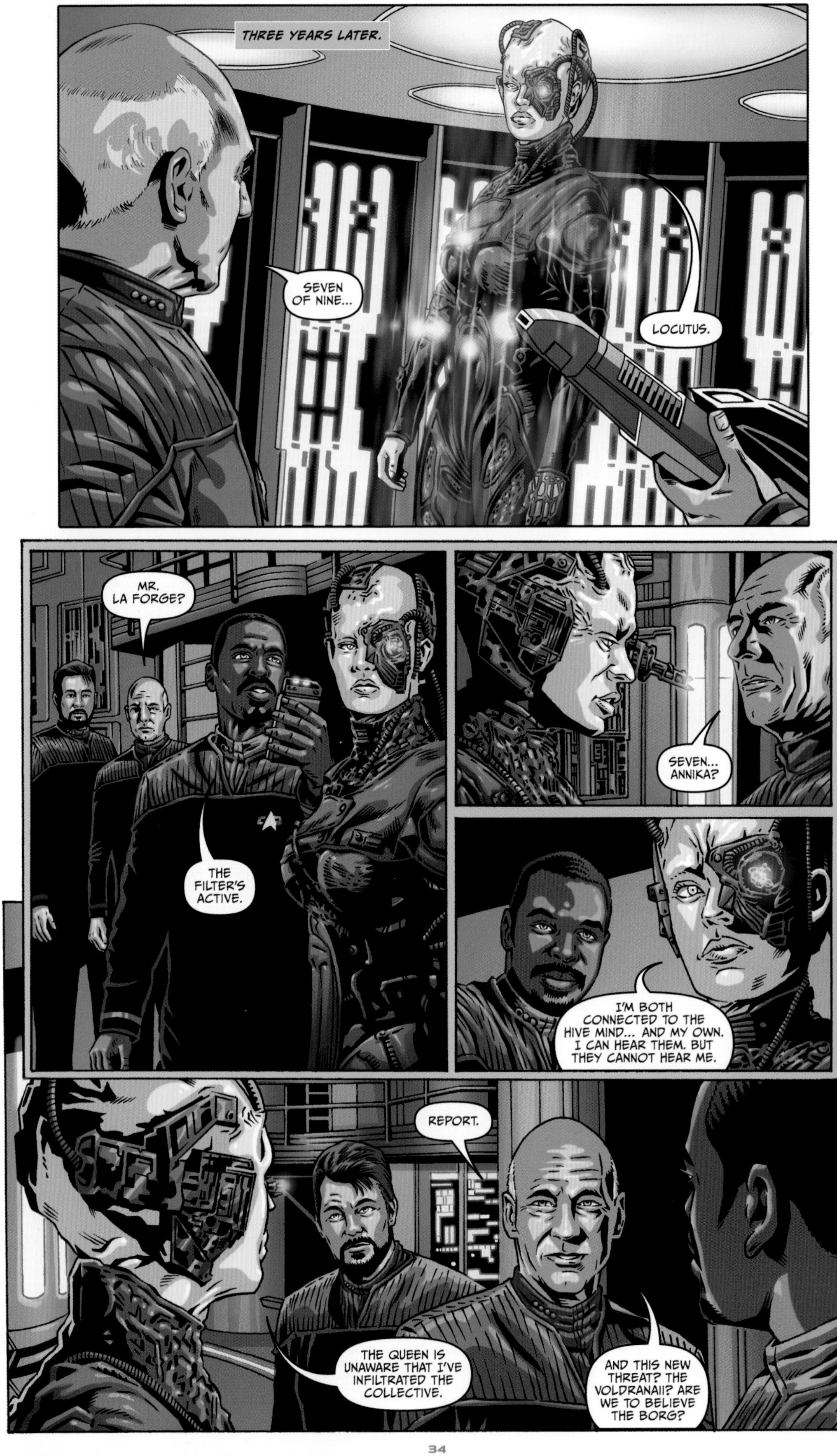

THREE YEARS LATER.
SEVEN OF NINE...
LOCUTUS.
MR. LA FORGE?
THE FILTER'S ACTIVE.
SEVEN... ANNIKA?
I'M BOTH CONNECTED TO THE HIVE MIND... AND MY OWN. I CAN HEAR THEM. BUT THEY CANNOT HEAR ME.
REPORT.
THE QUEEN IS UNAWARE THAT I'VE INFILTRATED THE COLLECTIVE.
AND THIS NEW THREAT? THE VOLDRANAII? ARE WE TO BELIEVE THE BORG?

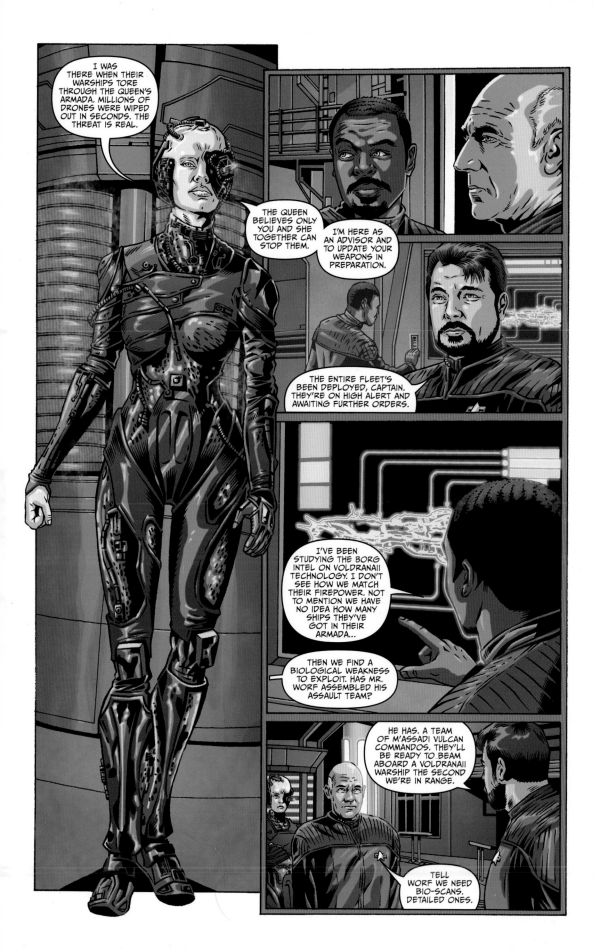

I WAS THERE WHEN THEIR WARSHIPS TORE THROUGH THE QUEEN'S ARMADA. MILLIONS OF DRONES WERE WIPED OUT IN SECONDS. THE THREAT IS REAL.

THE QUEEN BELIEVES ONLY YOU AND SHE TOGETHER CAN STOP THEM.

I'M HERE AS AN ADVISOR AND TO UPDATE YOUR WEAPONS IN PREPARATION.

THE ENTIRE FLEET'S BEEN DEPLOYED, CAPTAIN. THEY'RE ON HIGH ALERT AND AWAITING FURTHER ORDERS.

I'VE BEEN STUDYING THE BORG INTEL ON VOLDRANAII TECHNOLOGY. I DON'T SEE HOW WE MATCH THEIR FIREPOWER. NOT TO MENTION WE HAVE NO IDEA HOW MANY SHIPS THEY'VE GOT IN THEIR ARMADA...

THEN WE FIND A BIOLOGICAL WEAKNESS TO EXPLOIT. HAS MR. WORF ASSEMBLED HIS ASSAULT TEAM?

HE HAS. A TEAM OF M'ASSADI VULCAN COMMANDOS. THEY'LL BE READY TO BEAM ABOARD A VOLDRANAII WARSHIP THE SECOND WE'RE IN RANGE.

TELL WORF WE NEED BIO-SCANS. DETAILED ONES.

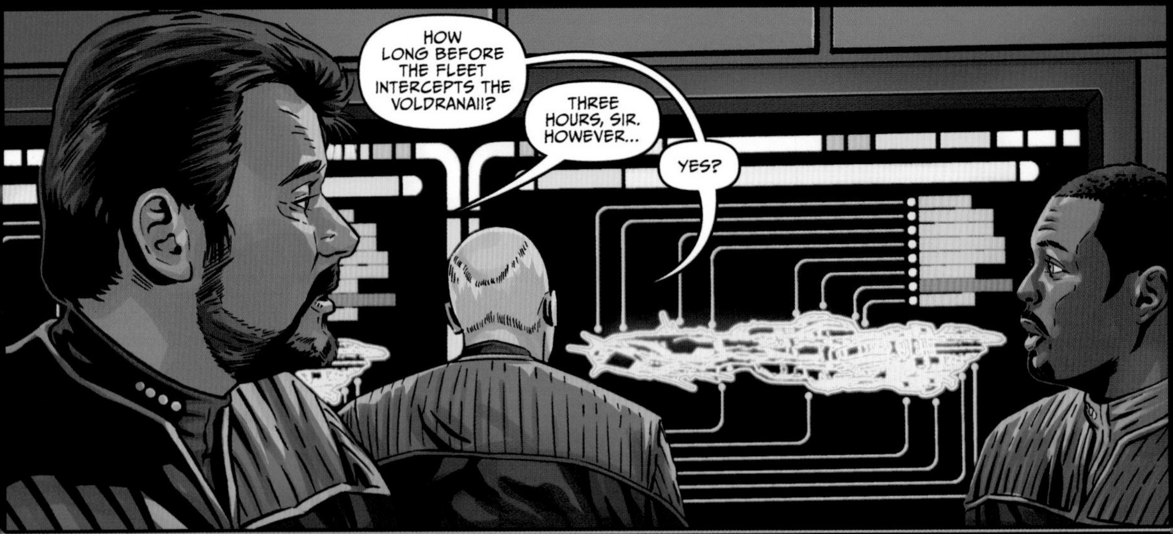
HOW LONG BEFORE THE FLEET INTERCEPTS THE VOLDRANAII?
THREE HOURS, SIR. HOWEVER...
YES?

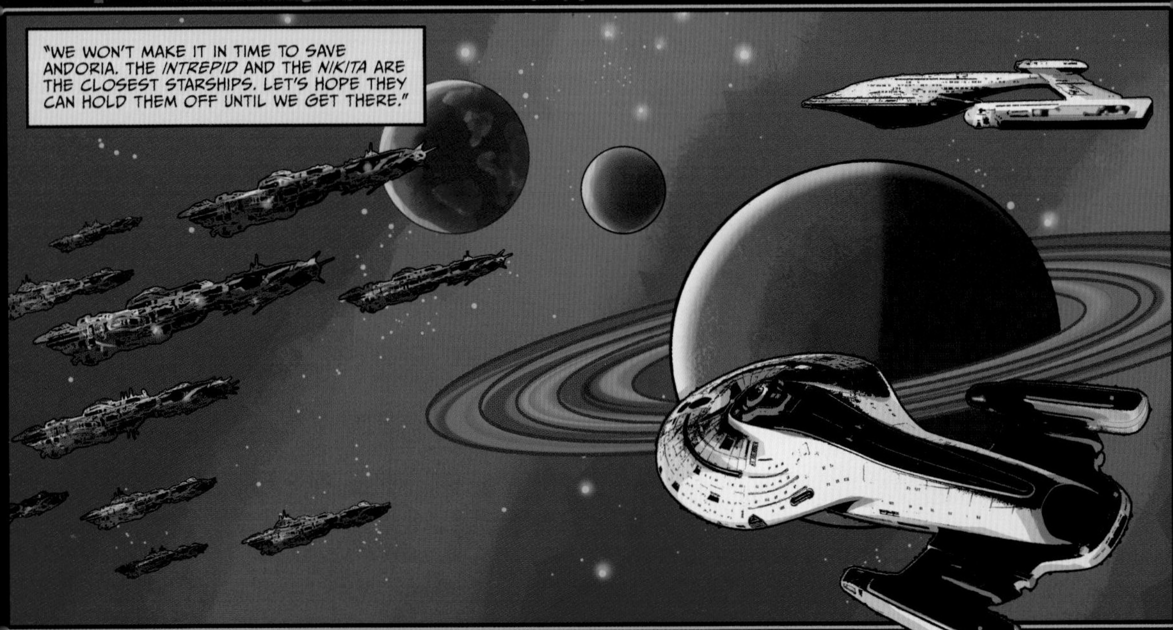
"WE WON'T MAKE IT IN TIME TO SAVE ANDORIA. THE *INTREPID* AND THE *NIKITA* ARE THE CLOSEST STARSHIPS. LET'S HOPE THEY CAN HOLD THEM OFF UNTIL WE GET THERE."

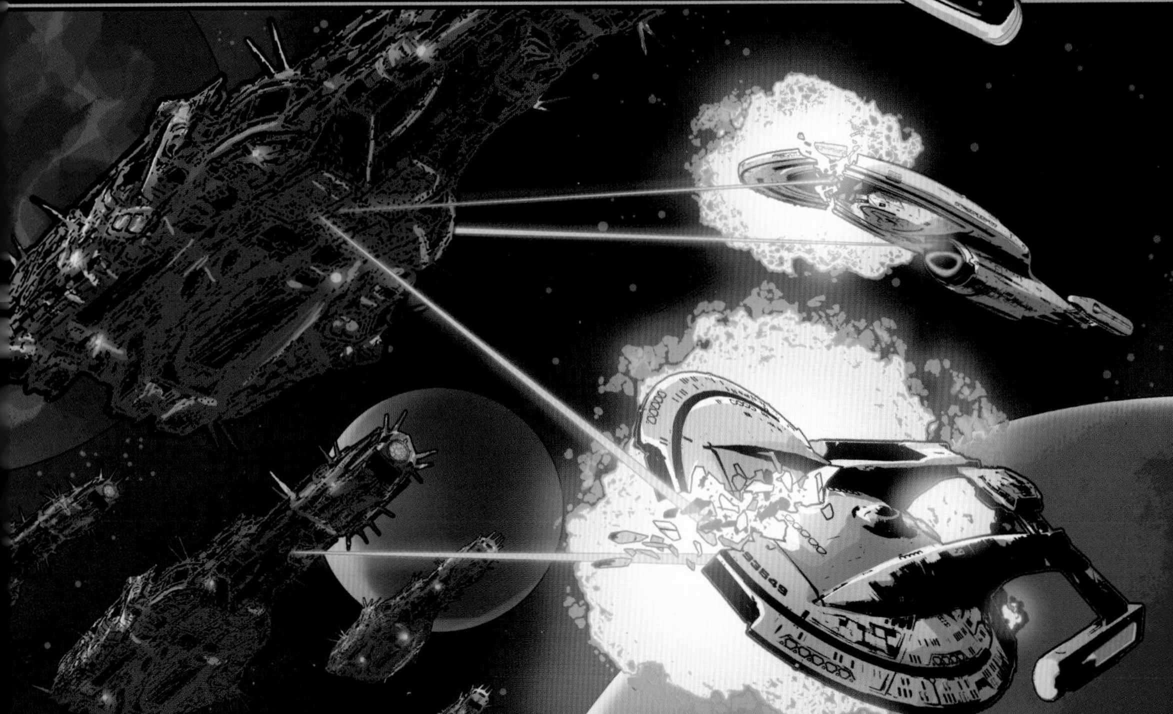

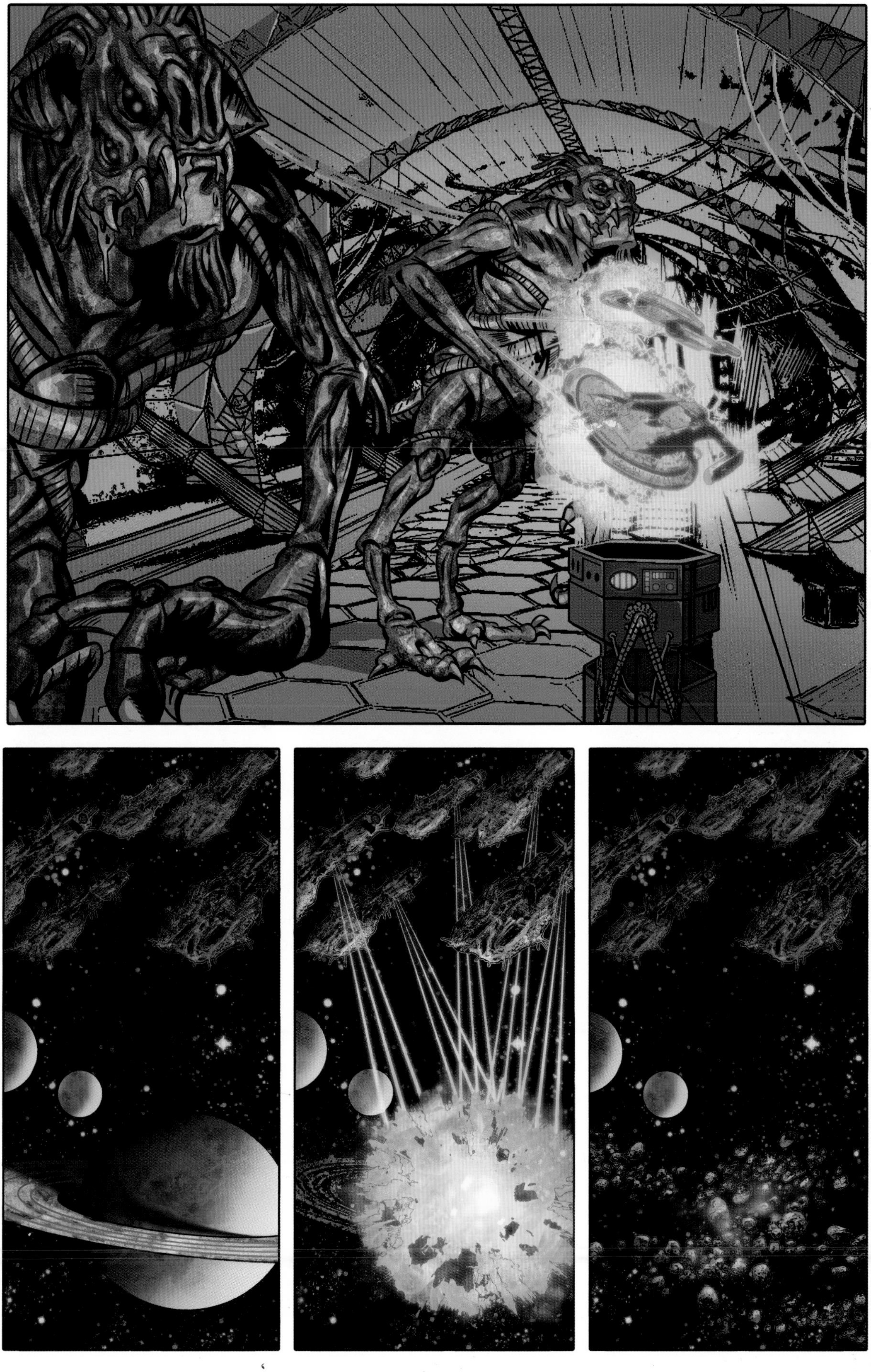

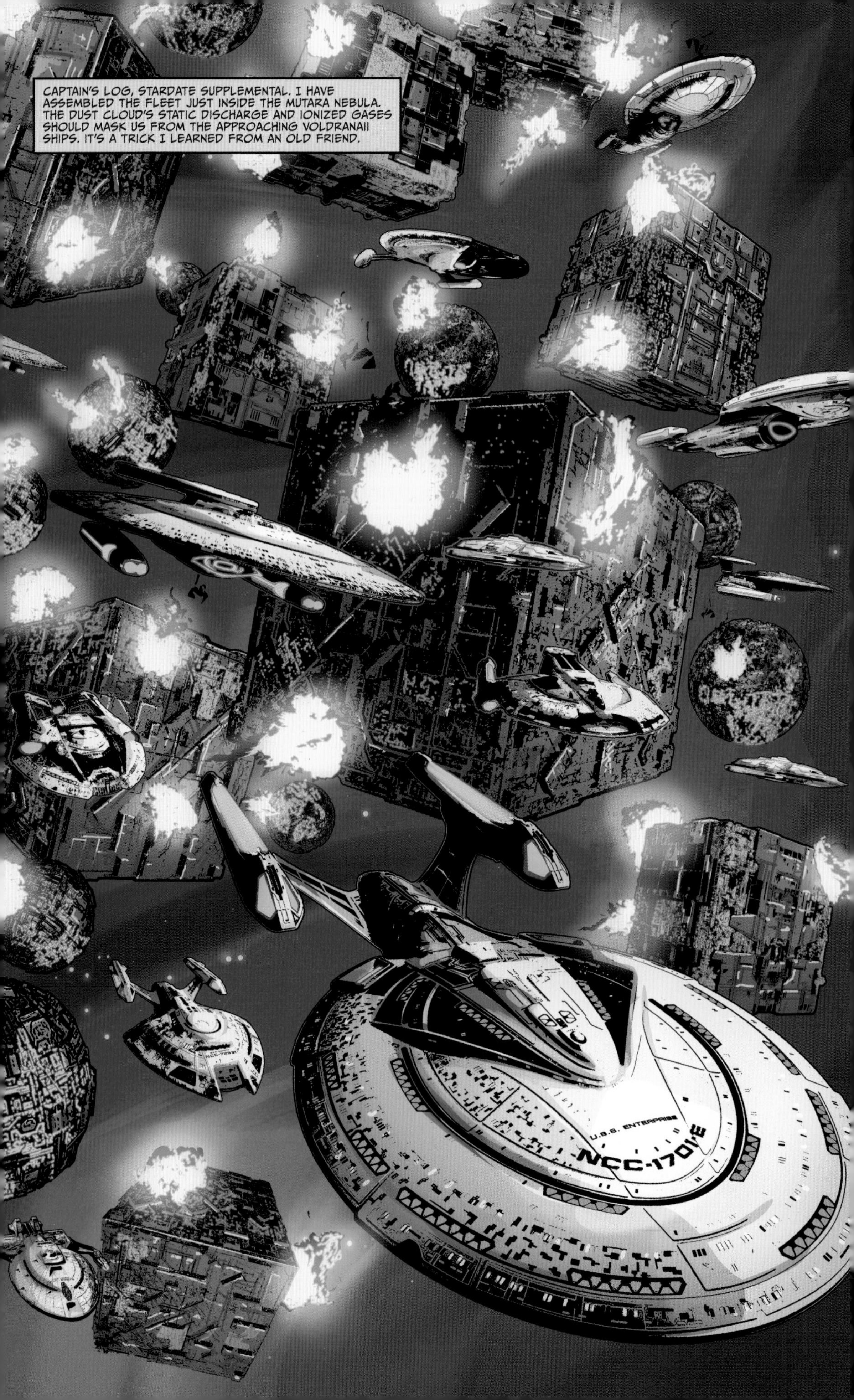
CAPTAIN'S LOG, STARDATE SUPPLEMENTAL. I HAVE ASSEMBLED THE FLEET JUST INSIDE THE MUTARA NEBULA. THE DUST CLOUD'S STATIC DISCHARGE AND IONIZED GASES SHOULD MASK US FROM THE APPROACHING VOLDRANAII SHIPS. IT'S A TRICK I LEARNED FROM AN OLD FRIEND.
U.S.S. ENTERPRISE
NCC-1701-E

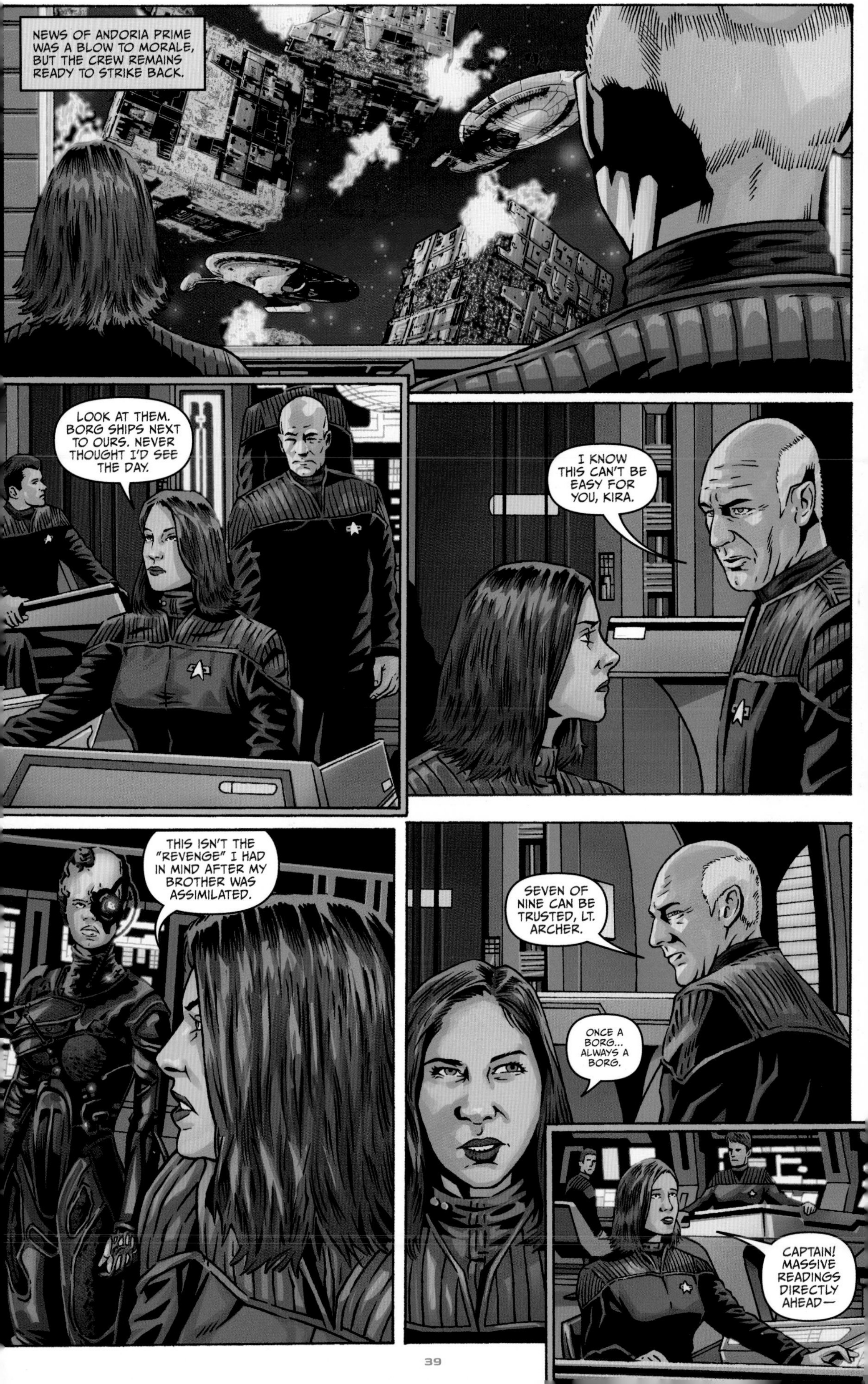
NEWS OF ANDORIA PRIME WAS A BLOW TO MORALE, BUT THE CREW REMAINS READY TO STRIKE BACK.
LOOK AT THEM. BORG SHIPS NEXT TO OURS. NEVER THOUGHT I'D SEE THE DAY.
I KNOW THIS CAN'T BE EASY FOR YOU, KIRA.
THIS ISN'T THE "REVENGE" I HAD IN MIND AFTER MY BROTHER WAS ASSIMILATED.
SEVEN OF NINE CAN BE TRUSTED, LT. ARCHER.
ONCE A BORG... ALWAYS A BORG.
CAPTAIN! MASSIVE READINGS DIRECTLY AHEAD—

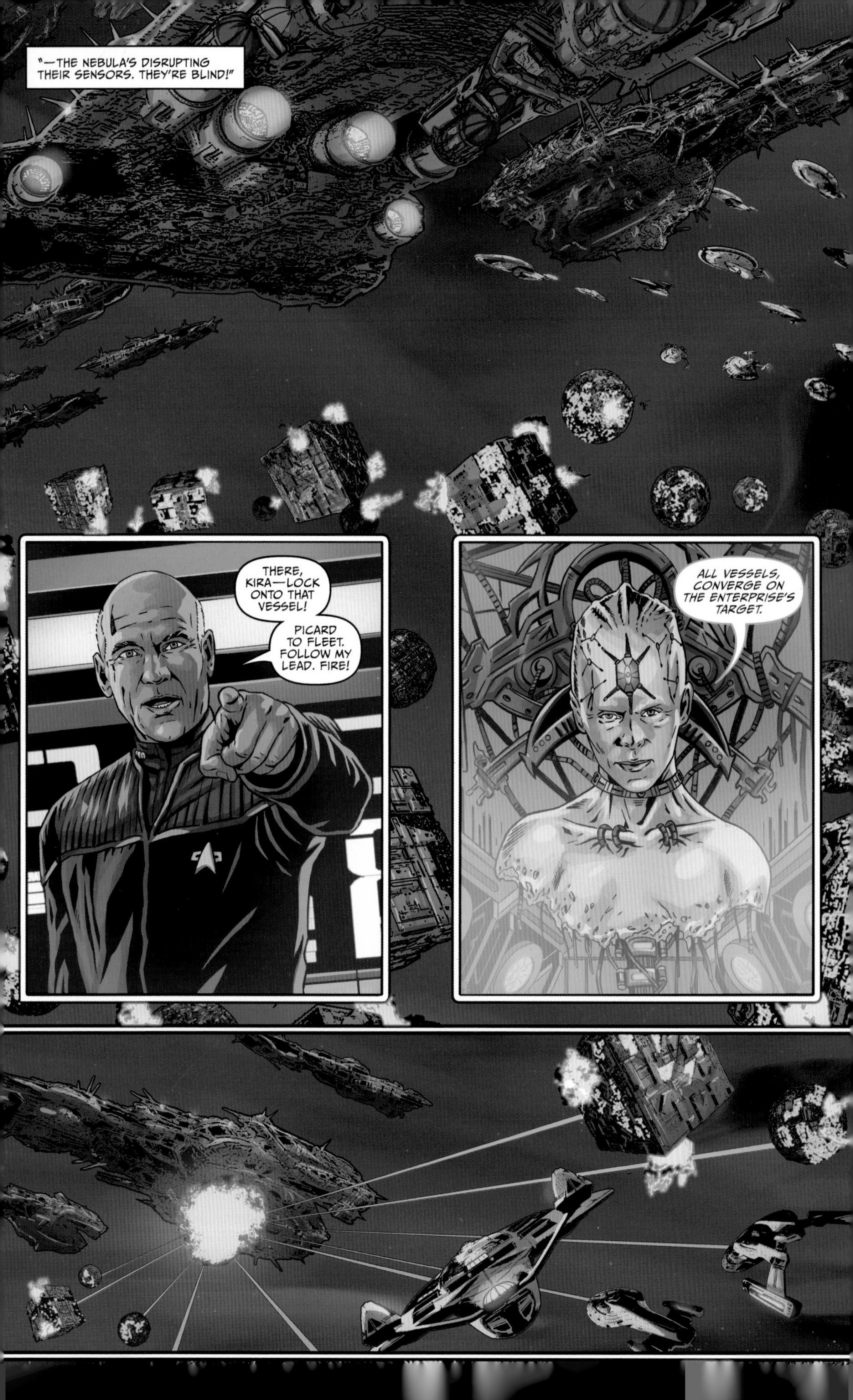
"—THE NEBULA'S DISRUPTING THEIR SENSORS. THEY'RE BLIND!"
THERE, KIRA—LOCK ONTO THAT VESSEL!
PICARD TO FLEET. FOLLOW MY LEAD. FIRE!
ALL VESSELS, CONVERGE ON THE ENTERPRISE'S TARGET.

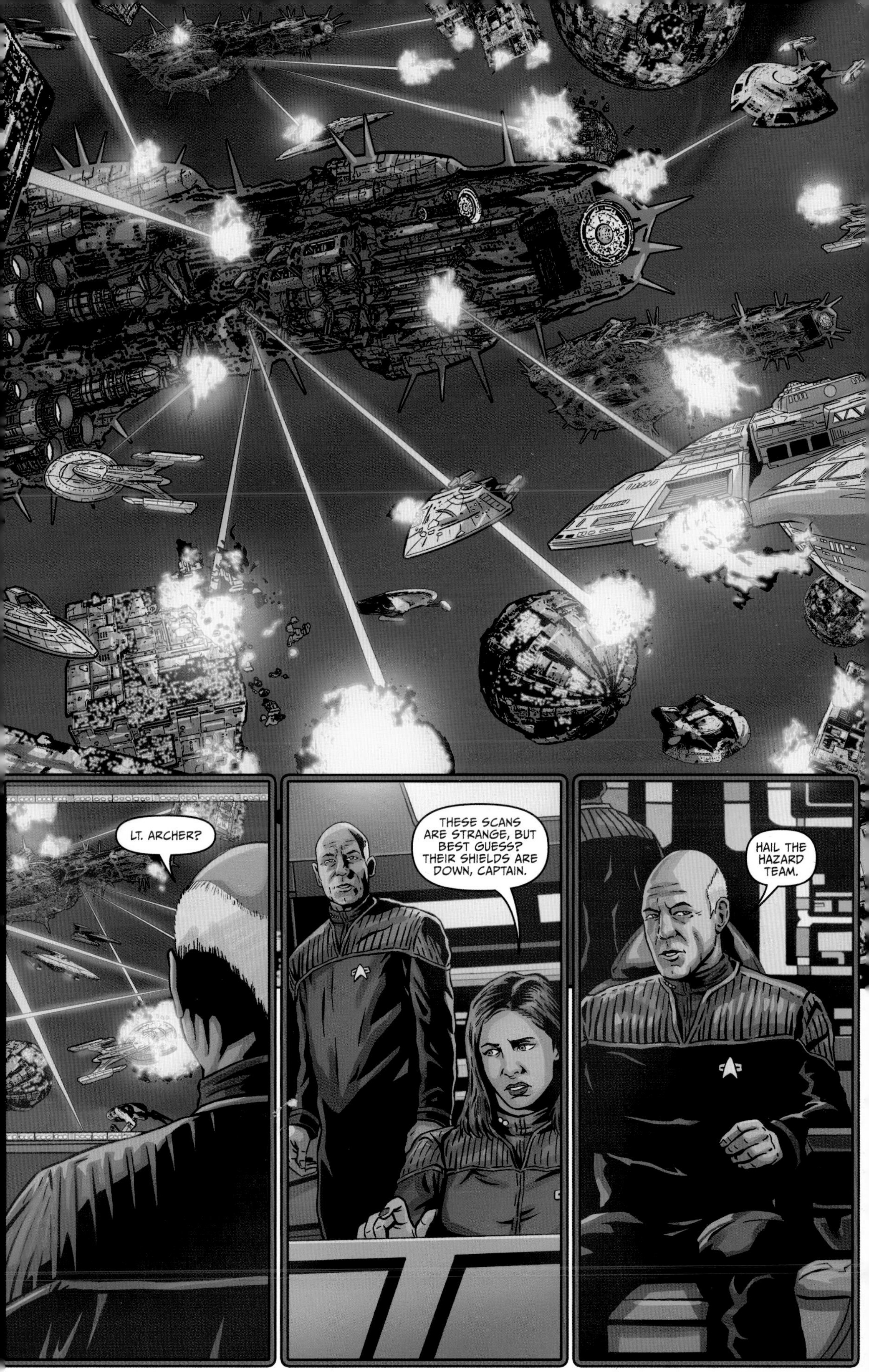
LT. ARCHER?
THESE SCANS ARE STRANGE, BUT BEST GUESS? THEIR SHIELDS ARE DOWN, CAPTAIN.
HAIL THE HAZARD TEAM.

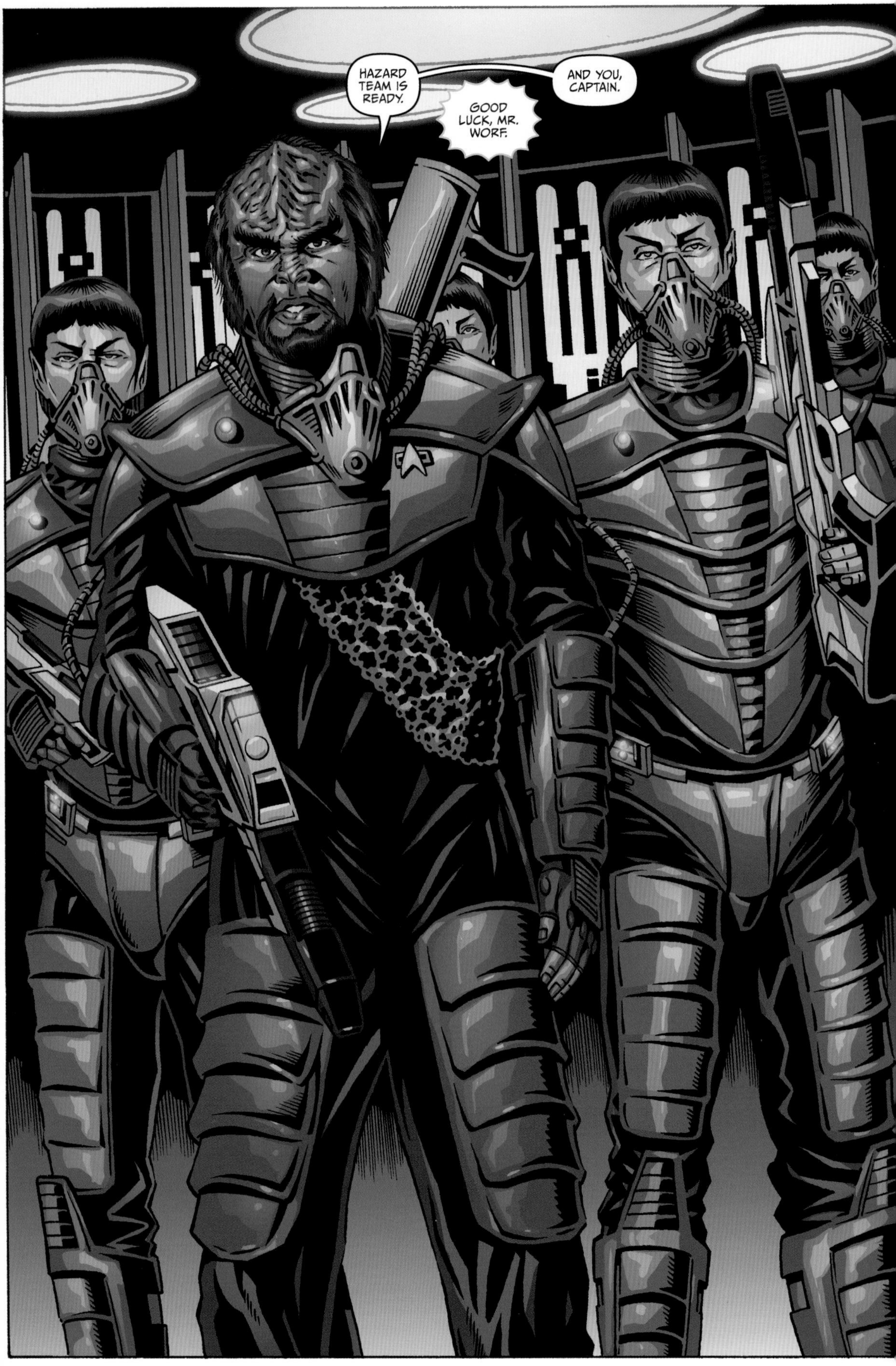
HAZARD TEAM IS READY.
GOOD LUCK, MR. WORF.
AND YOU, CAPTAIN.

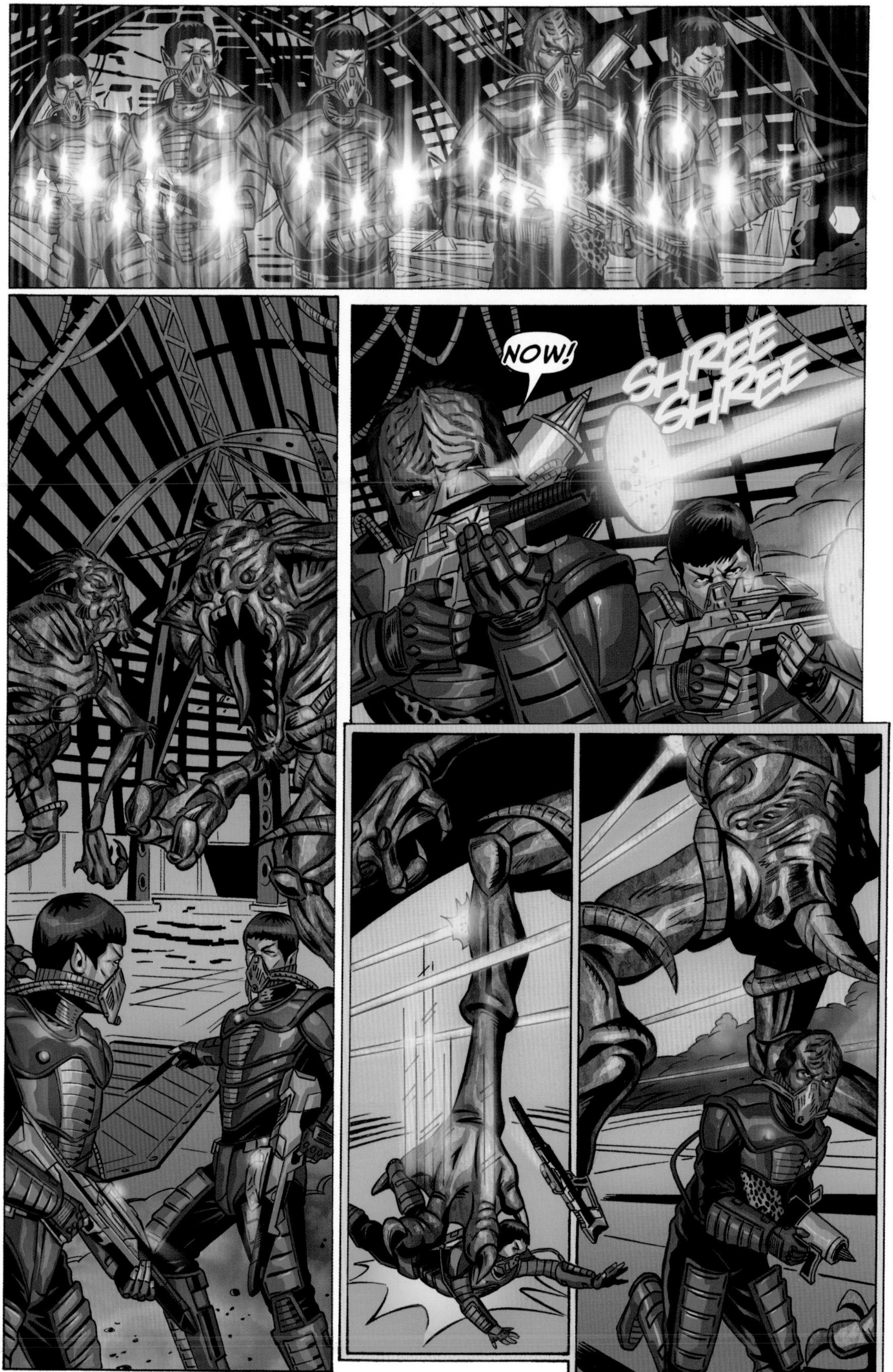
NOW!
SHREE
SHREE

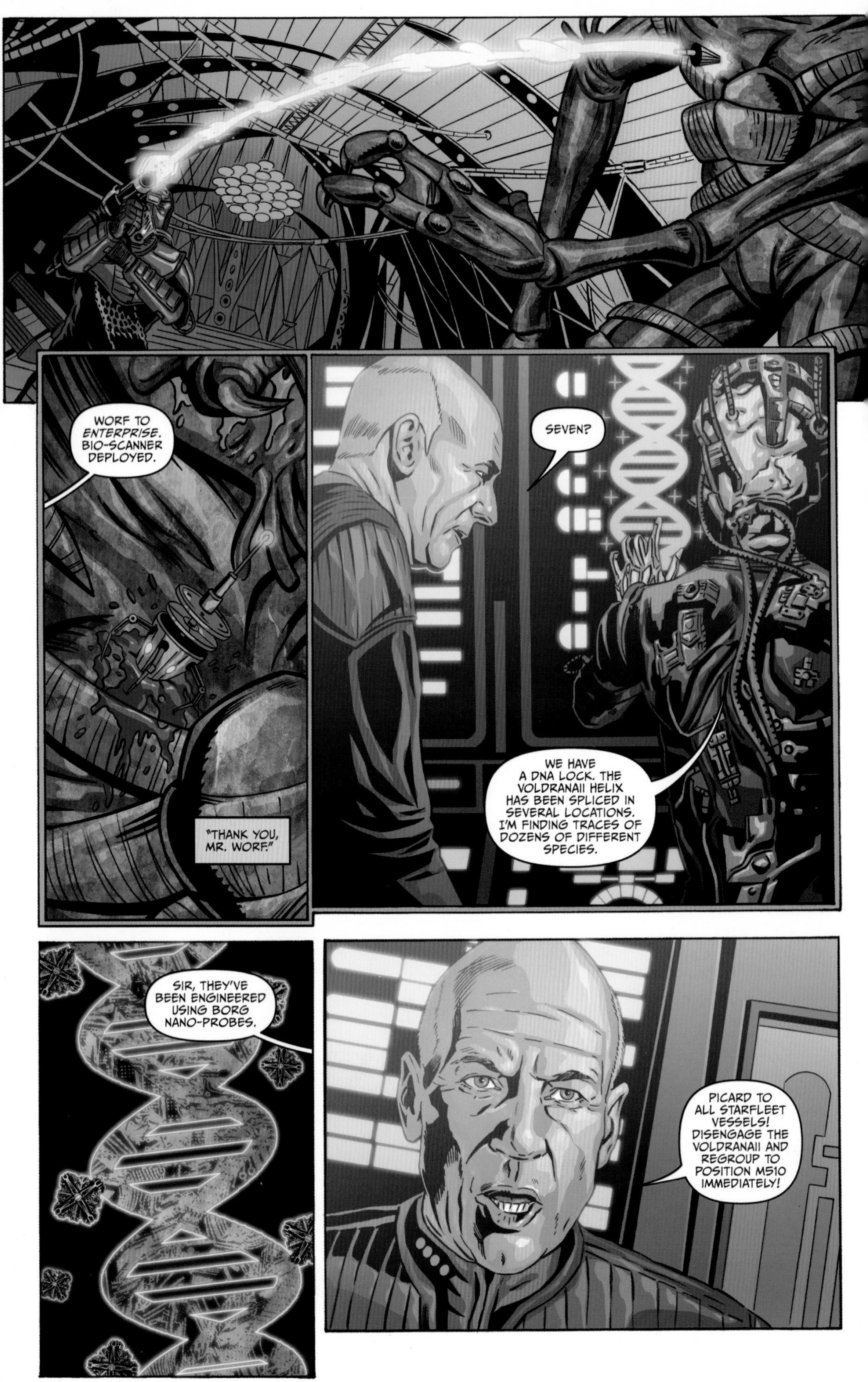
WORF TO ENTERPRISE. BIO-SCANNER DEPLOYED.
"THANK YOU, MR. WORF."
SEVEN?
WE HAVE A DNA LOCK. THE VOLDRANAII HELIX HAS BEEN SPLICED IN SEVERAL LOCATIONS. I'M FINDING TRACES OF DOZENS OF DIFFERENT SPECIES.
SIR, THEY'VE BEEN ENGINEERED USING BORG NANO-PROBES.
PICARD TO ALL STARFLEET VESSELS! DISENGAGE THE VOLDRANAII AND REGROUP TO POSITION M510 IMMEDIATELY!

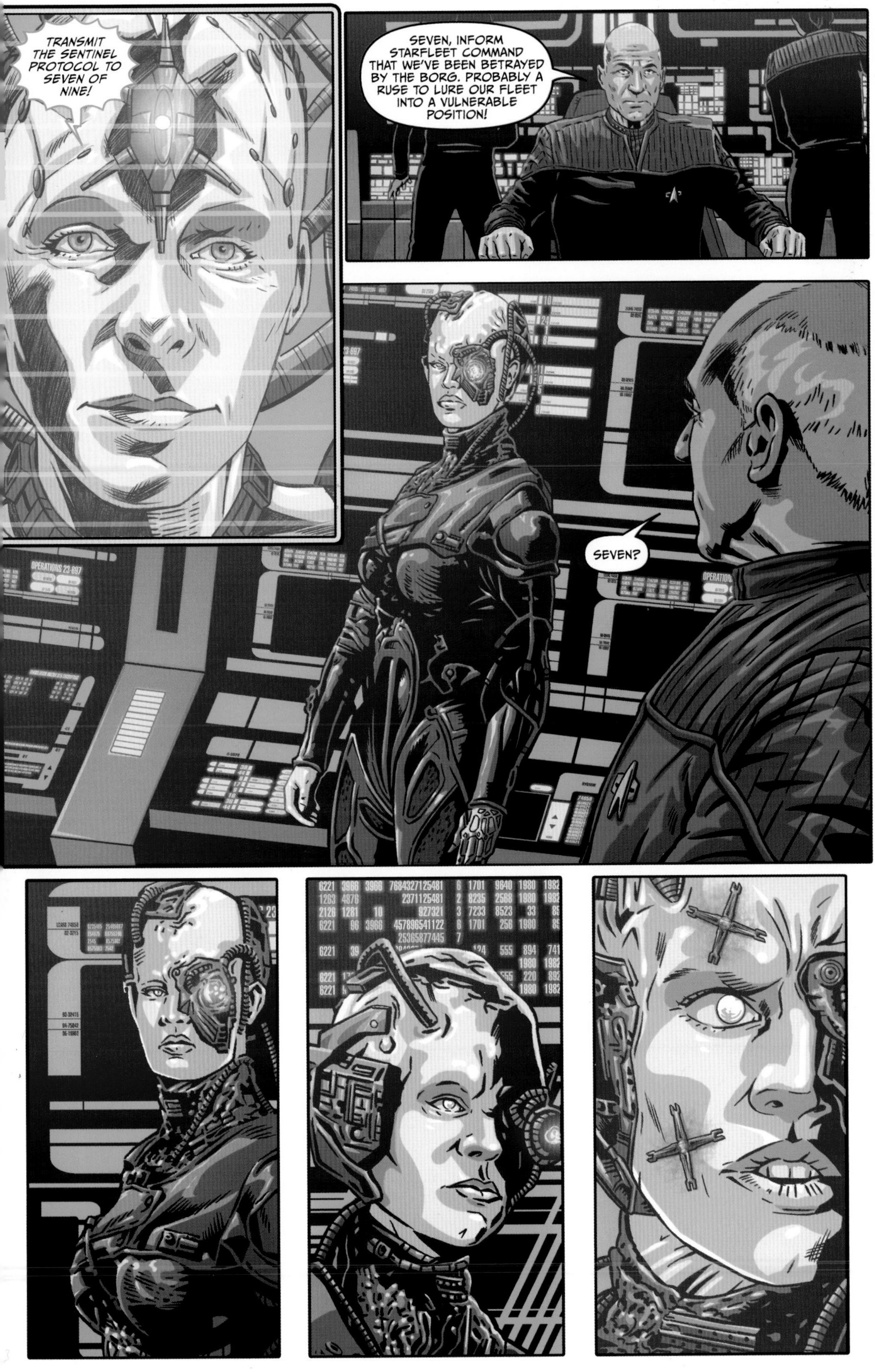
TRANSMIT THE SENTINEL PROTOCOL TO SEVEN OF NINE!
SEVEN, INFORM STARFLEET COMMAND THAT WE'VE BEEN BETRAYED BY THE BORG. PROBABLY A RUSE TO LURE OUR FLEET INTO A VULNERABLE POSITION!
SEVEN?

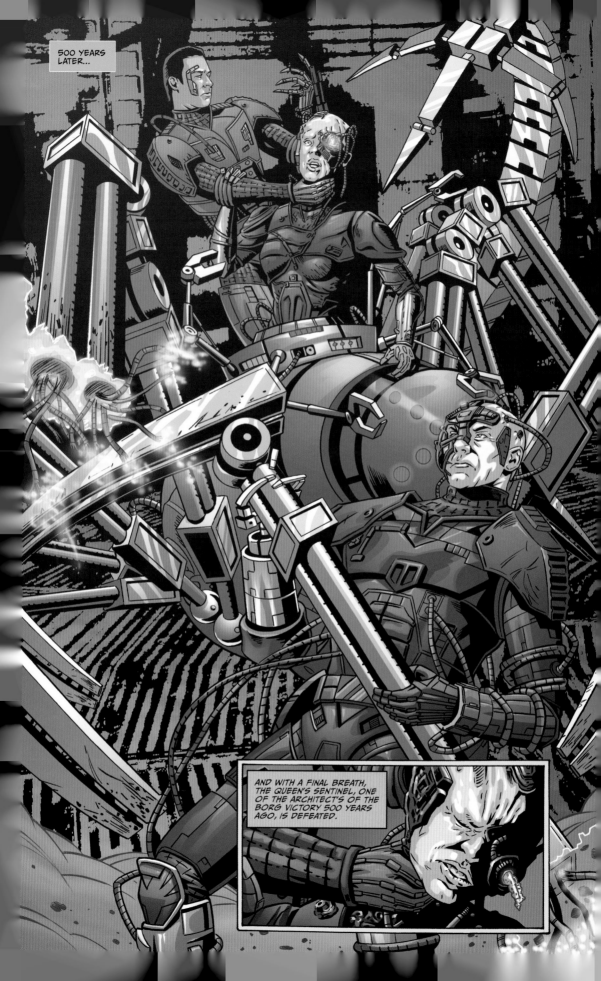

500 YEARS
LATER...

AND WITH A FINAL BREATH,
THE QUEEN'S SENTINEL, ONE
OF THE ARCHITECT'S OF THE
BORG VICTORY 500 YEARS
AGO, IS DEFEATED.

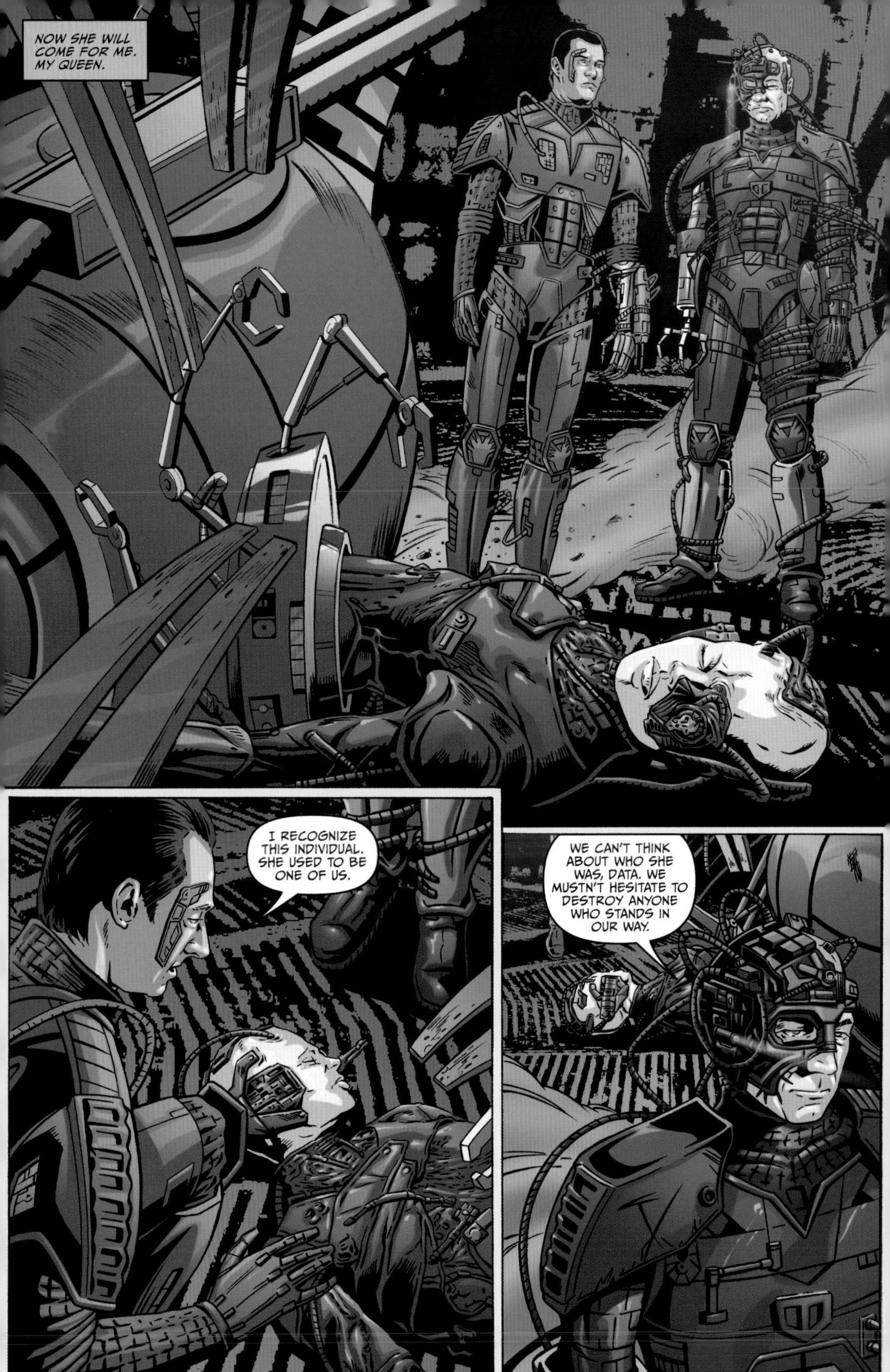
NOW SHE WILL COME FOR ME. MY QUEEN.
I RECOGNIZE THIS INDIVIDUAL. SHE USED TO BE ONE OF US.
WE CAN'T THINK ABOUT WHO SHE WAS, DATA. WE MUSTN'T HESITATE TO DESTROY ANYONE WHO STANDS IN OUR WAY.

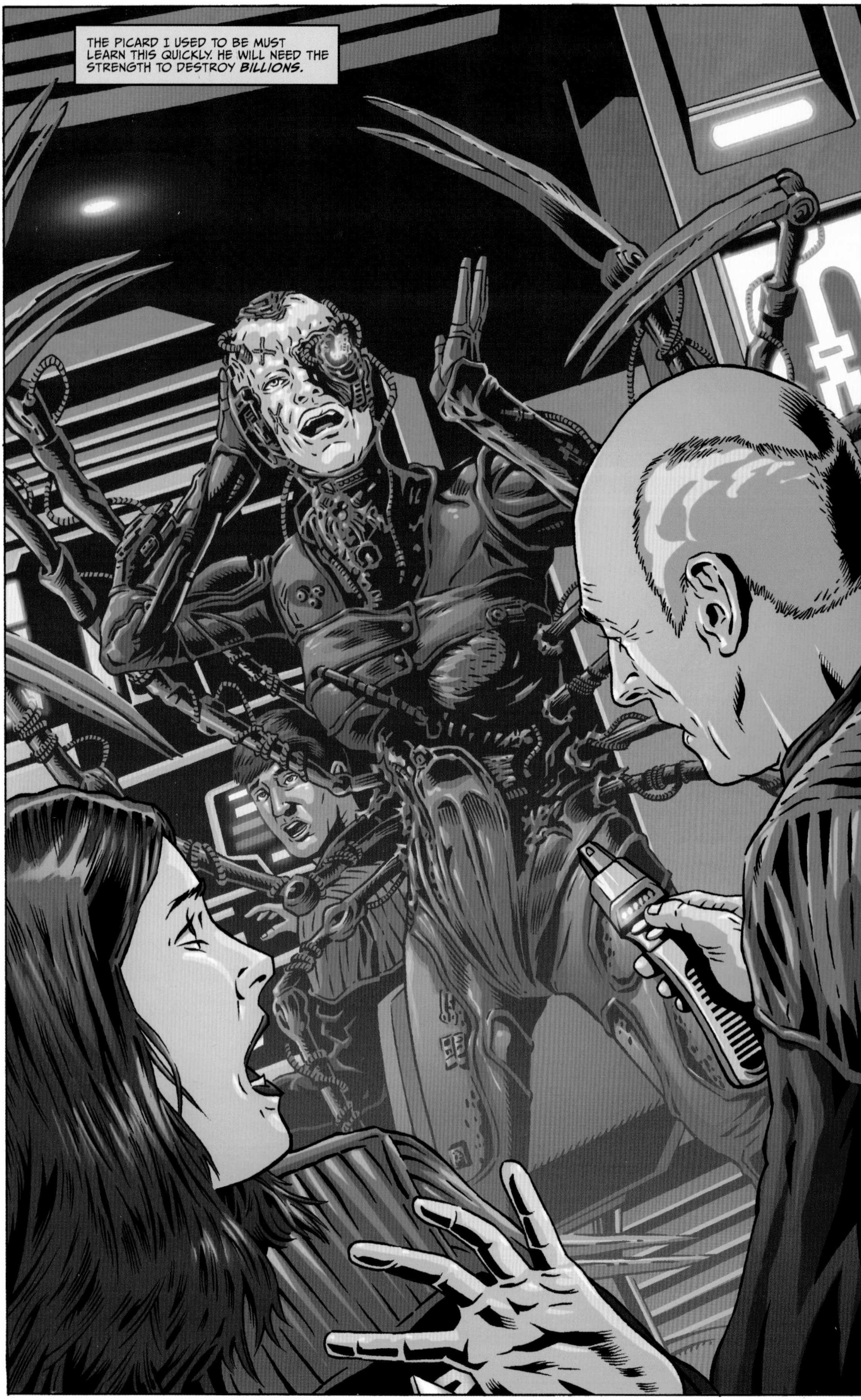
THE PICARD I USED TO BE MUST LEARN THIS QUICKLY. HE WILL NEED THE STRENGTH TO DESTROY *BILLIONS.*

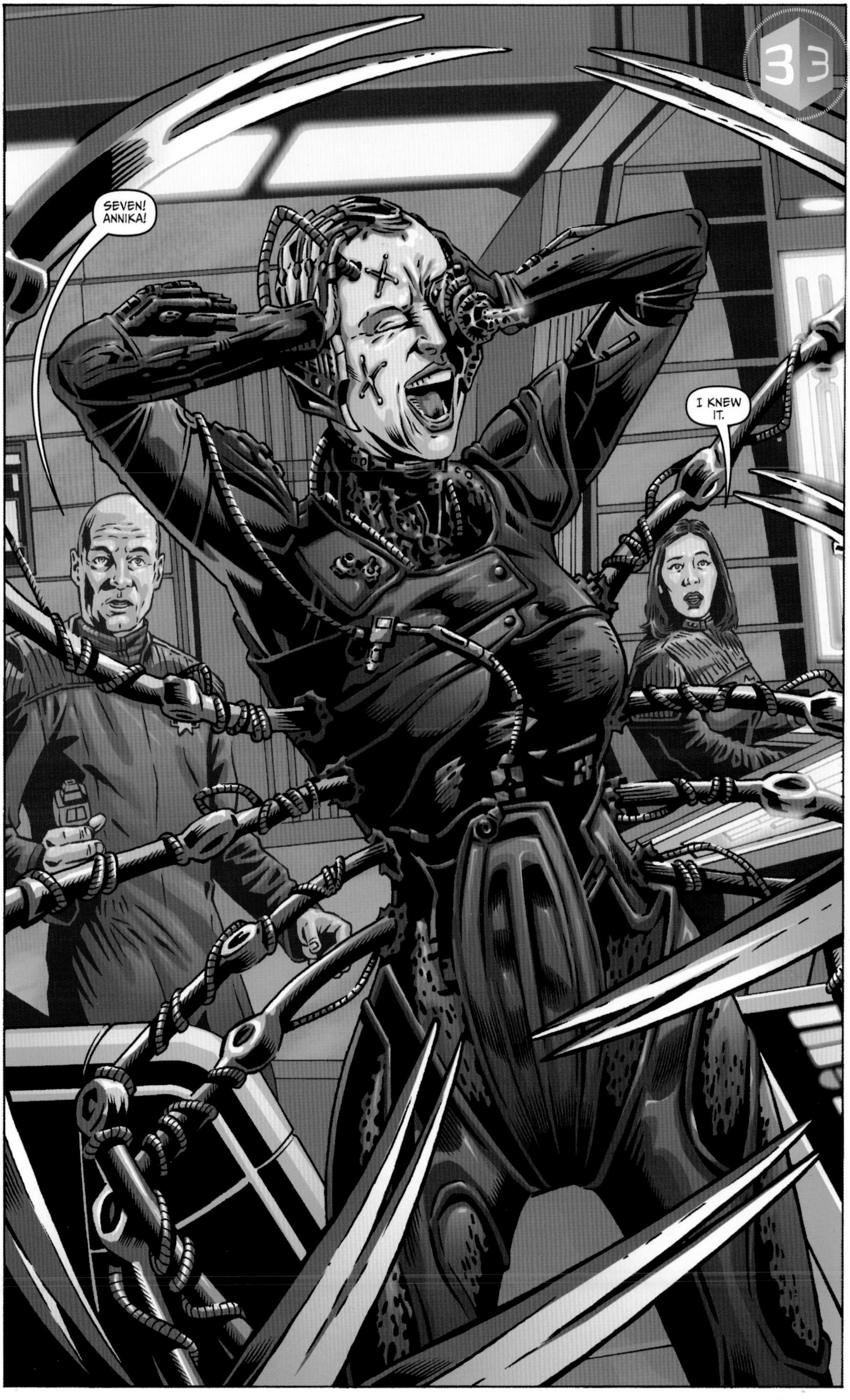
33
SEVEN! ANNIKA!
I KNEW IT.

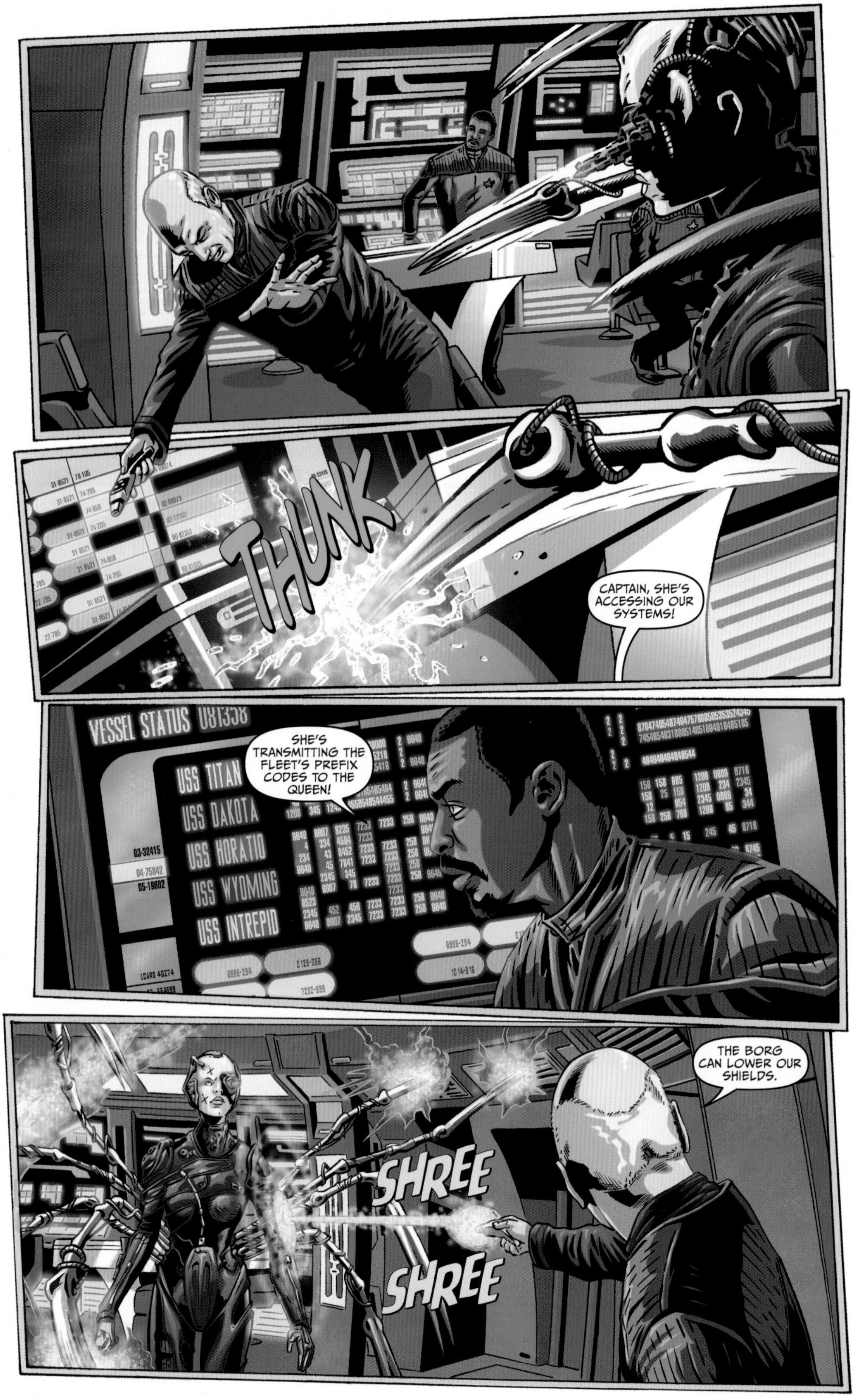
THUNK
CAPTAIN, SHE'S ACCESSING OUR SYSTEMS!
VESSEL STATUS 081358
USS TITAN
USS DAKOTA
USS HORATIO
USS WYOMING
USS INTREPID
SHE'S TRANSMITTING THE FLEET'S PREFIX CODES TO THE QUEEN!
THE BORG CAN LOWER OUR SHIELDS.
SHREE
SHREE

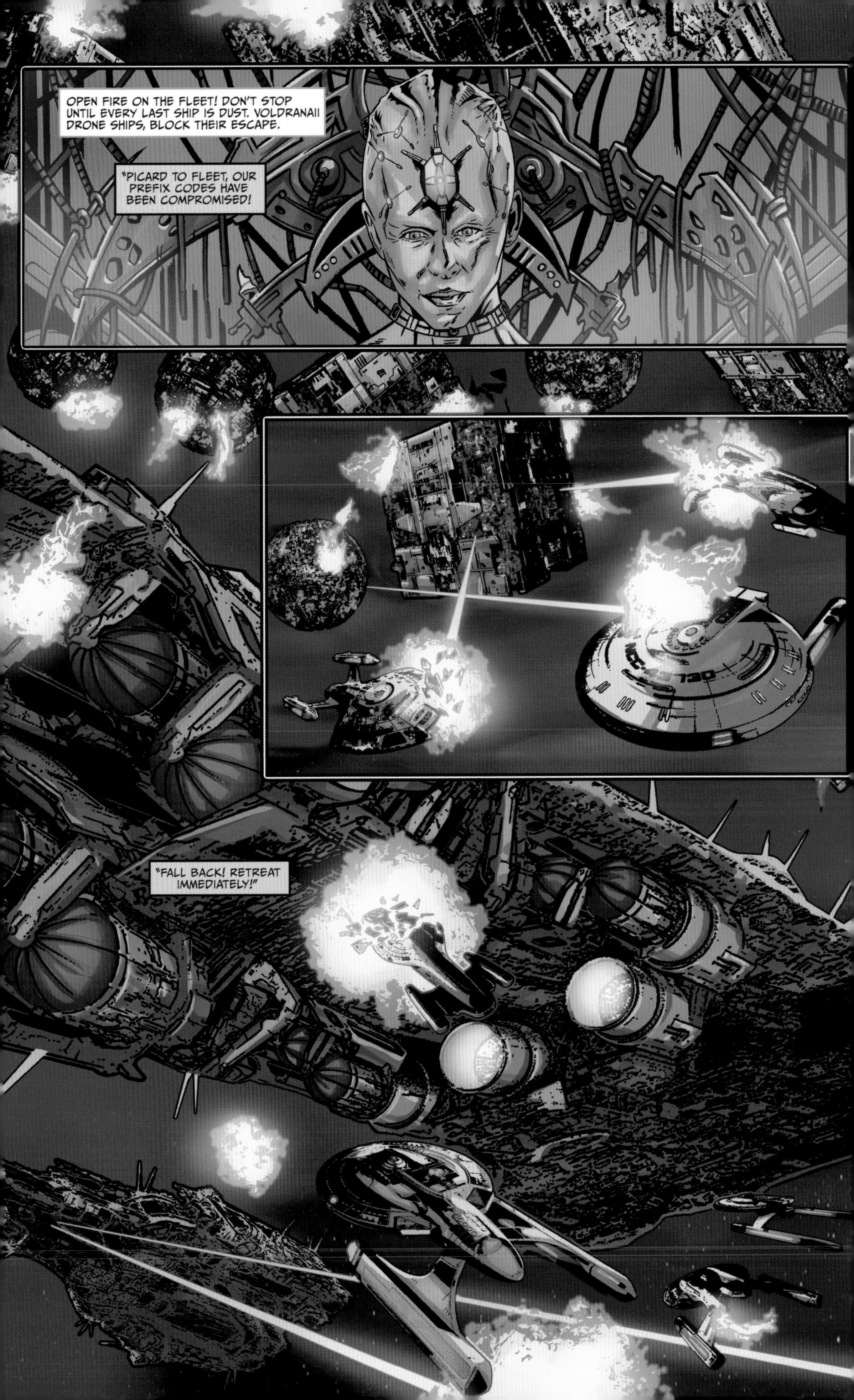
OPEN FIRE ON THE FLEET! DON'T STOP UNTIL EVERY LAST SHIP IS DUST. VOLDRANAII DRONE SHIPS, BLOCK THEIR ESCAPE.
"PICARD TO FLEET, OUR PREFIX CODES HAVE BEEN COMPROMISED!
NCC-43730
"FALL BACK! RETREAT IMMEDIATELY!"

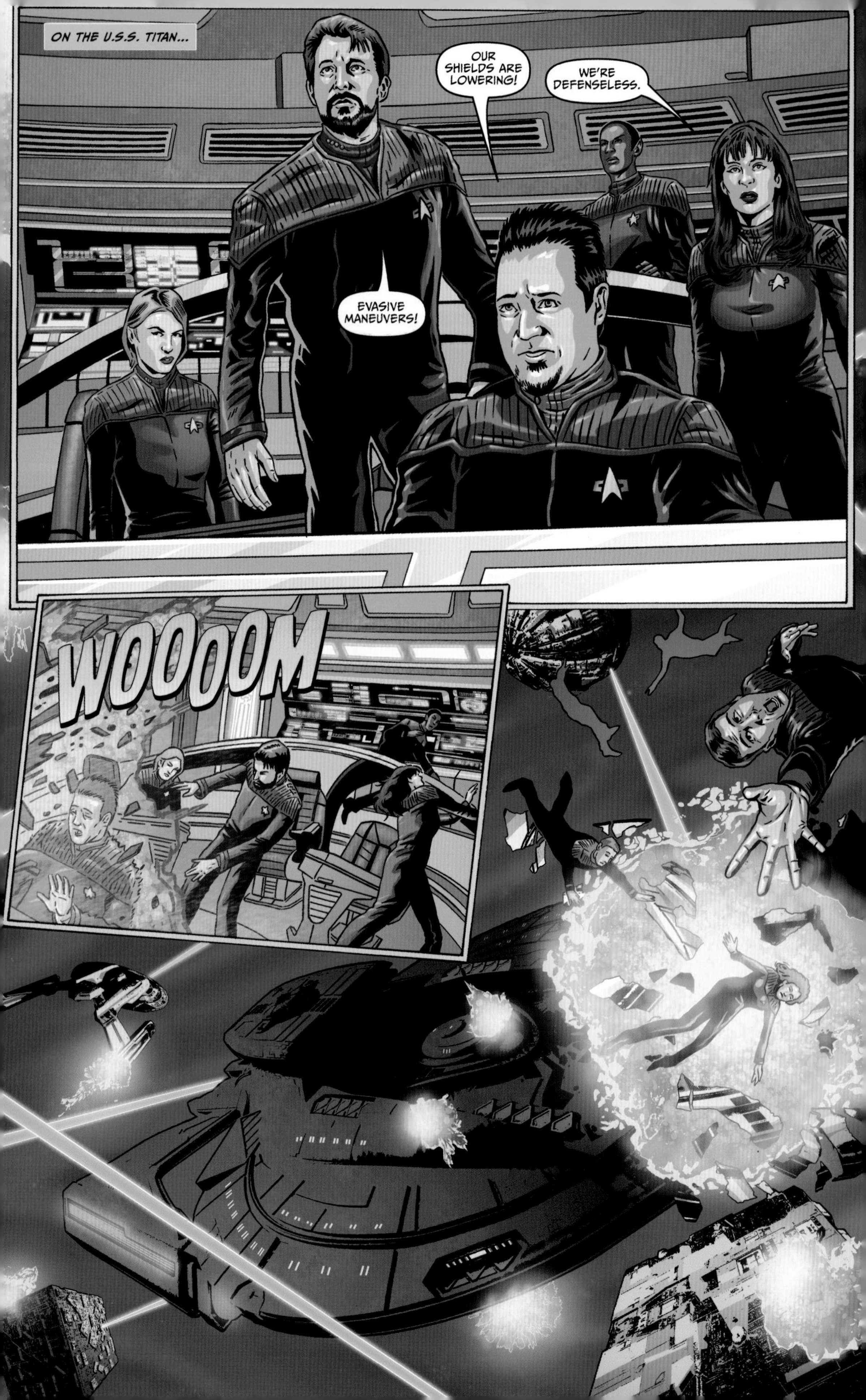
ON THE U.S.S. TITAN...
OUR SHIELDS ARE LOWERING!
WE'RE DEFENSELESS.
EVASIVE MANEUVERS!
WOOOOM

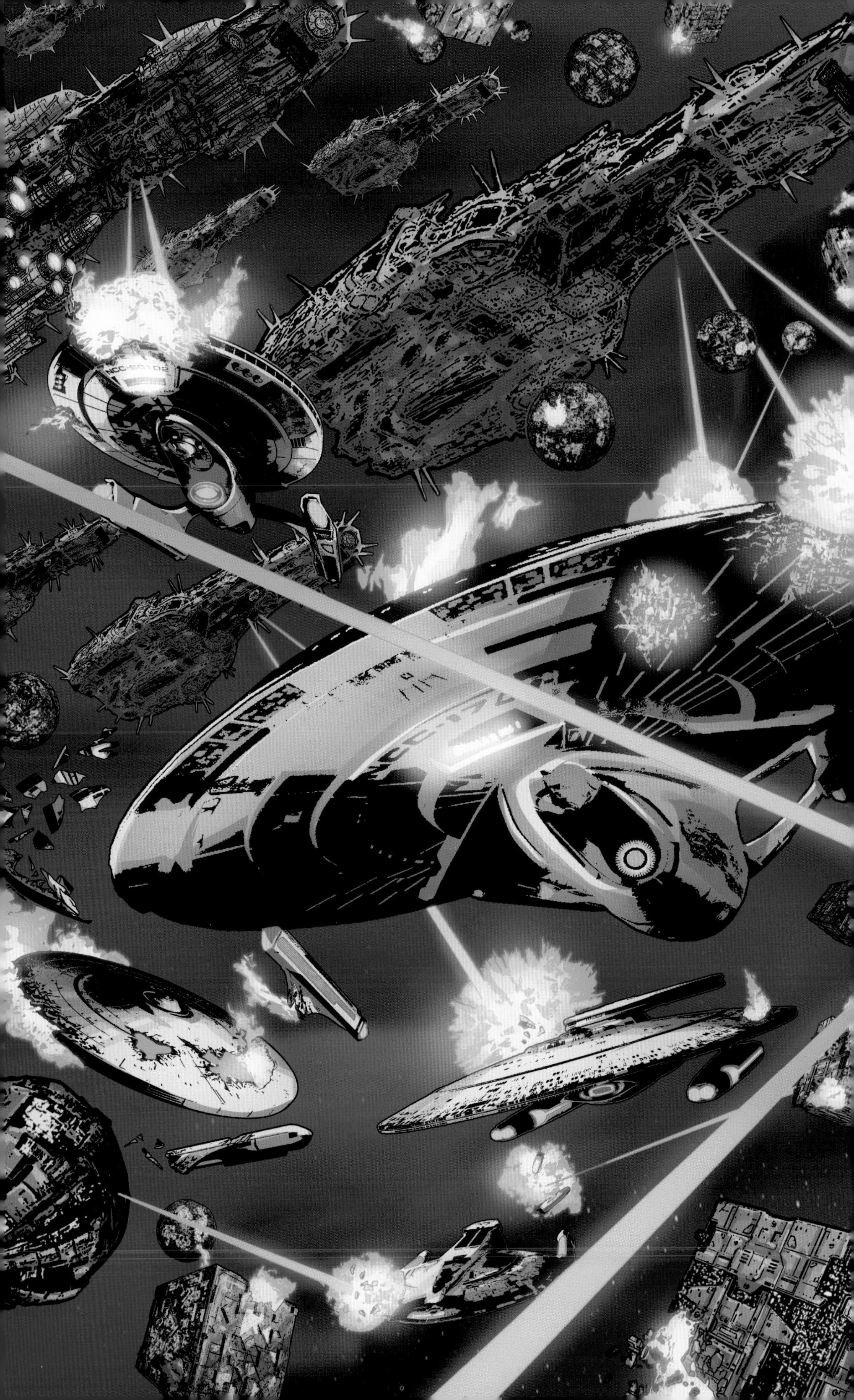

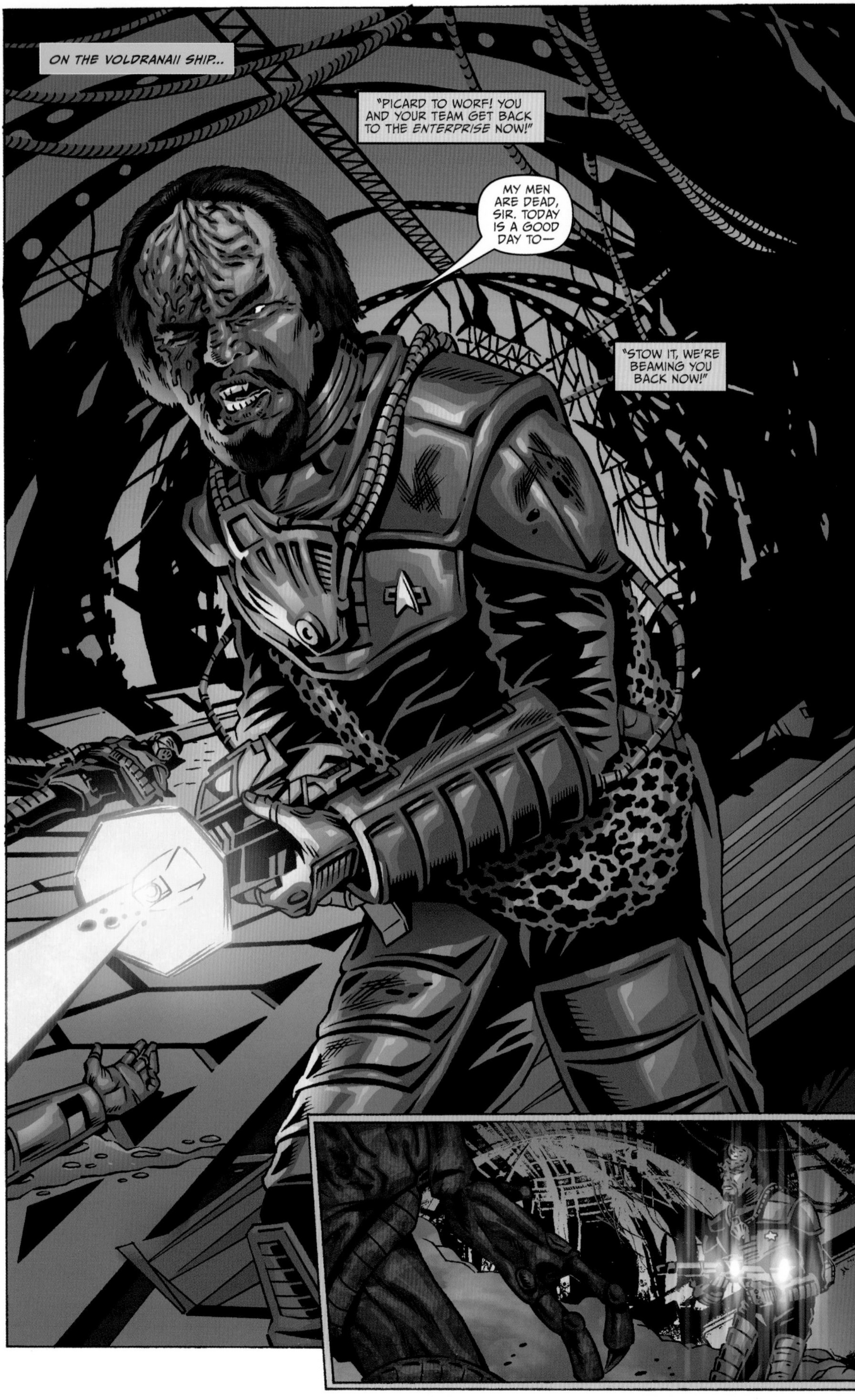
ON THE VOLDRANAII SHIP...
"PICARD TO WORF! YOU AND YOUR TEAM GET BACK TO THE ENTERPRISE NOW!"
MY MEN ARE DEAD, SIR. TODAY IS A GOOD DAY TO—
"STOW IT, WE'RE BEAMING YOU BACK NOW!"

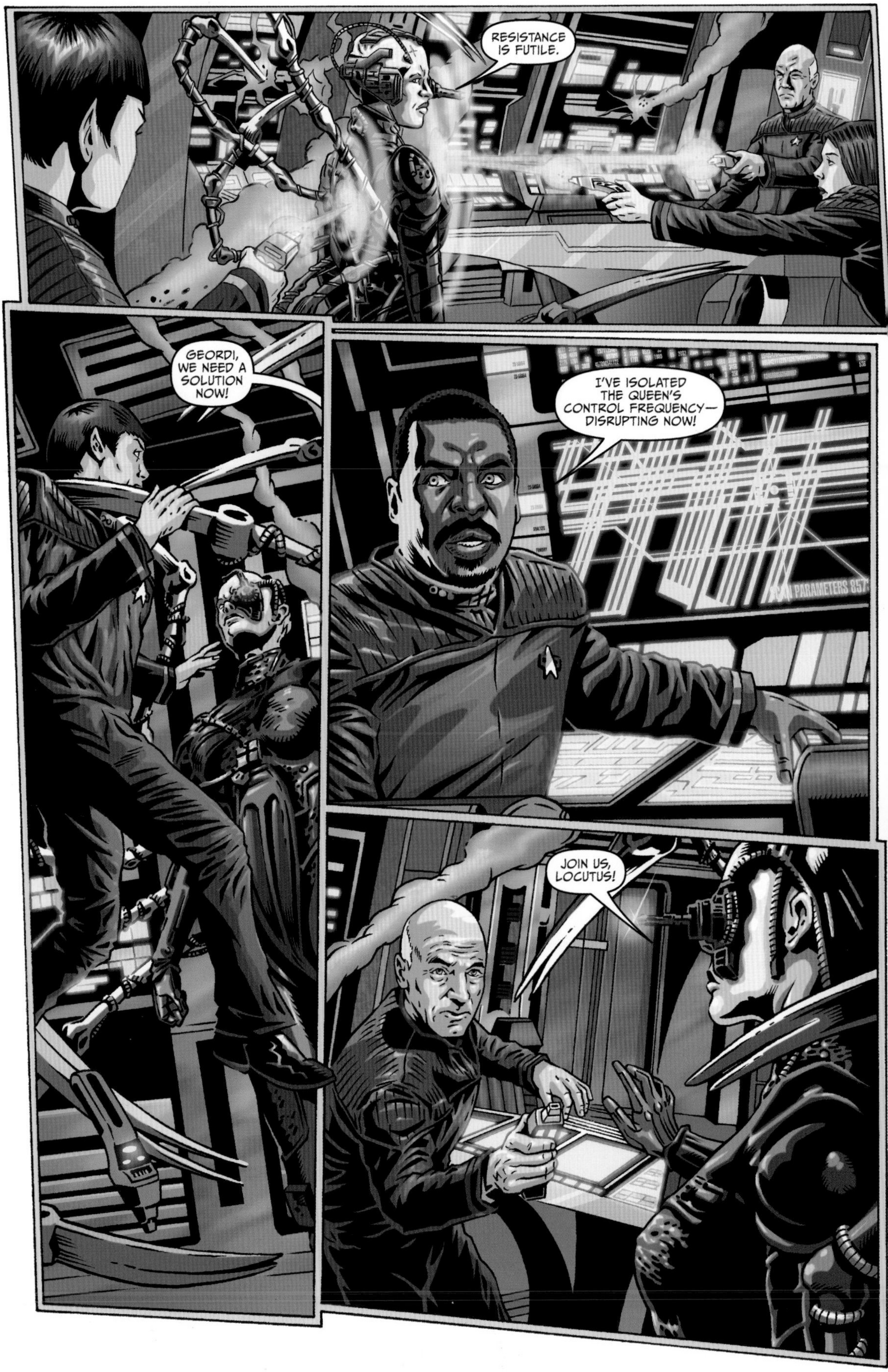
RESISTANCE IS FUTILE.
GEORDI, WE NEED A SOLUTION NOW!
I'VE ISOLATED THE QUEEN'S CONTROL FREQUENCY— DISRUPTING NOW!
SCAN PARAMETERS 857
JOIN US, LOCUTUS!

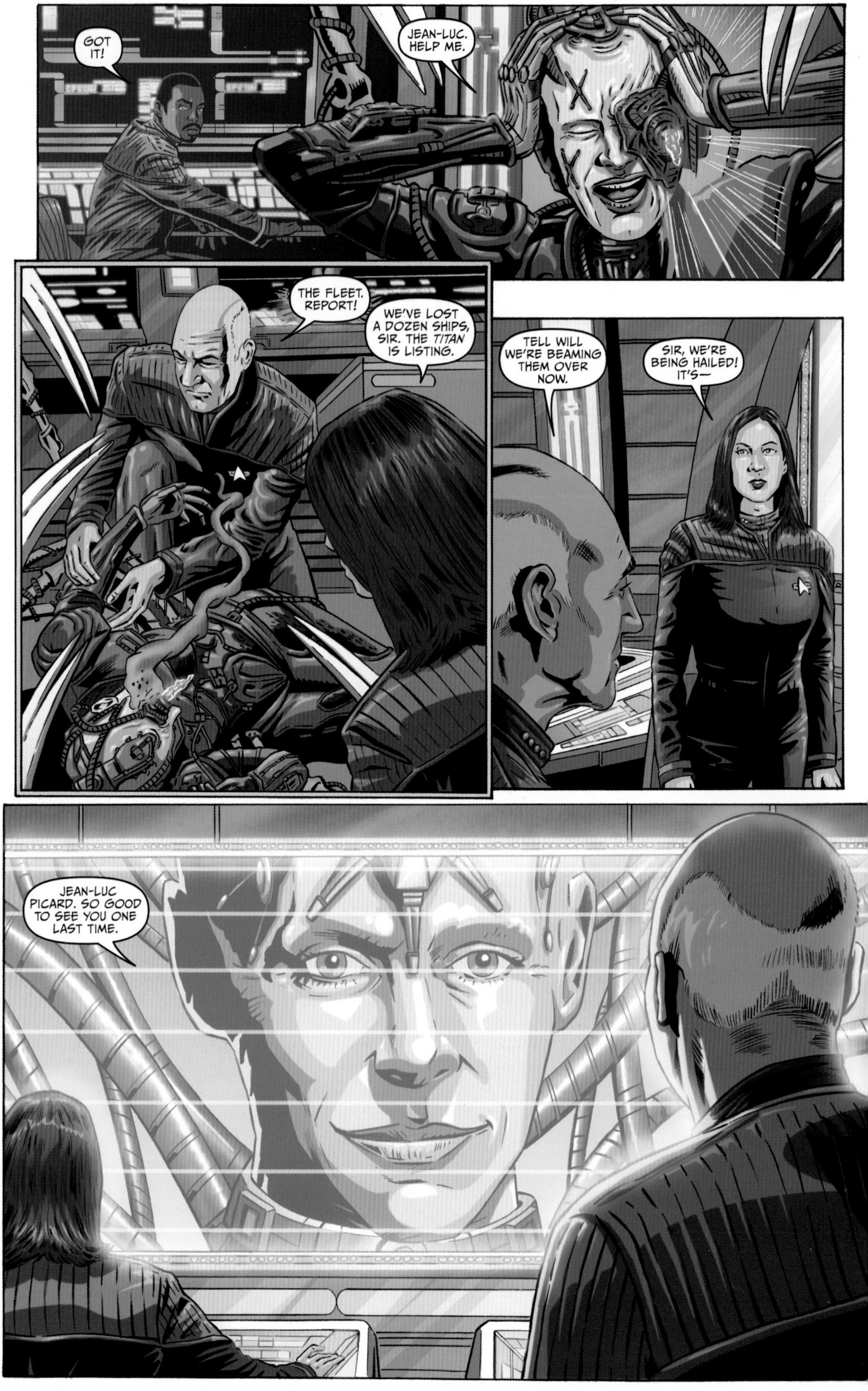
GOT IT!
JEAN-LUC. HELP ME.
THE FLEET. REPORT!
WE'VE LOST A DOZEN SHIPS, SIR. THE *TITAN* IS LISTING.
TELL WILL WE'RE BEAMING THEM OVER NOW.
SIR, WE'RE BEING HAILED! IT'S—
JEAN-LUC PICARD. SO GOOD TO SEE YOU ONE LAST TIME.

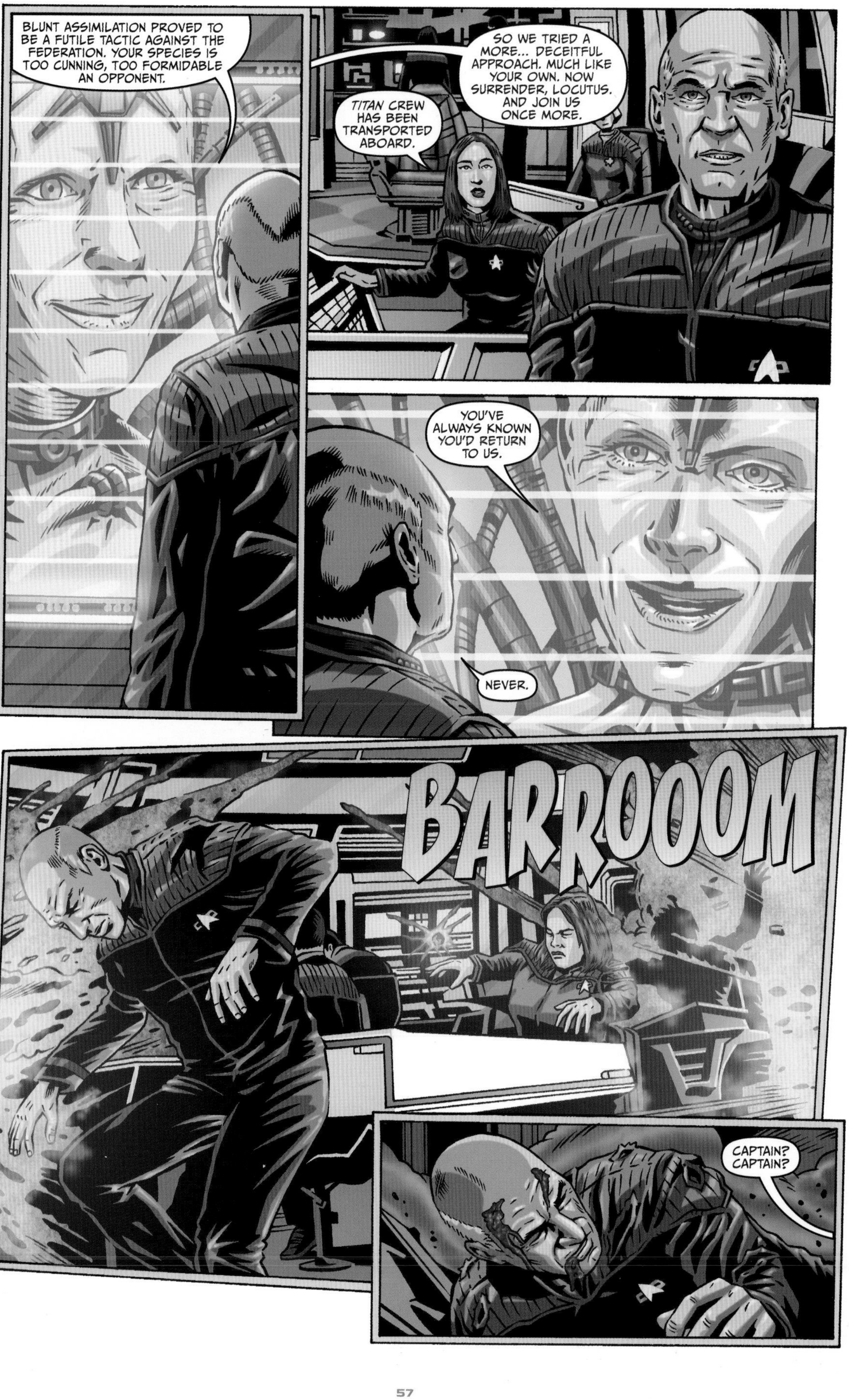
BLUNT ASSIMILATION PROVED TO BE A FUTILE TACTIC AGAINST THE FEDERATION. YOUR SPECIES IS TOO CUNNING, TOO FORMIDABLE AN OPPONENT.
SO WE TRIED A MORE... DECEITFUL APPROACH. MUCH LIKE YOUR OWN. NOW SURRENDER, LOCUTUS. AND JOIN US ONCE MORE.
TITAN CREW HAS BEEN TRANSPORTED ABOARD.
YOU'VE ALWAYS KNOWN YOU'D RETURN TO US.
NEVER.
BARROOOM
CAPTAIN? CAPTAIN?

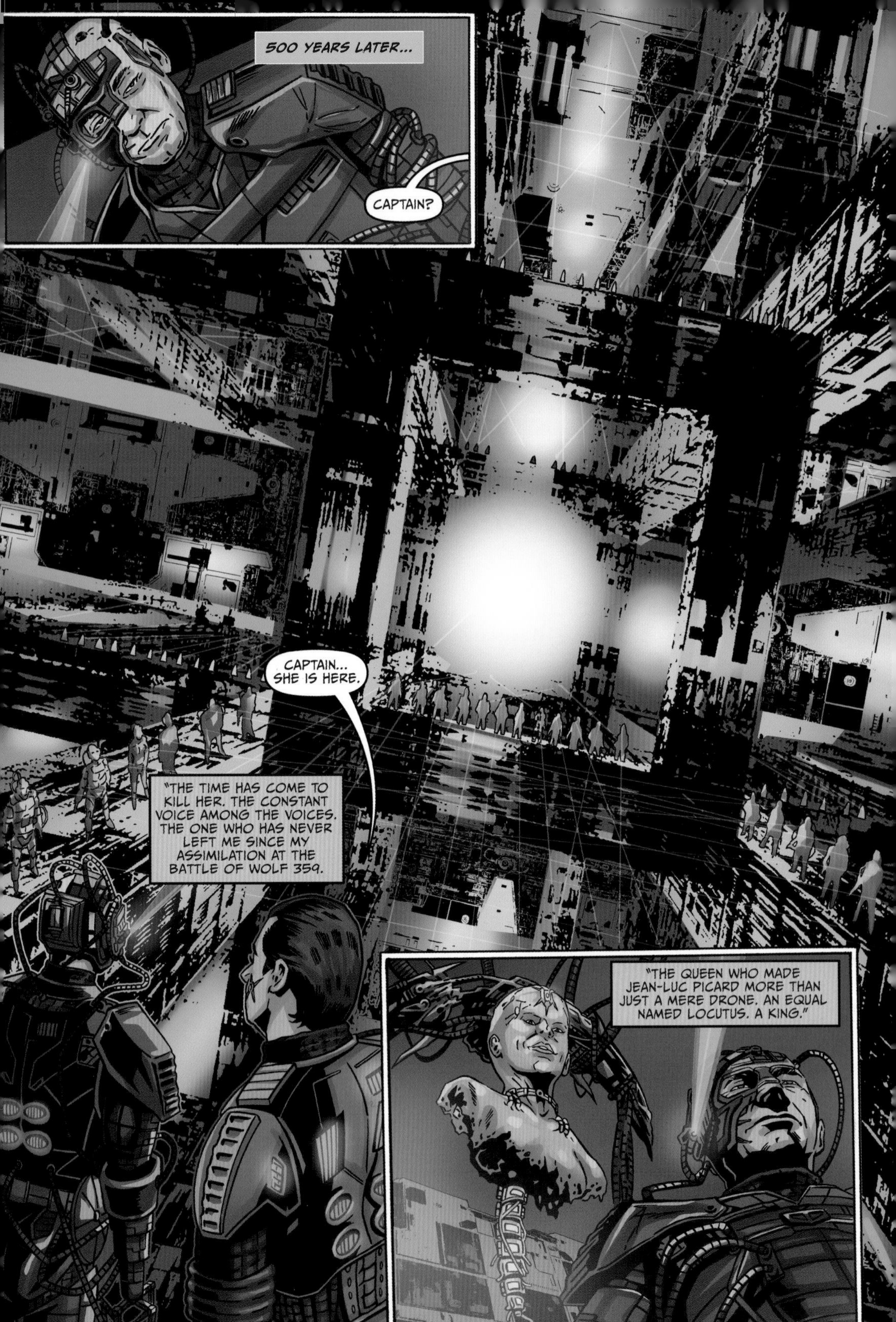
500 YEARS LATER...
CAPTAIN?
CAPTAIN... SHE IS HERE.
"THE TIME HAS COME TO KILL HER. THE CONSTANT VOICE AMONG THE VOICES. THE ONE WHO HAS NEVER LEFT ME SINCE MY ASSIMILATION AT THE BATTLE OF WOLF 359.
"THE QUEEN WHO MADE JEAN-LUC PICARD MORE THAN JUST A MERE DRONE. AN EQUAL NAMED LOCUTUS. A KING."

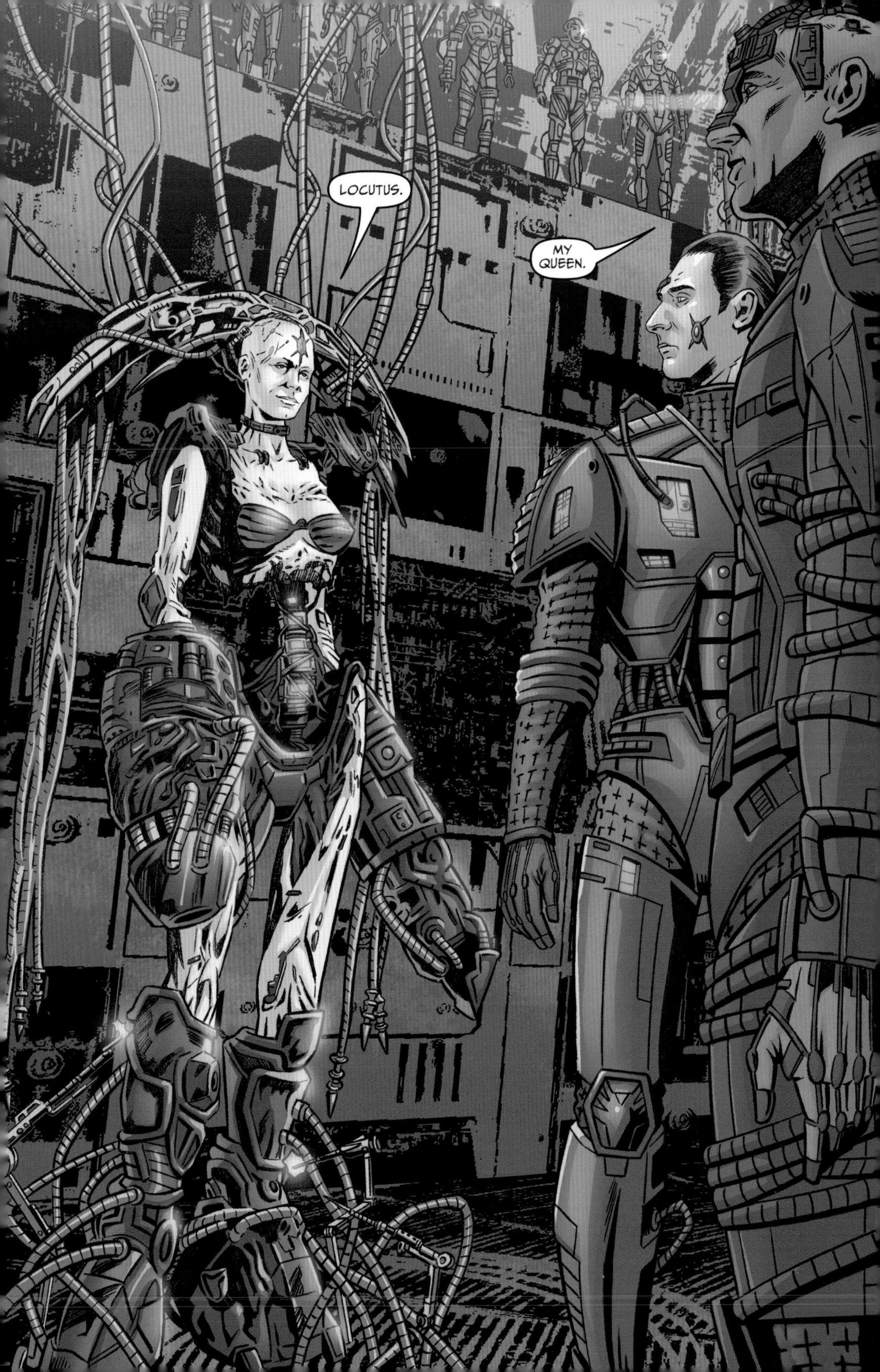
LOCUTUS.
MY QUEEN.

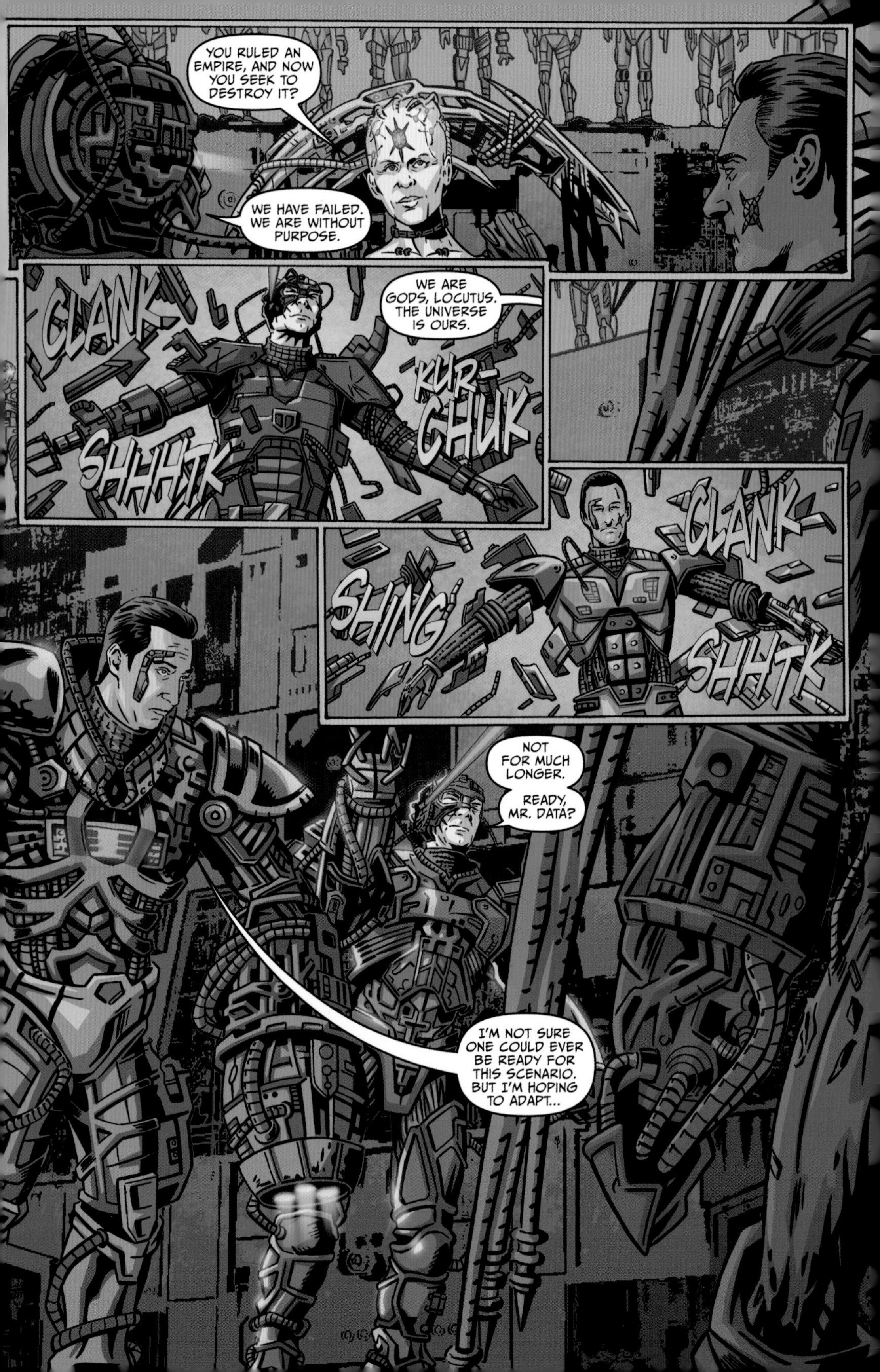
YOU RULED AN EMPIRE, AND NOW YOU SEEK TO DESTROY IT?
WE HAVE FAILED. WE ARE WITHOUT PURPOSE.
CLANK
WE ARE GODS, LOCUTUS. THE UNIVERSE IS OURS.
KUR-CHUK
SHHHTK
CLANK
SHING
SHHTK
NOT FOR MUCH LONGER.
READY, MR. DATA?
I'M NOT SURE ONE COULD EVER BE READY FOR THIS SCENARIO. BUT I'M HOPING TO ADAPT...

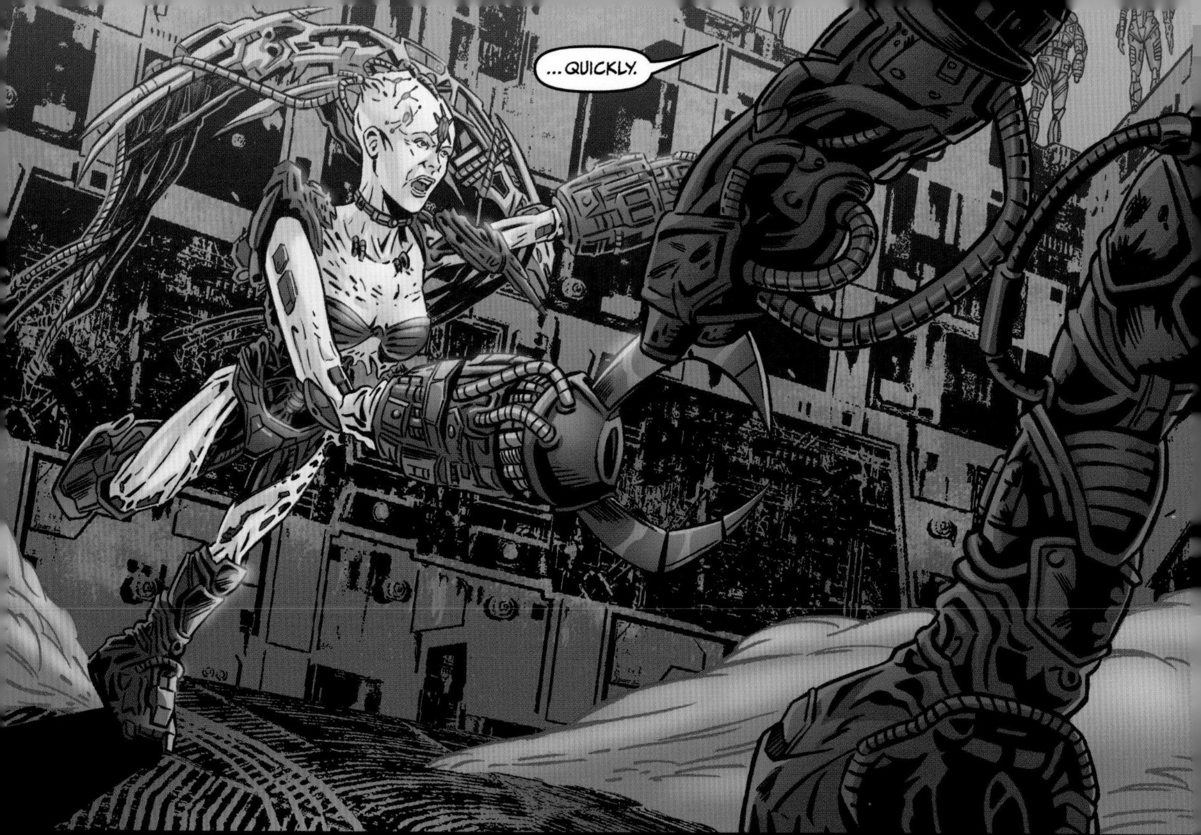
...QUICKLY.

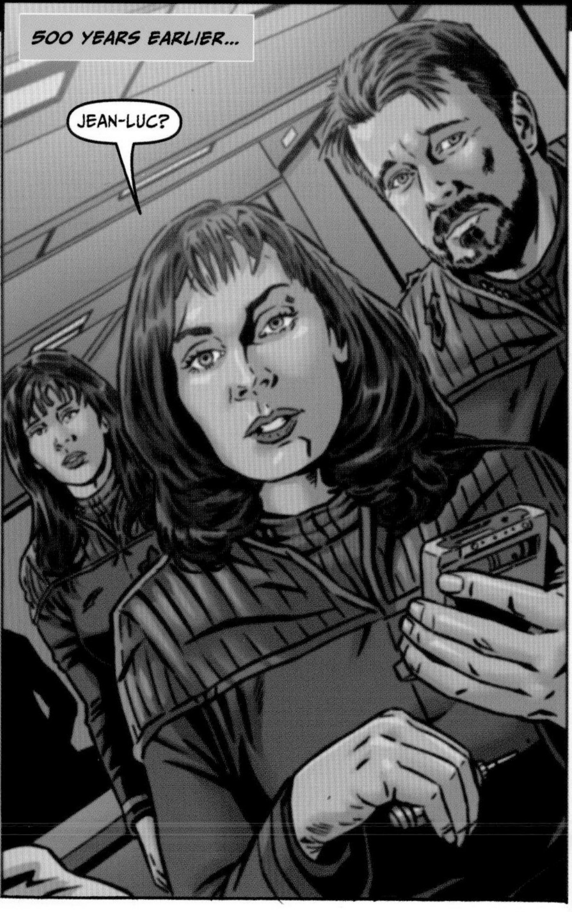
500 YEARS EARLIER...
JEAN-LUC?

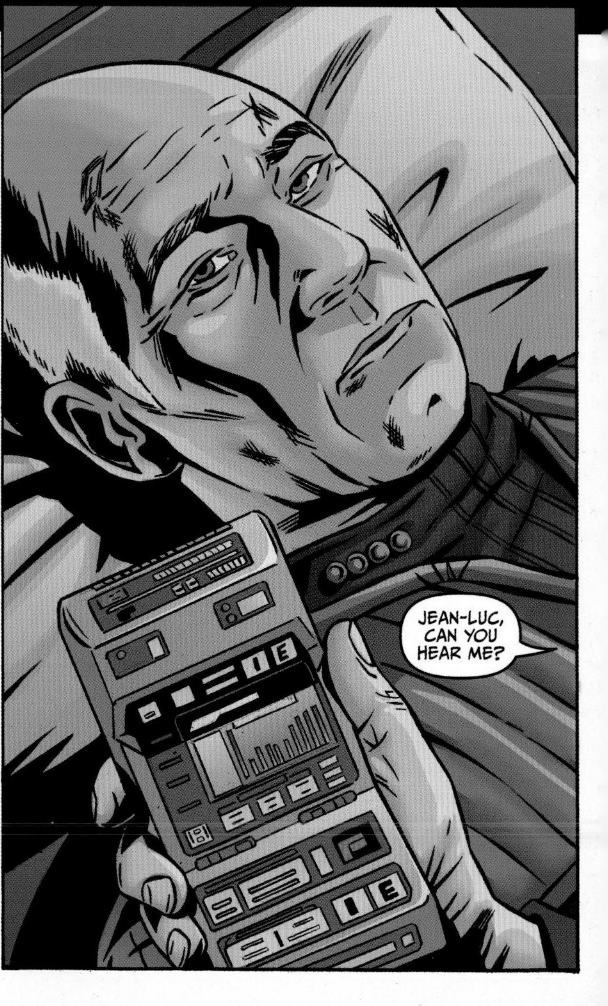
JEAN-LUC, CAN YOU HEAR ME?

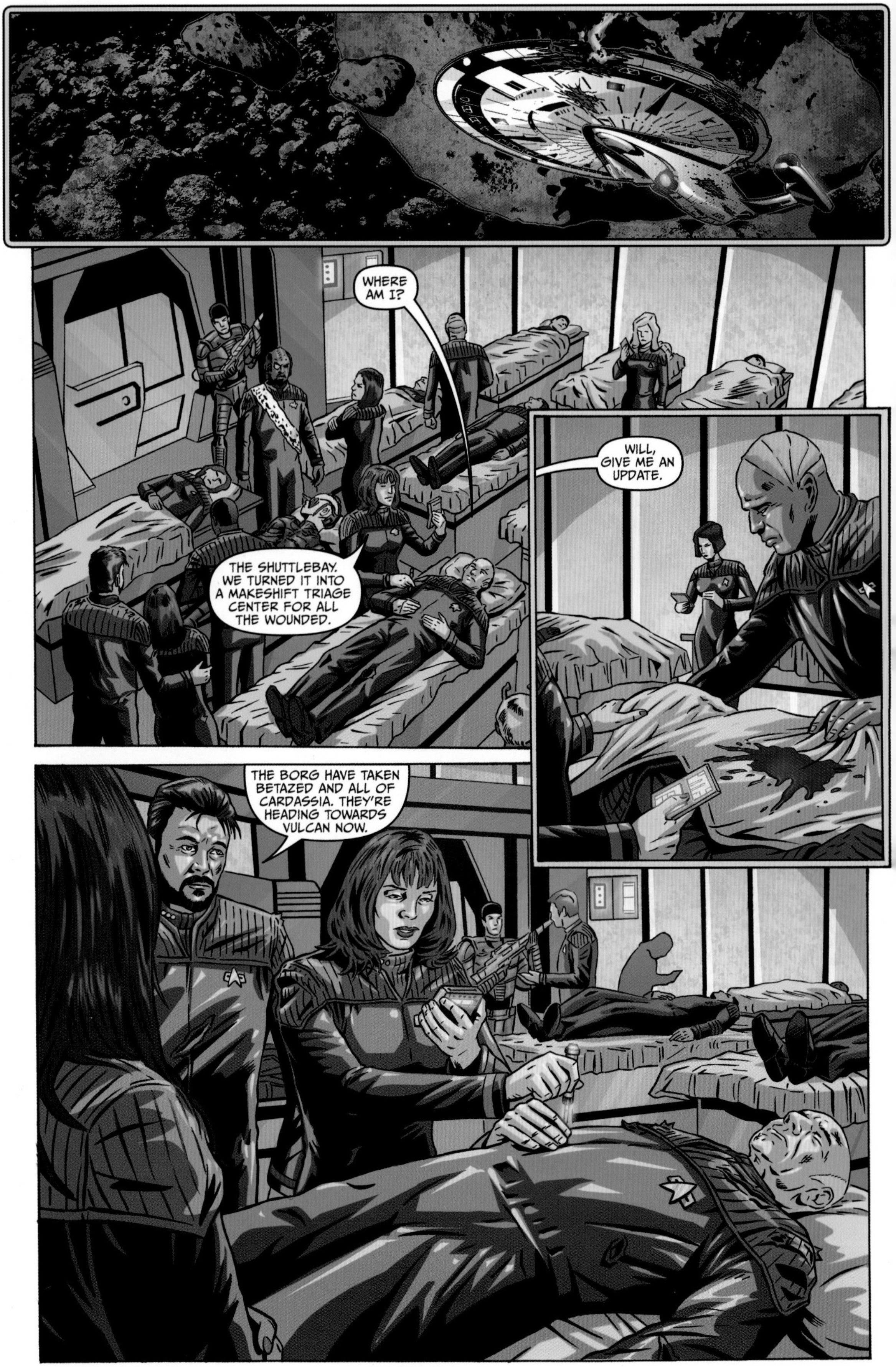
WHERE AM I?
THE SHUTTLEBAY. WE TURNED IT INTO A MAKESHIFT TRIAGE CENTER FOR ALL THE WOUNDED.
WILL, GIVE ME AN UPDATE.
THE BORG HAVE TAKEN BETAZED AND ALL OF CARDASSIA. THEY'RE HEADING TOWARDS VULCAN NOW.

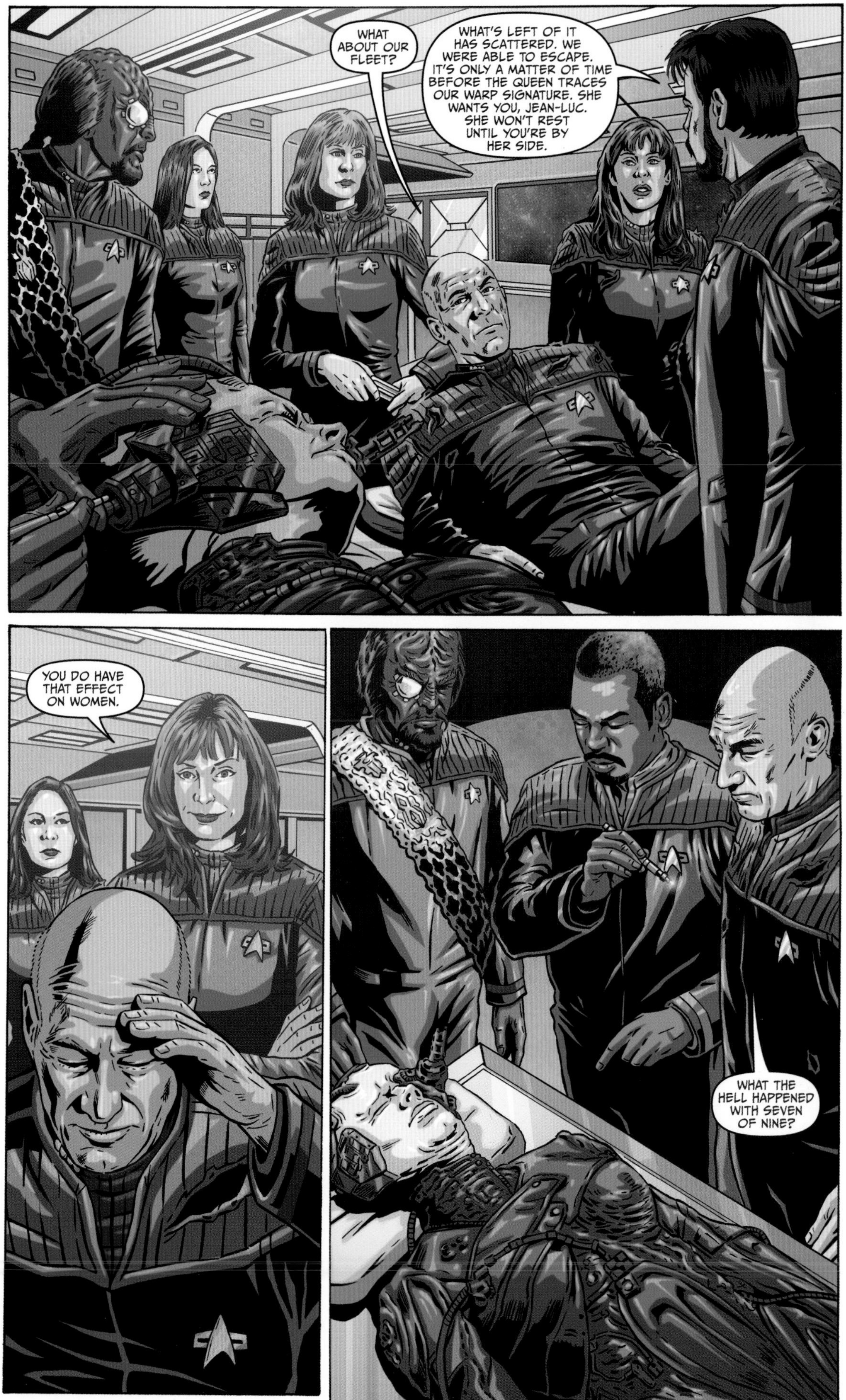
WHAT ABOUT OUR FLEET?
WHAT'S LEFT OF IT HAS SCATTERED. WE WERE ABLE TO ESCAPE. IT'S ONLY A MATTER OF TIME BEFORE THE QUEEN TRACES OUR WARP SIGNATURE. SHE WANTS YOU, JEAN-LUC. SHE WON'T REST UNTIL YOU'RE BY HER SIDE.
YOU DO HAVE THAT EFFECT ON WOMEN.
WHAT THE HELL HAPPENED WITH SEVEN OF NINE?

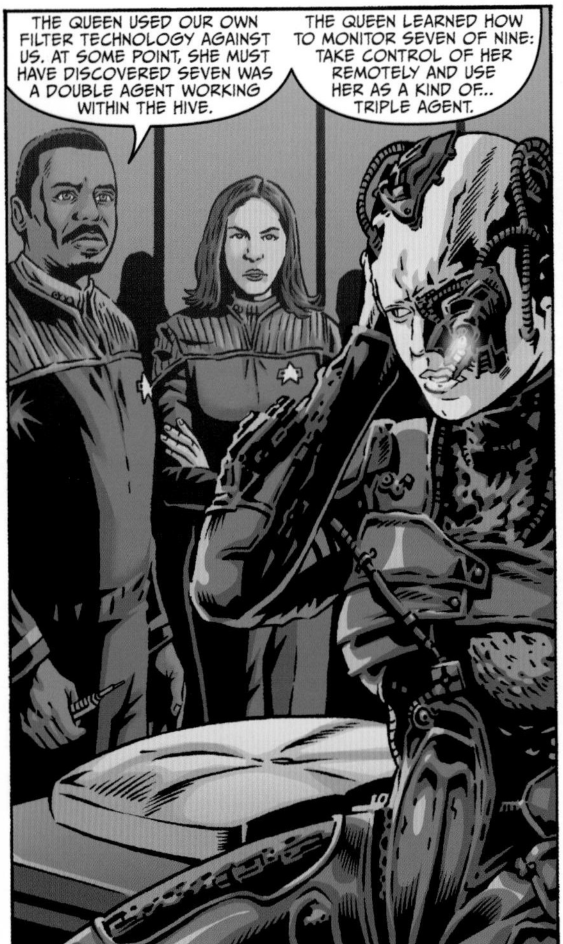
THE QUEEN USED OUR OWN FILTER TECHNOLOGY AGAINST US. AT SOME POINT, SHE MUST HAVE DISCOVERED SEVEN WAS A DOUBLE AGENT WORKING WITHIN THE HIVE.
THE QUEEN LEARNED HOW TO MONITOR SEVEN OF NINE: TAKE CONTROL OF HER REMOTELY AND USE HER AS A KIND OF... TRIPLE AGENT.

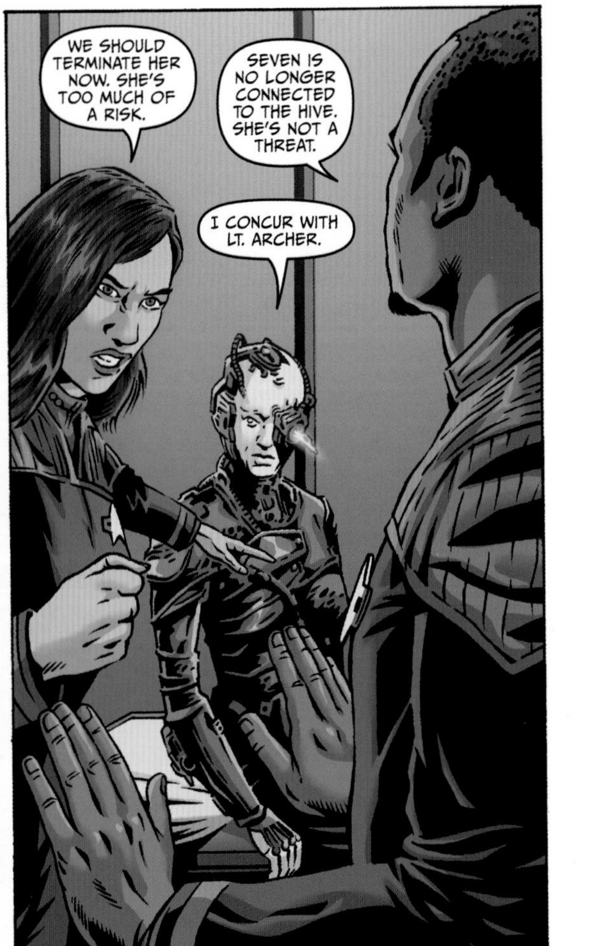
WE SHOULD TERMINATE HER NOW. SHE'S TOO MUCH OF A RISK.
SEVEN IS NO LONGER CONNECTED TO THE HIVE. SHE'S NOT A THREAT.
I CONCUR WITH LT. ARCHER.

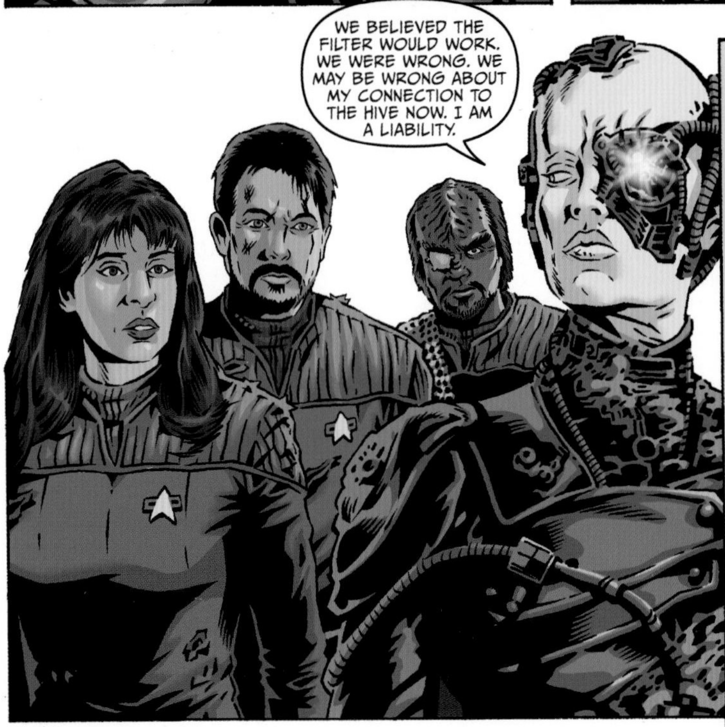
WE BELIEVED THE FILTER WOULD WORK. WE WERE WRONG. WE MAY BE WRONG ABOUT MY CONNECTION TO THE HIVE NOW. I AM A LIABILITY.

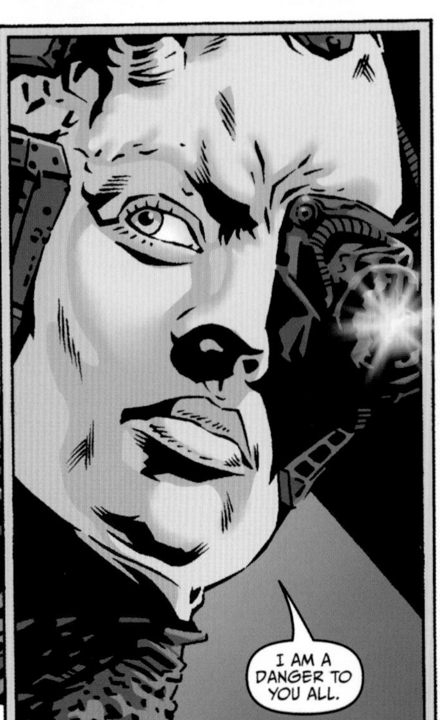
I AM A DANGER TO YOU ALL.

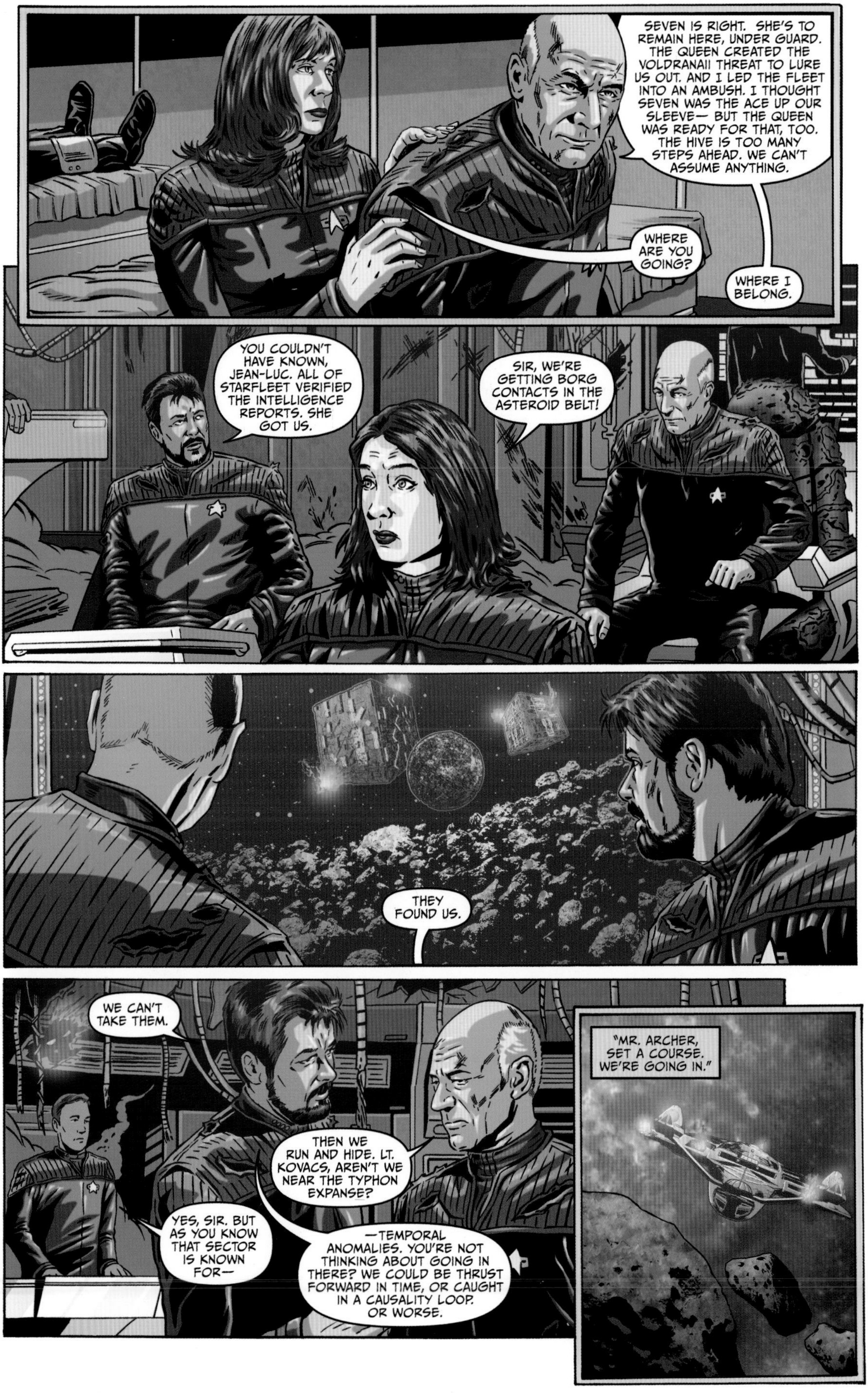
SEVEN IS RIGHT. SHE'S TO REMAIN HERE, UNDER GUARD. THE QUEEN CREATED THE VOLDRANAII THREAT TO LURE US OUT. AND I LED THE FLEET INTO AN AMBUSH. I THOUGHT SEVEN WAS THE ACE UP OUR SLEEVE— BUT THE QUEEN WAS READY FOR THAT, TOO. THE HIVE IS TOO MANY STEPS AHEAD. WE CAN'T ASSUME ANYTHING.
WHERE ARE YOU GOING?
WHERE I BELONG.
YOU COULDN'T HAVE KNOWN, JEAN-LUC. ALL OF STARFLEET VERIFIED THE INTELLIGENCE REPORTS. SHE GOT US.
SIR, WE'RE GETTING BORG CONTACTS IN THE ASTEROID BELT!
THEY FOUND US.
WE CAN'T TAKE THEM.
THEN WE RUN AND HIDE. LT. KOVACS, AREN'T WE NEAR THE TYPHON EXPANSE?
YES, SIR. BUT AS YOU KNOW THAT SECTOR IS KNOWN FOR—
—TEMPORAL ANOMALIES. YOU'RE NOT THINKING ABOUT GOING IN THERE? WE COULD BE THRUST FORWARD IN TIME, OR CAUGHT IN A CAUSALITY LOOP. OR WORSE.
"MR. ARCHER, SET A COURSE. WE'RE GOING IN."

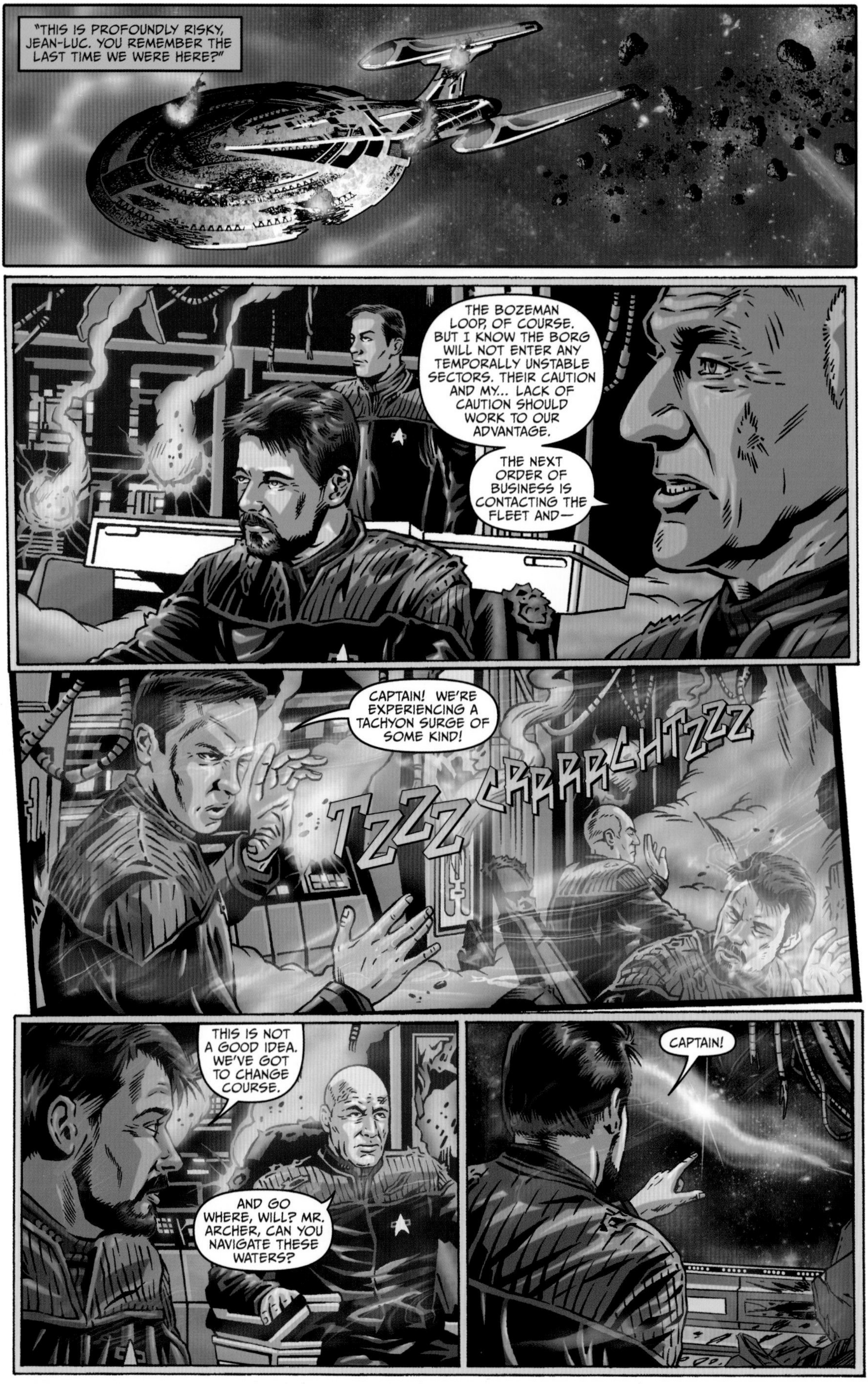
"THIS IS PROFOUNDLY RISKY, JEAN-LUC. YOU REMEMBER THE LAST TIME WE WERE HERE?"
THE BOZEMAN LOOP, OF COURSE. BUT I KNOW THE BORG WILL NOT ENTER ANY TEMPORALLY UNSTABLE SECTORS. THEIR CAUTION AND MY... LACK OF CAUTION SHOULD WORK TO OUR ADVANTAGE.
THE NEXT ORDER OF BUSINESS IS CONTACTING THE FLEET AND—
CAPTAIN! WE'RE EXPERIENCING A TACHYON SURGE OF SOME KIND!
TZZZ CRRRRCHTZZZ
THIS IS NOT A GOOD IDEA. WE'VE GOT TO CHANGE COURSE.
AND GO WHERE, WILL? MR. ARCHER, CAN YOU NAVIGATE THESE WATERS?
CAPTAIN!

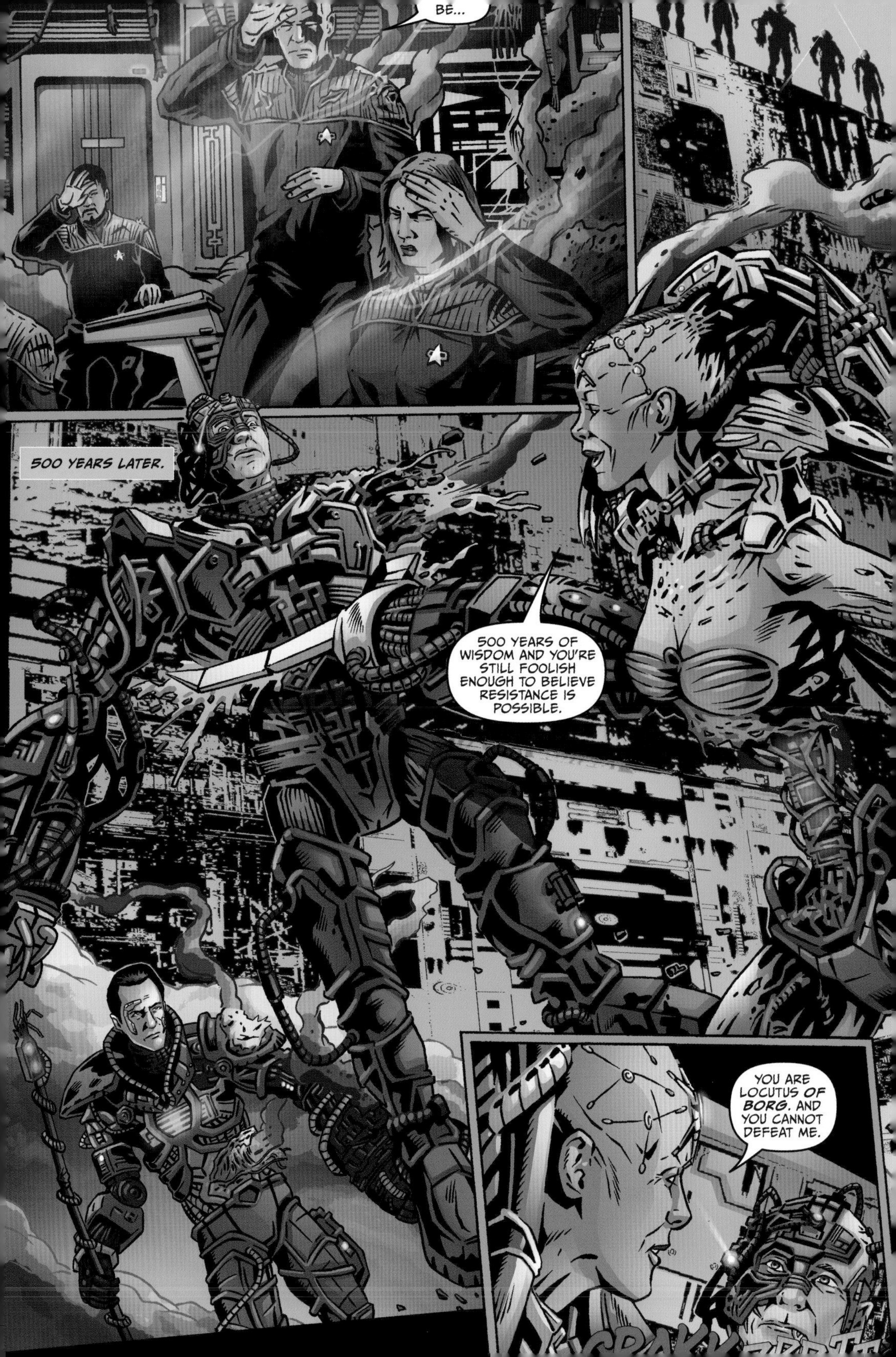
BE...
500 YEARS LATER.
500 YEARS OF WISDOM AND YOU'RE STILL FOOLISH ENOUGH TO BELIEVE RESISTANCE IS POSSIBLE.
YOU ARE LOCUTUS *OF BORG*. AND YOU CANNOT DEFEAT ME.

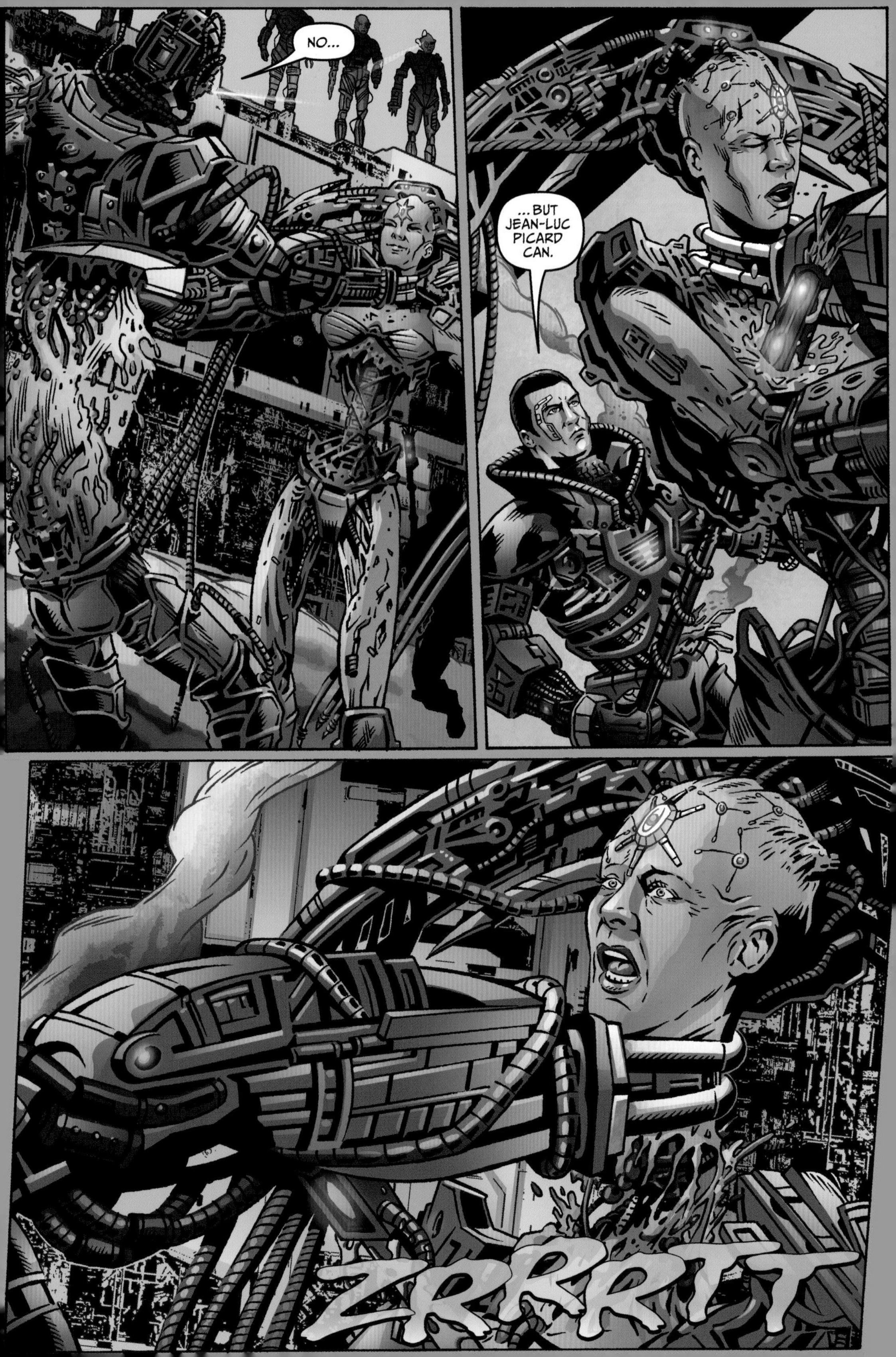
NO...
...BUT JEAN-LUC PICARD CAN.
ZRRRTT

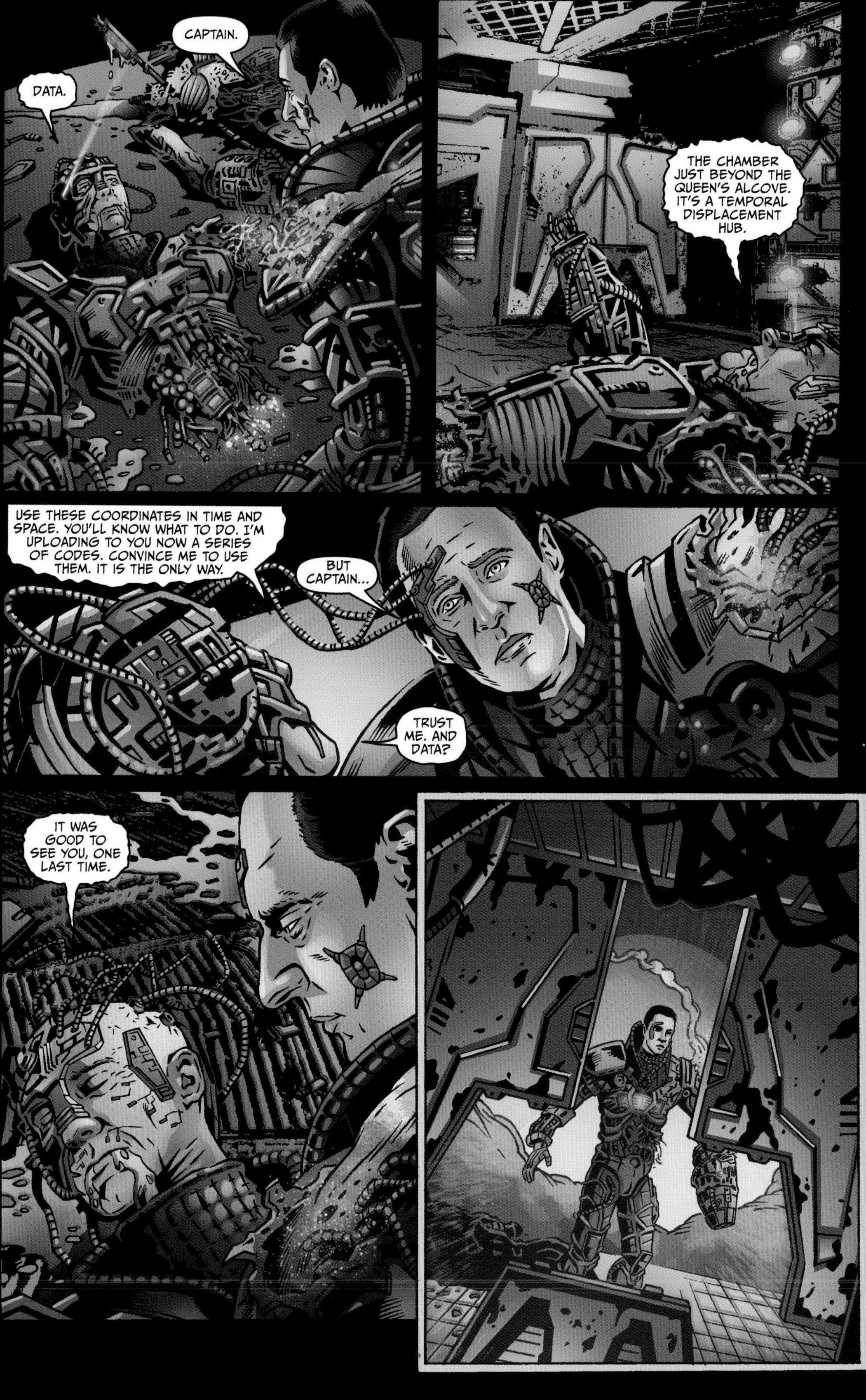
CAPTAIN.
DATA.
THE CHAMBER JUST BEYOND THE QUEEN'S ALCOVE. IT'S A TEMPORAL DISPLACEMENT HUB.
USE THESE COORDINATES IN TIME AND SPACE. YOU'LL KNOW WHAT TO DO. I'M UPLOADING TO YOU NOW A SERIES OF CODES. CONVINCE ME TO USE THEM. IT IS THE ONLY WAY.
BUT CAPTAIN...
TRUST ME. AND DATA?
IT WAS GOOD TO SEE YOU, ONE LAST TIME.

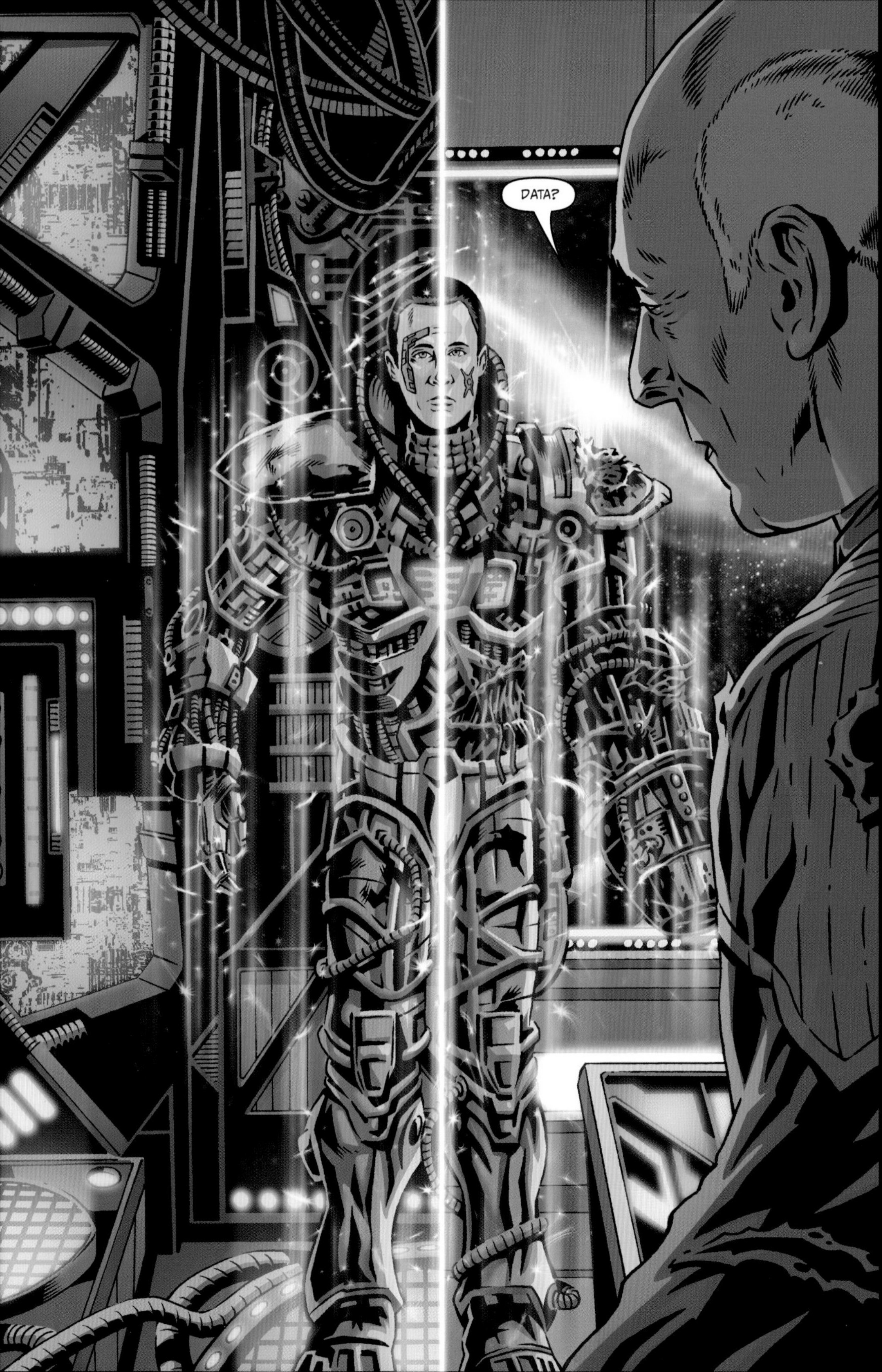
DATA?

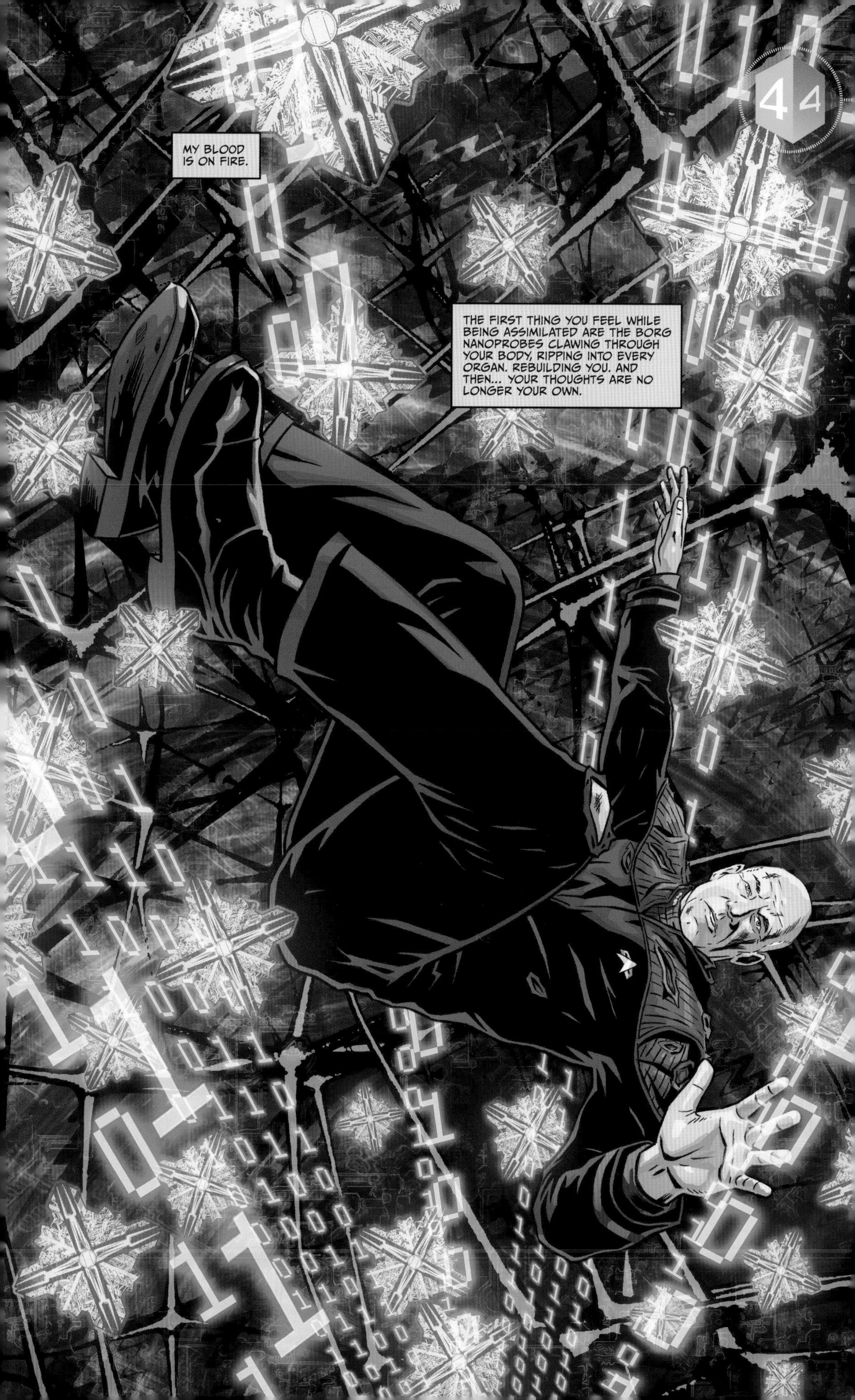
MY BLOOD IS ON FIRE.
THE FIRST THING YOU FEEL WHILE BEING ASSIMILATED ARE THE BORG NANOPROBES CLAWING THROUGH YOUR BODY, RIPPING INTO EVERY ORGAN. REBUILDING YOU. AND THEN... YOUR THOUGHTS ARE NO LONGER YOUR OWN.

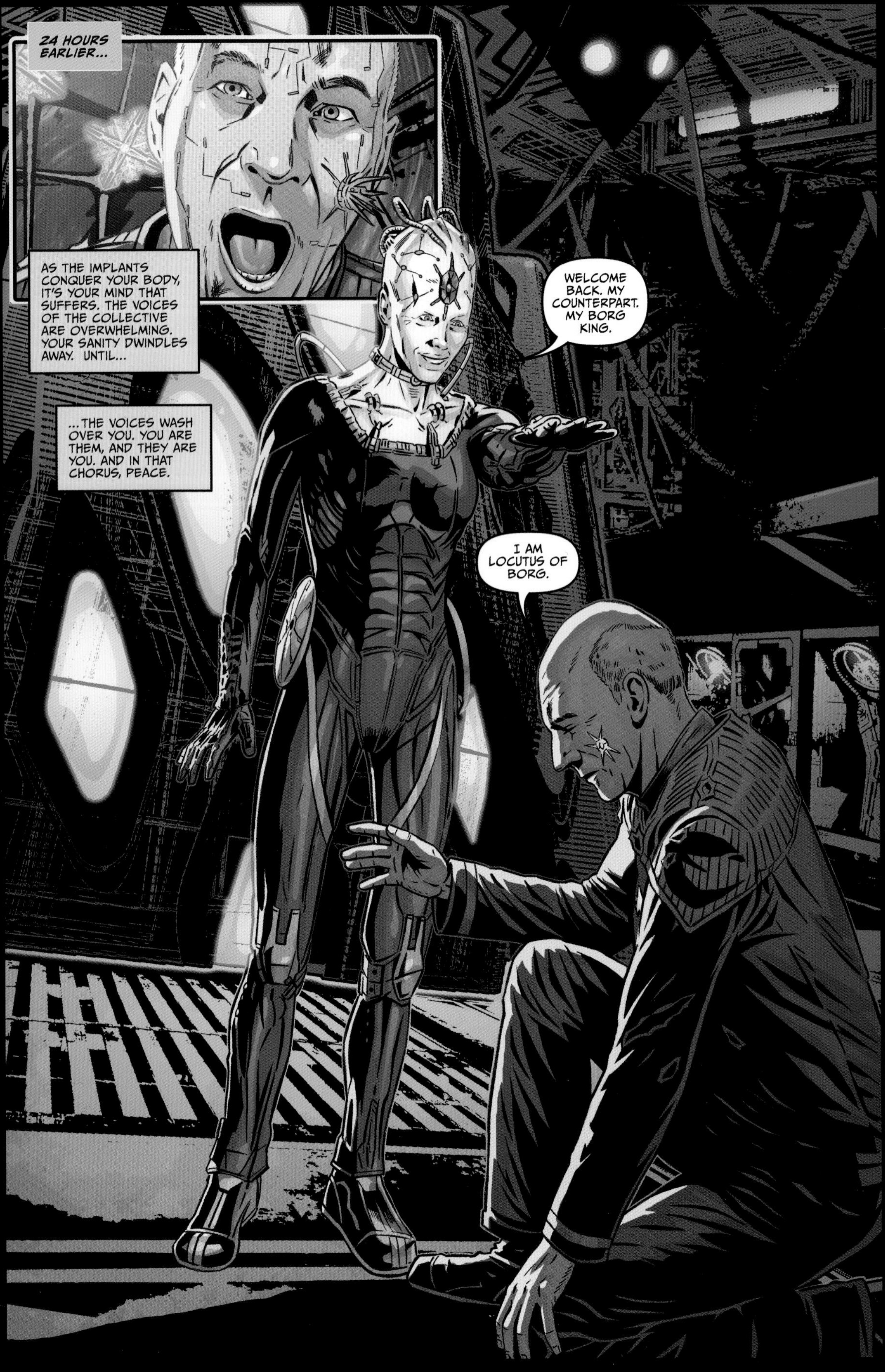
24 HOURS EARLIER...
AS THE IMPLANTS CONQUER YOUR BODY, IT'S YOUR MIND THAT SUFFERS. THE VOICES OF THE COLLECTIVE ARE OVERWHELMING. YOUR SANITY DWINDLES AWAY. UNTIL...
WELCOME BACK. MY COUNTERPART. MY BORG KING.
...THE VOICES WASH OVER YOU. YOU ARE THEM, AND THEY ARE YOU. AND IN THAT CHORUS, PEACE.
I AM LOCUTUS OF BORG.

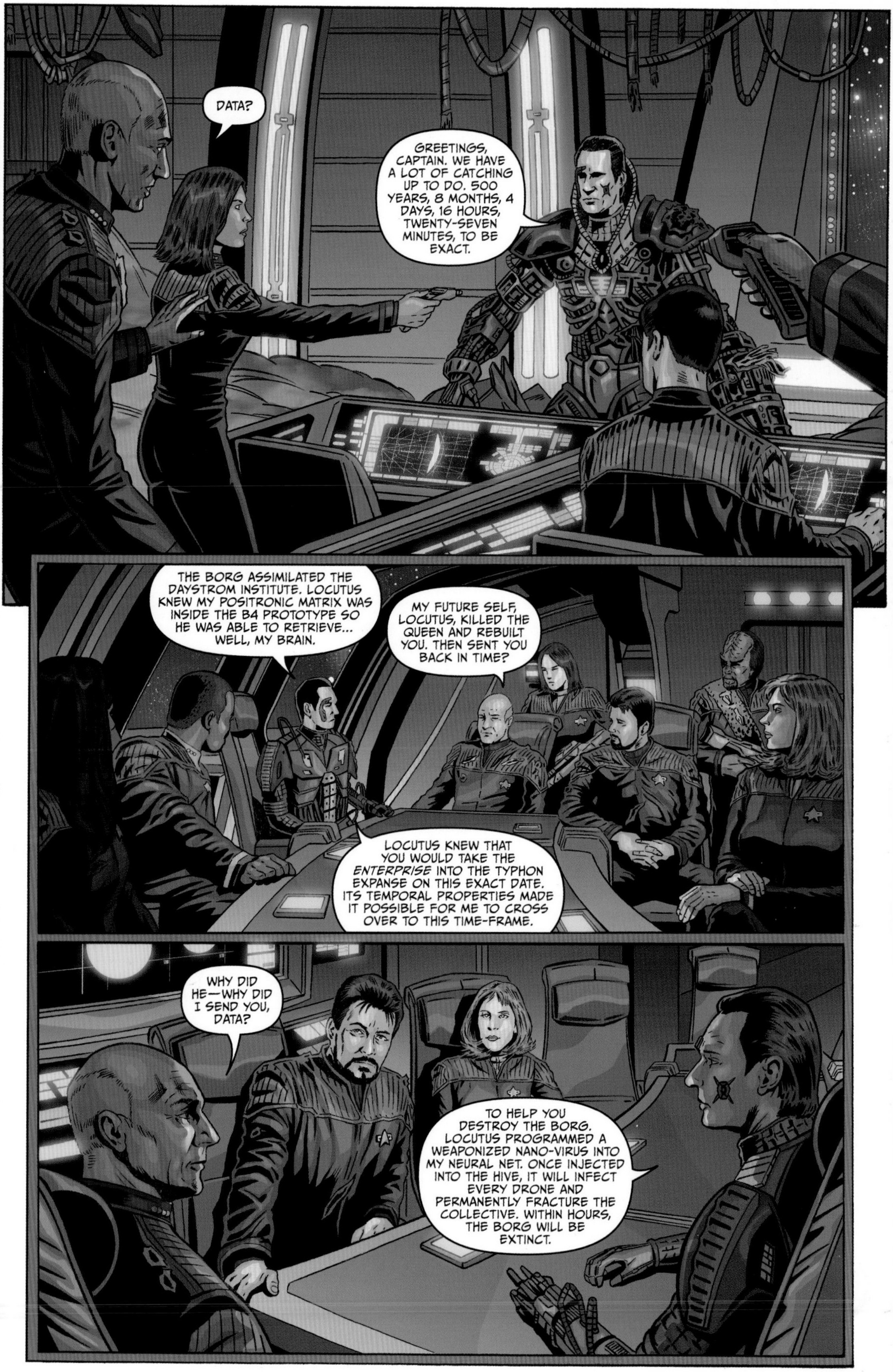
DATA?
GREETINGS, CAPTAIN. WE HAVE A LOT OF CATCHING UP TO DO. 500 YEARS, 8 MONTHS, 4 DAYS, 16 HOURS, TWENTY-SEVEN MINUTES, TO BE EXACT.
THE BORG ASSIMILATED THE DAYSTROM INSTITUTE. LOCUTUS KNEW MY POSITRONIC MATRIX WAS INSIDE THE B4 PROTOTYPE SO HE WAS ABLE TO RETRIEVE... WELL, MY BRAIN.
MY FUTURE SELF, LOCUTUS, KILLED THE QUEEN AND REBUILT YOU. THEN SENT YOU BACK IN TIME?
LOCUTUS KNEW THAT YOU WOULD TAKE THE *ENTERPRISE* INTO THE TYPHON EXPANSE ON THIS EXACT DATE. ITS TEMPORAL PROPERTIES MADE IT POSSIBLE FOR ME TO CROSS OVER TO THIS TIME-FRAME.
WHY DID HE—WHY DID I SEND YOU, DATA?
TO HELP YOU DESTROY THE BORG. LOCUTUS PROGRAMMED A WEAPONIZED NANO-VIRUS INTO MY NEURAL NET. ONCE INJECTED INTO THE HIVE, IT WILL INFECT EVERY DRONE AND PERMANENTLY FRACTURE THE COLLECTIVE. WITHIN HOURS, THE BORG WILL BE EXTINCT.

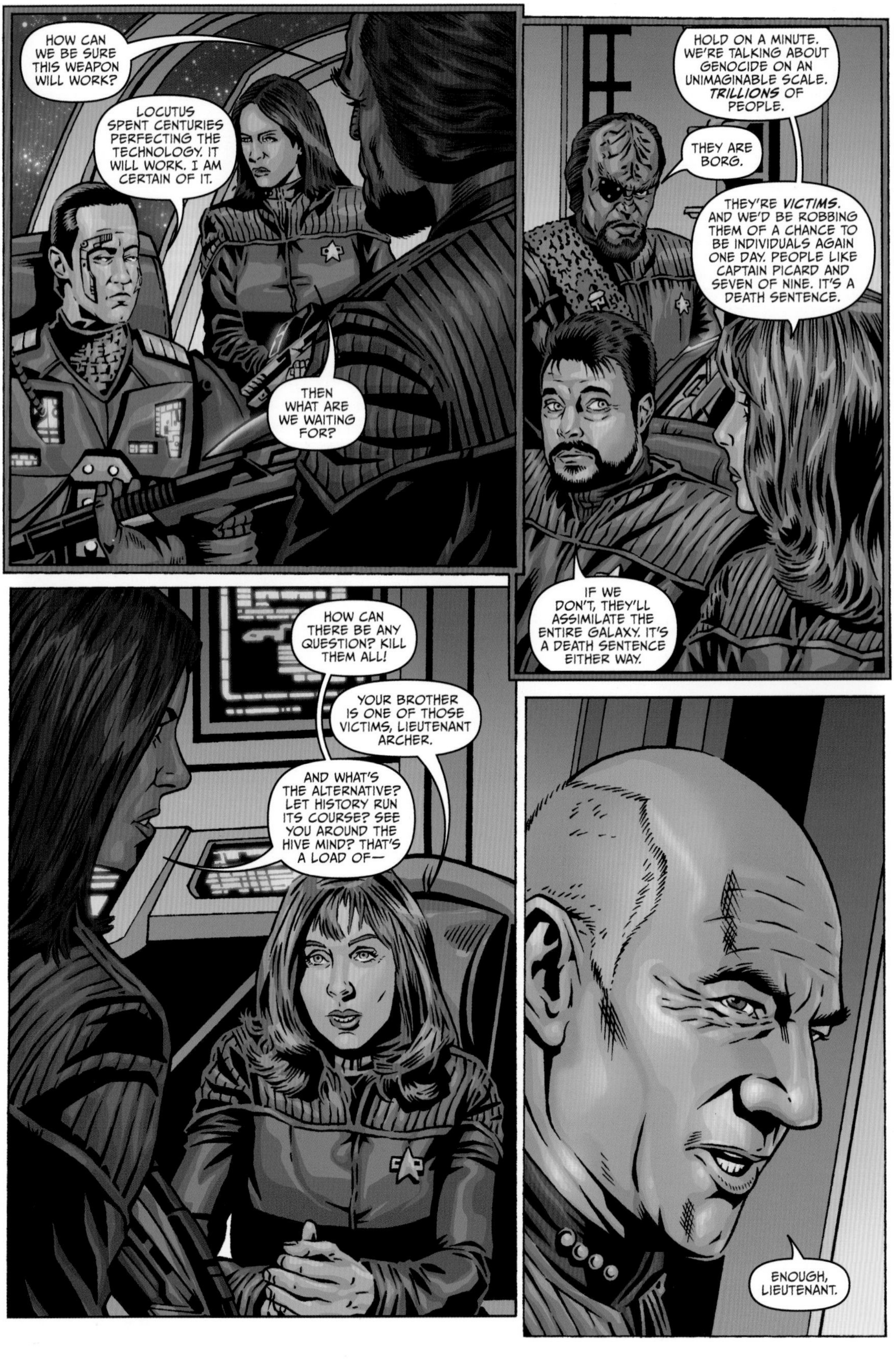
HOW CAN WE BE SURE THIS WEAPON WILL WORK?
LOCUTUS SPENT CENTURIES PERFECTING THE TECHNOLOGY. IT WILL WORK. I AM CERTAIN OF IT.
THEN WHAT ARE WE WAITING FOR?
HOLD ON A MINUTE. WE'RE TALKING ABOUT GENOCIDE ON AN UNIMAGINABLE SCALE. *TRILLIONS* OF PEOPLE.
THEY ARE BORG.
THEY'RE *VICTIMS*. AND WE'D BE ROBBING THEM OF A CHANCE TO BE INDIVIDUALS AGAIN ONE DAY. PEOPLE LIKE CAPTAIN PICARD AND SEVEN OF NINE. IT'S A DEATH SENTENCE.
IF WE DON'T, THEY'LL ASSIMILATE THE ENTIRE GALAXY. IT'S A DEATH SENTENCE EITHER WAY.
HOW CAN THERE BE ANY QUESTION? KILL THEM ALL!
YOUR BROTHER IS ONE OF THOSE VICTIMS, LIEUTENANT ARCHER.
AND WHAT'S THE ALTERNATIVE? LET HISTORY RUN ITS COURSE? SEE YOU AROUND THE HIVE MIND? THAT'S A LOAD OF—
ENOUGH, LIEUTENANT.

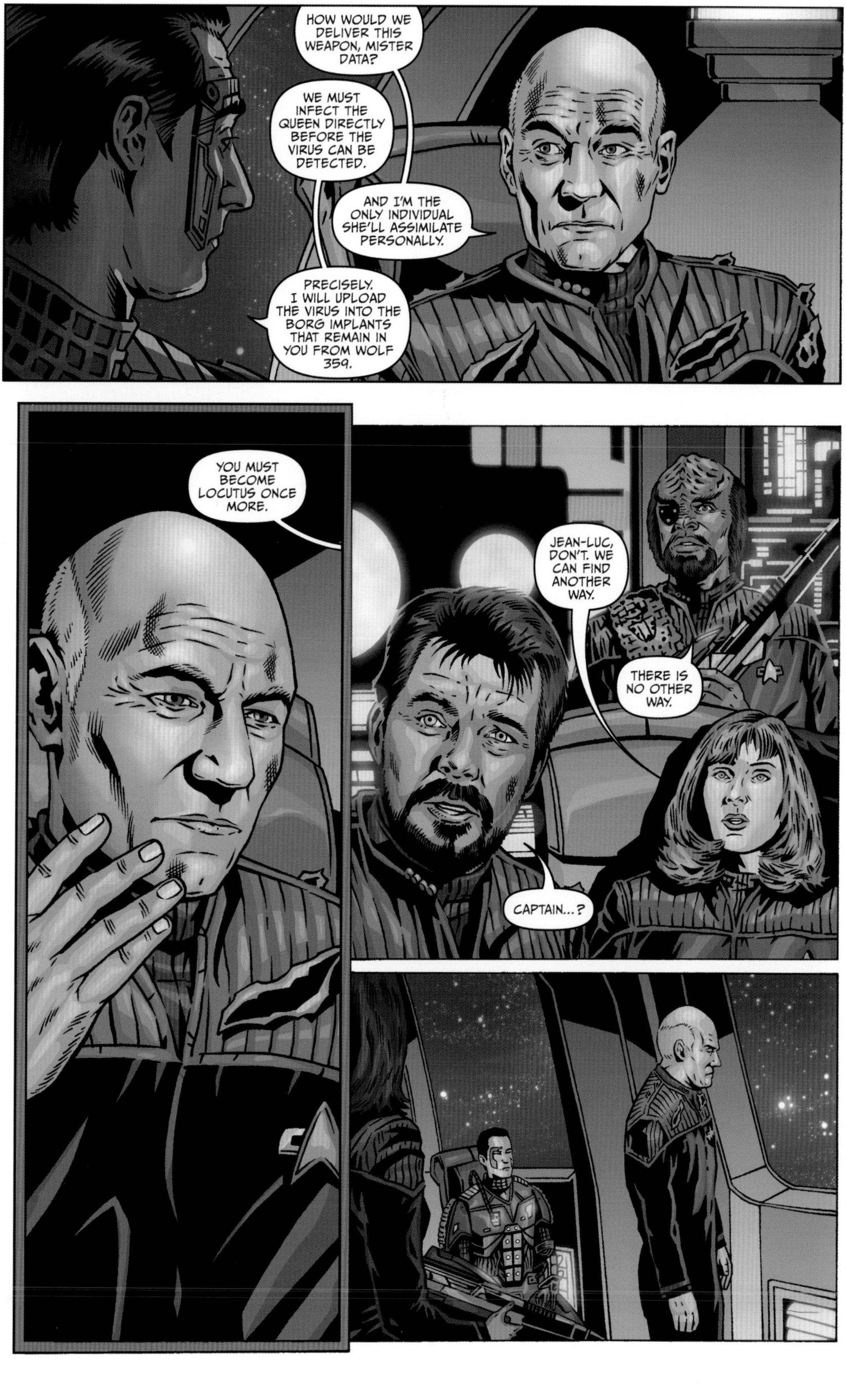
HOW WOULD WE DELIVER THIS WEAPON, MISTER DATA?
WE MUST INFECT THE QUEEN DIRECTLY BEFORE THE VIRUS CAN BE DETECTED.
AND I'M THE ONLY INDIVIDUAL SHE'LL ASSIMILATE PERSONALLY.
PRECISELY. I WILL UPLOAD THE VIRUS INTO THE BORG IMPLANTS THAT REMAIN IN YOU FROM WOLF 359.
YOU MUST BECOME LOCUTUS ONCE MORE.
JEAN-LUC, DON'T. WE CAN FIND ANOTHER WAY.
THERE IS NO OTHER WAY.
CAPTAIN...?

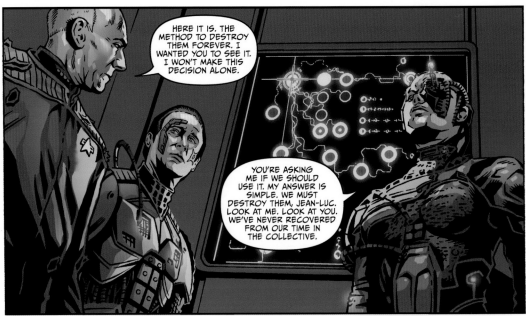

HERE IT IS. THE METHOD TO DESTROY THEM FOREVER. I WANTED YOU TO SEE IT. I WON'T MAKE THIS DECISION ALONE.

YOU'RE ASKING ME IF WE SHOULD USE IT. MY ANSWER IS SIMPLE. WE MUST DESTROY THEM, JEAN-LUC. LOOK AT ME. LOOK AT YOU. WE'VE NEVER RECOVERED FROM OUR TIME IN THE COLLECTIVE.

WE MISS IT. WE NEED IT. THE VOICES OF THE HIVE CALL US STILL.

THE VOICES, YES.

ARE YOU THINKING WHAT I'M THINKING? FIGURATIVELY SPEAKING, OF COURSE.

I BELIEVE SO, CAPTAIN.

SIR?

WHEN SEVEN WAS UNDERCOVER IN THE COLLECTIVE, SHE USED A NEURO-CORTICAL FILTER TO CONCEAL HER THOUGHTS FROM THE OTHER DRONES. I BELIEVE WE CAN USE IT AGAIN.

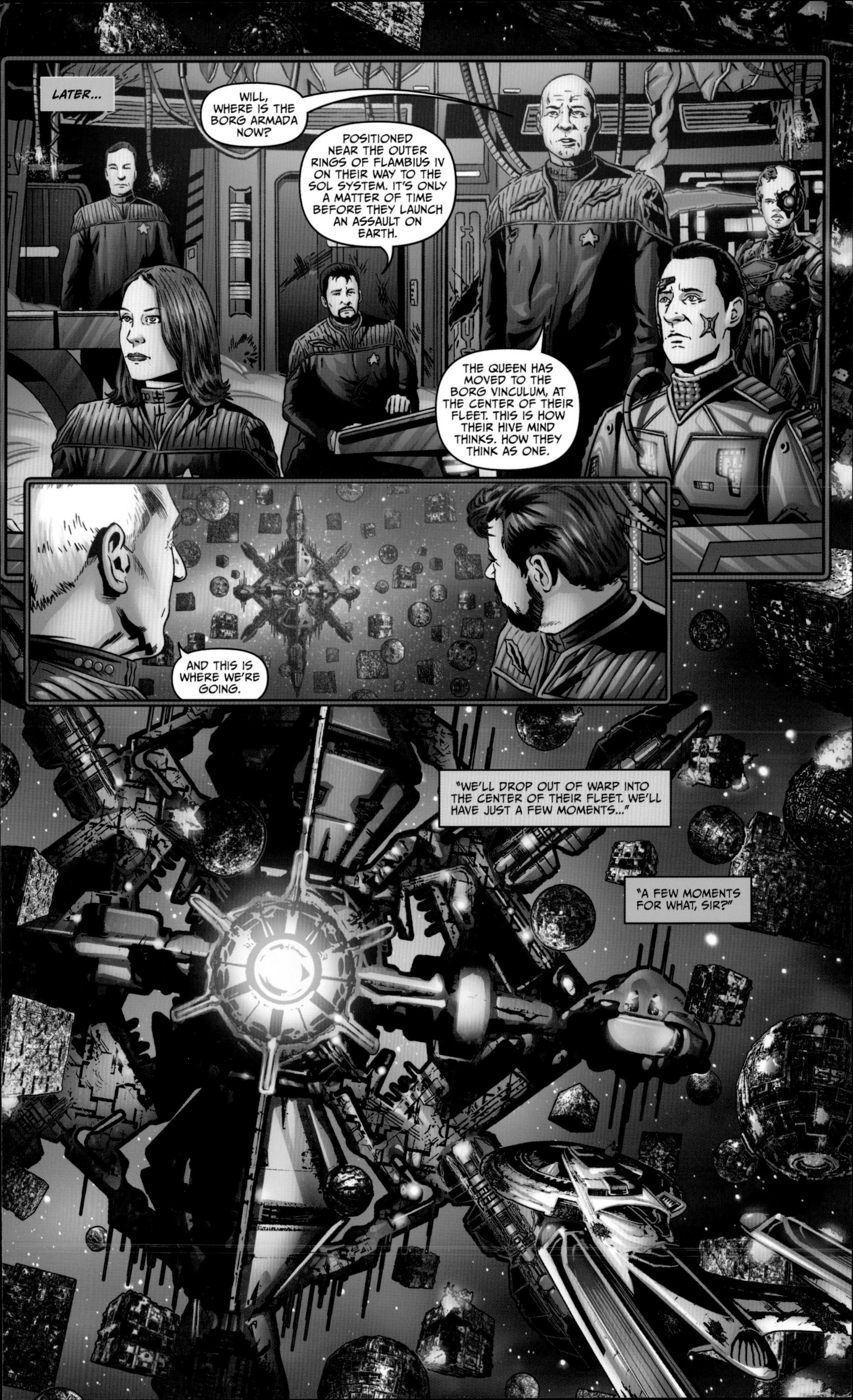
LATER...
WILL, WHERE IS THE BORG ARMADA NOW?
POSITIONED NEAR THE OUTER RINGS OF FLAMBIUS IV ON THEIR WAY TO THE SOL SYSTEM. IT'S ONLY A MATTER OF TIME BEFORE THEY LAUNCH AN ASSAULT ON EARTH.
THE QUEEN HAS MOVED TO THE BORG VINCULUM, AT THE CENTER OF THEIR FLEET. THIS IS HOW THEIR HIVE MIND THINKS. HOW THEY THINK AS ONE.
AND THIS IS WHERE WE'RE GOING.
"WE'LL DROP OUT OF WARP INTO THE CENTER OF THEIR FLEET. WE'LL HAVE JUST A FEW MOMENTS..."
"A FEW MOMENTS FOR WHAT, SIR?"

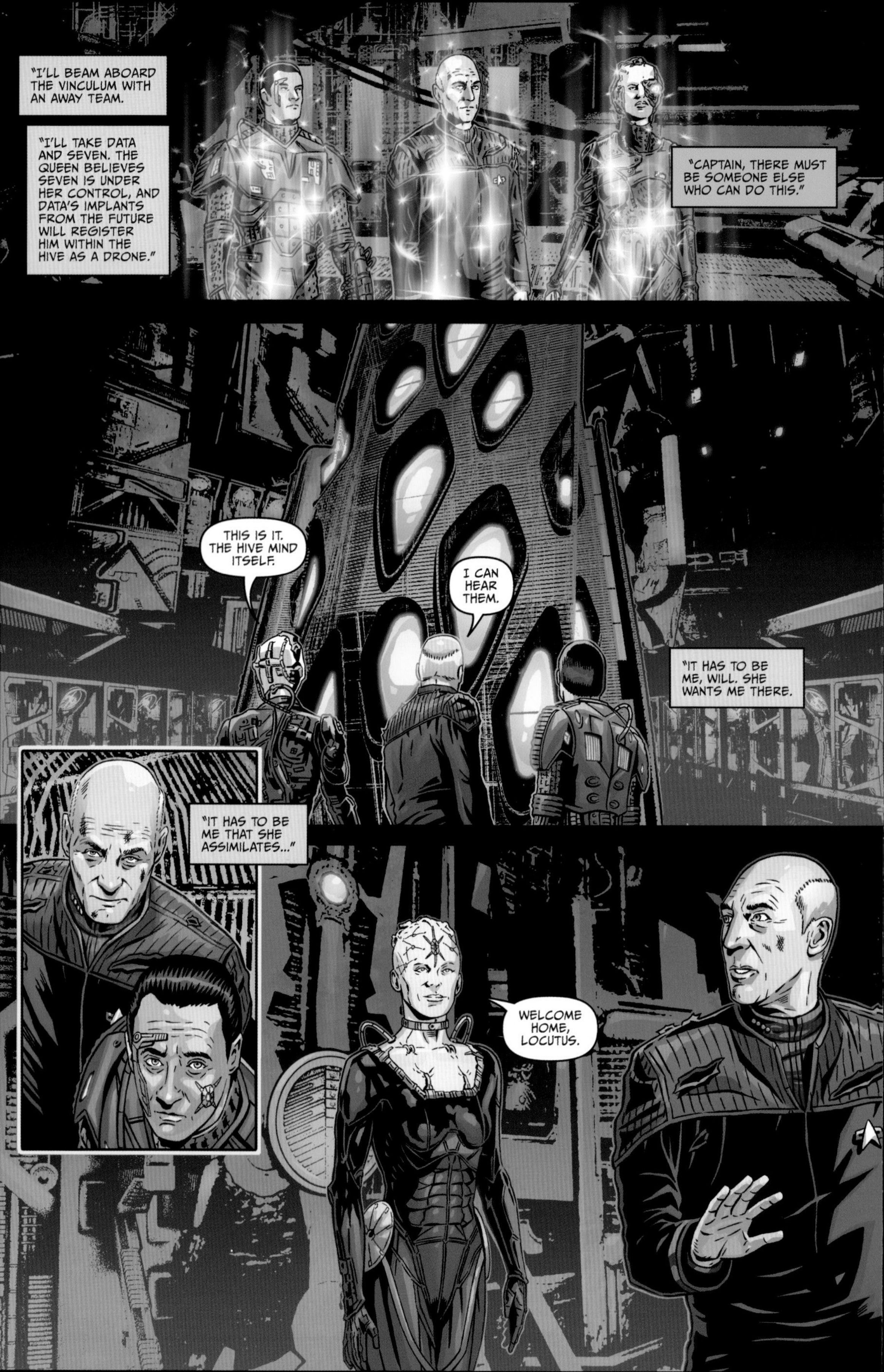
"I'LL BEAM ABOARD THE VINCULUM WITH AN AWAY TEAM.
"I'LL TAKE DATA AND SEVEN. THE QUEEN BELIEVES SEVEN IS UNDER HER CONTROL, AND DATA'S IMPLANTS FROM THE FUTURE WILL REGISTER HIM WITHIN THE HIVE AS A DRONE."
"CAPTAIN, THERE MUST BE SOMEONE ELSE WHO CAN DO THIS."
THIS IS IT. THE HIVE MIND ITSELF.
I CAN HEAR THEM.
"IT HAS TO BE ME, WILL. SHE WANTS ME THERE.
"IT HAS TO BE ME THAT SHE ASSIMILATES..."
WELCOME HOME, LOCUTUS.

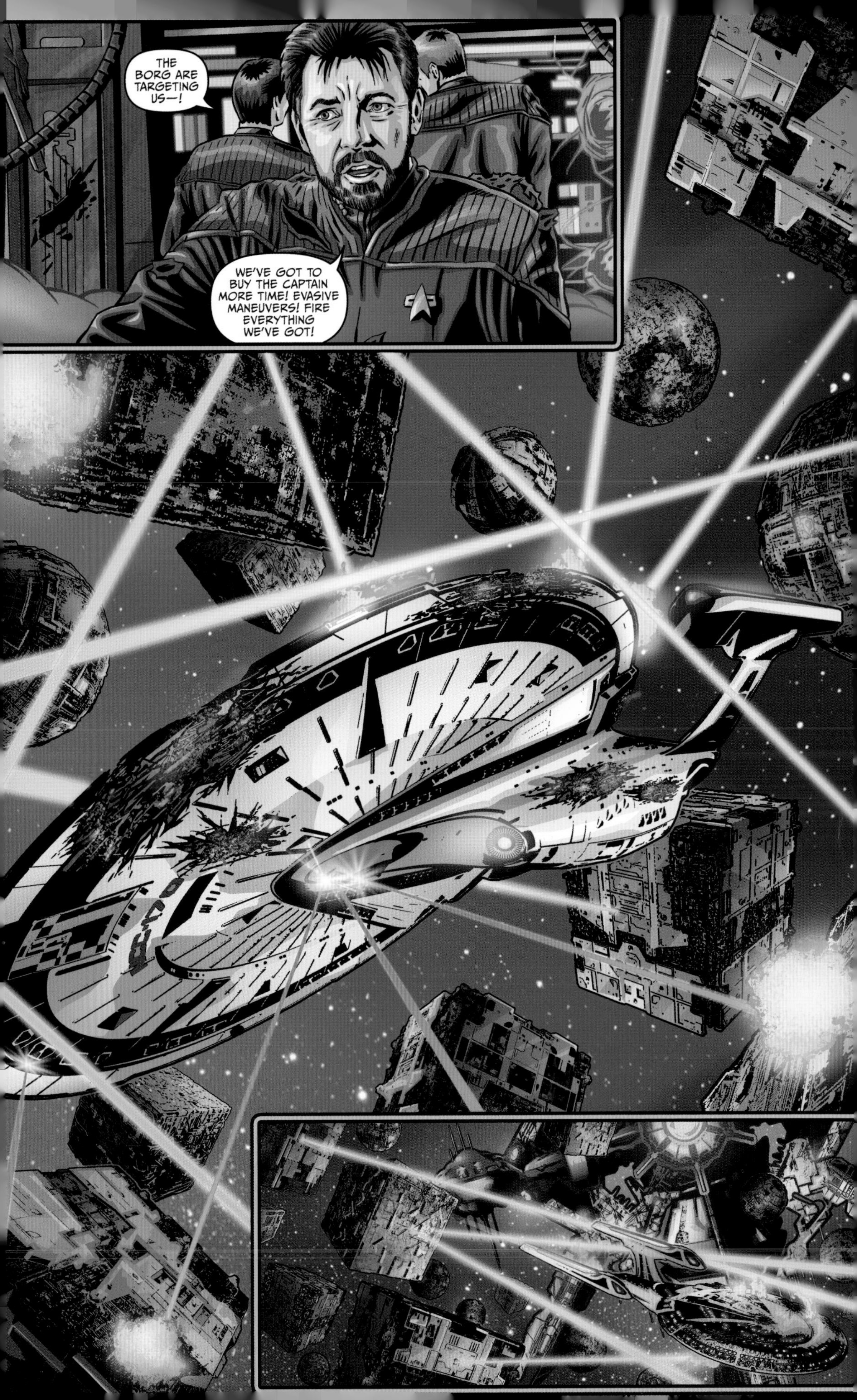
THE BORG ARE TARGETING US—!
WE'VE GOT TO BUY THE CAPTAIN MORE TIME! EVASIVE MANEUVERS! FIRE EVERYTHING WE'VE GOT!

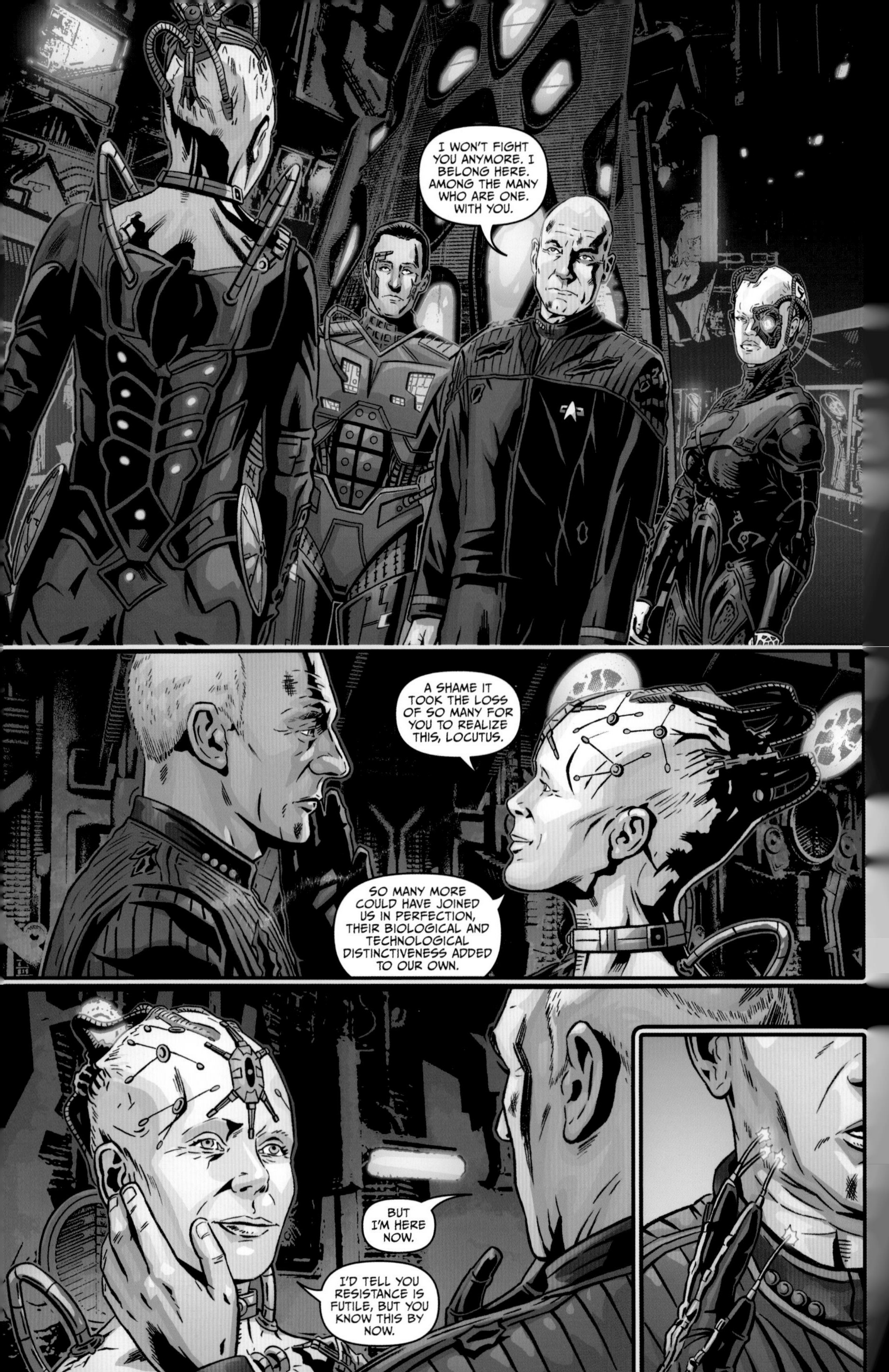
I WON'T FIGHT YOU ANYMORE. I BELONG HERE. AMONG THE MANY WHO ARE ONE. WITH YOU.
A SHAME IT TOOK THE LOSS OF SO MANY FOR YOU TO REALIZE THIS, LOCUTUS.
SO MANY MORE COULD HAVE JOINED US IN PERFECTION, THEIR BIOLOGICAL AND TECHNOLOGICAL DISTINCTIVENESS ADDED TO OUR OWN.
BUT I'M HERE NOW.
I'D TELL YOU RESISTANCE IS FUTILE, BUT YOU KNOW THIS BY NOW.

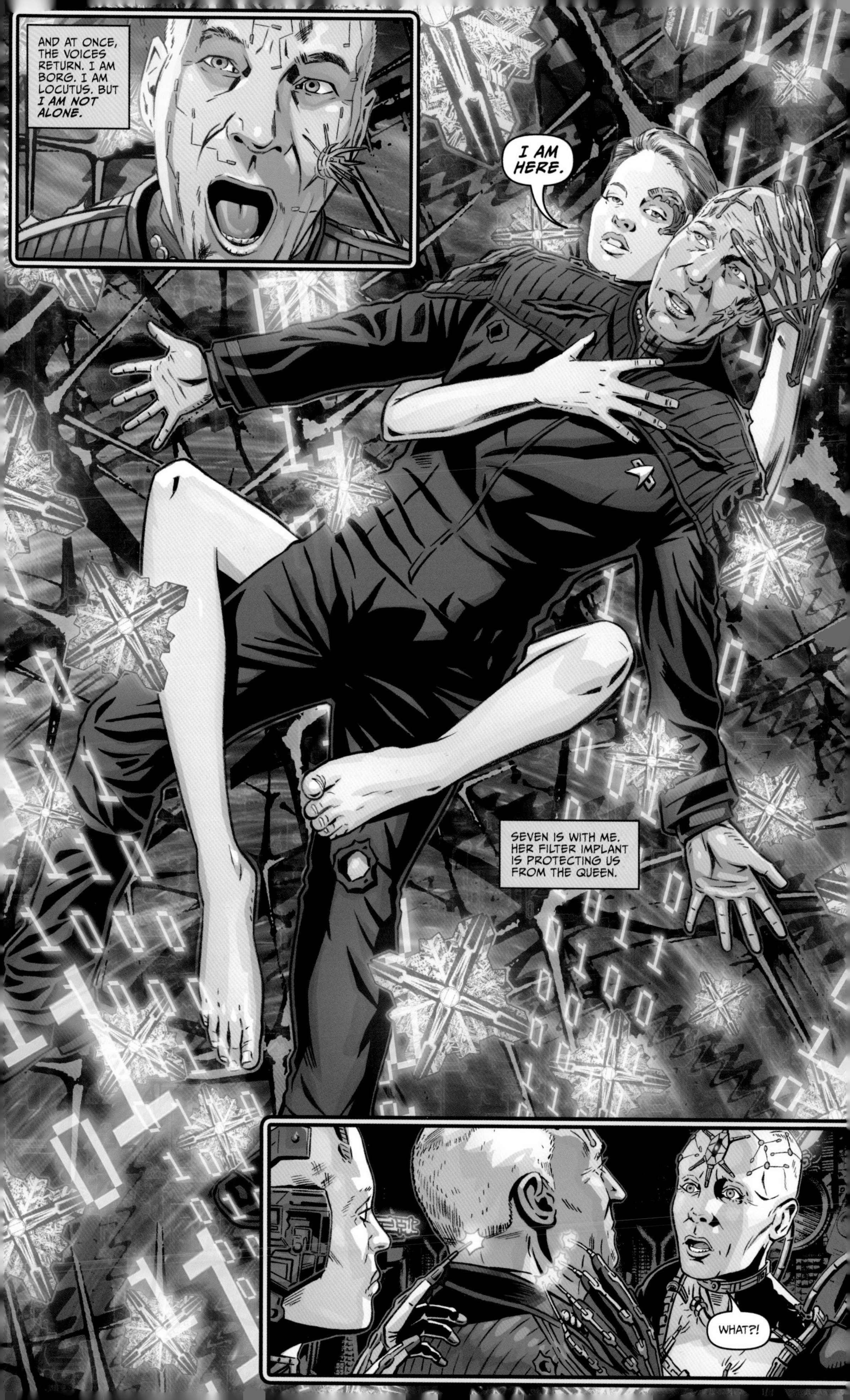
AND AT ONCE, THE VOICES RETURN. I AM BORG. I AM LOCUTUS. BUT *I AM NOT ALONE.*
I AM HERE.
SEVEN IS WITH ME. HER FILTER IMPLANT IS PROTECTING US FROM THE QUEEN.
WHAT?!

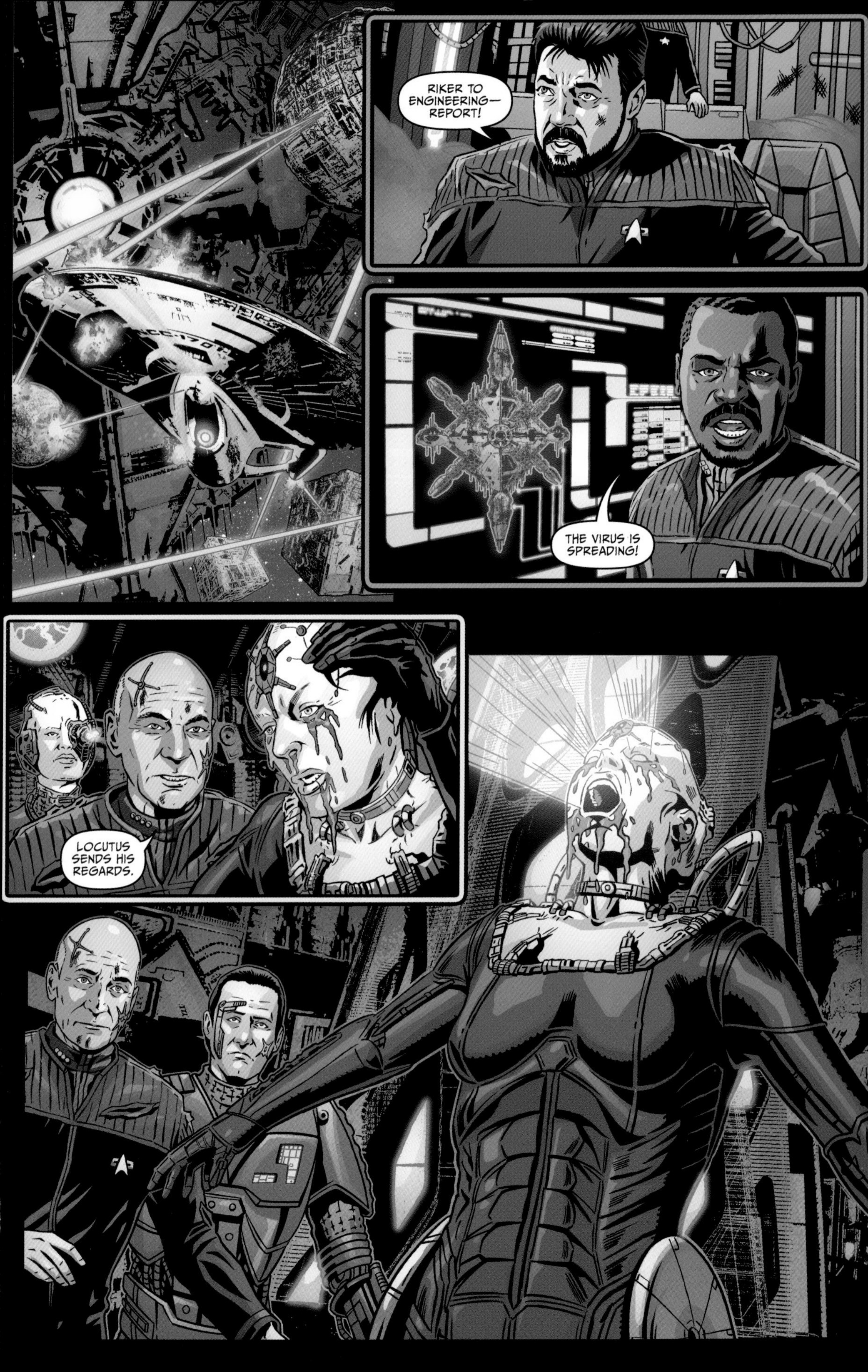
RIKER TO ENGINEERING— REPORT!
THE VIRUS IS SPREADING!
LOCUTUS SENDS HIS REGARDS.

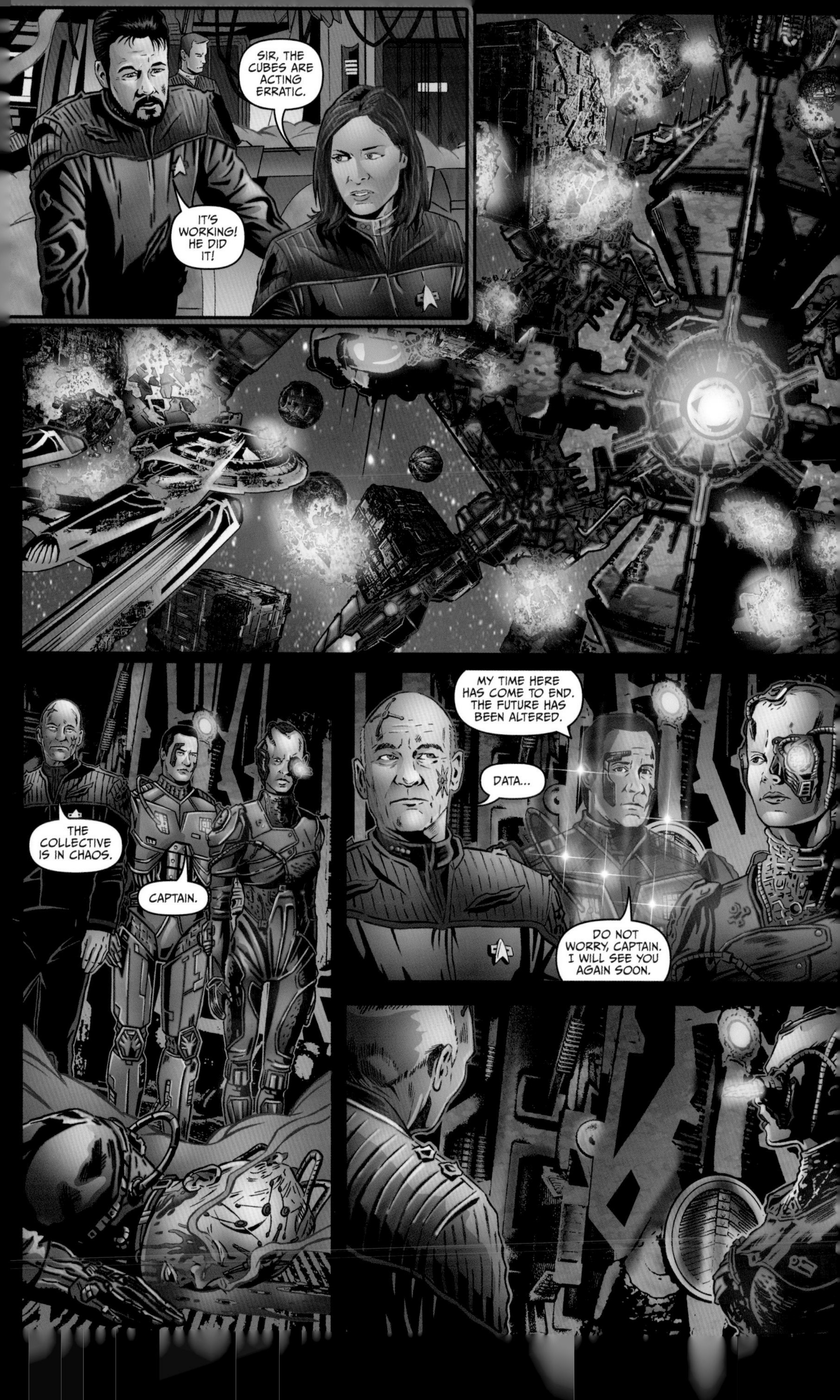
SIR, THE CUBES ARE ACTING ERRATIC.
IT'S WORKING! HE DID IT!
THE COLLECTIVE IS IN CHAOS.
CAPTAIN.
MY TIME HERE HAS COME TO END. THE FUTURE HAS BEEN ALTERED.
DATA...
DO NOT WORRY, CAPTAIN. I WILL SEE YOU AGAIN SOON.

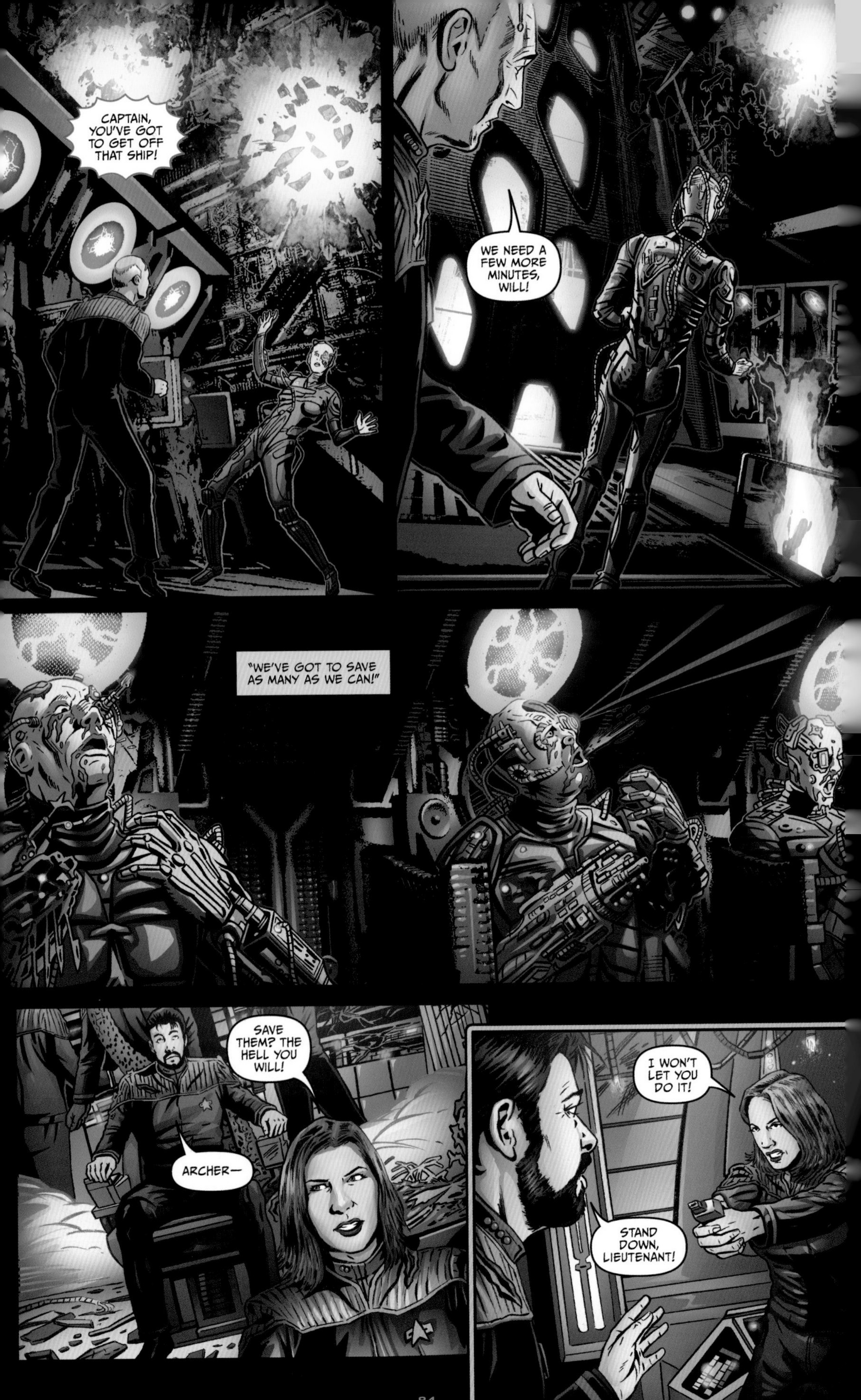
CAPTAIN, YOU'VE GOT TO GET OFF THAT SHIP!
WE NEED A FEW MORE MINUTES, WILL!
"WE'VE GOT TO SAVE AS MANY AS WE CAN!"
SAVE THEM? THE HELL YOU WILL!
ARCHER—
I WON'T LET YOU DO IT!
STAND DOWN, LIEUTENANT!

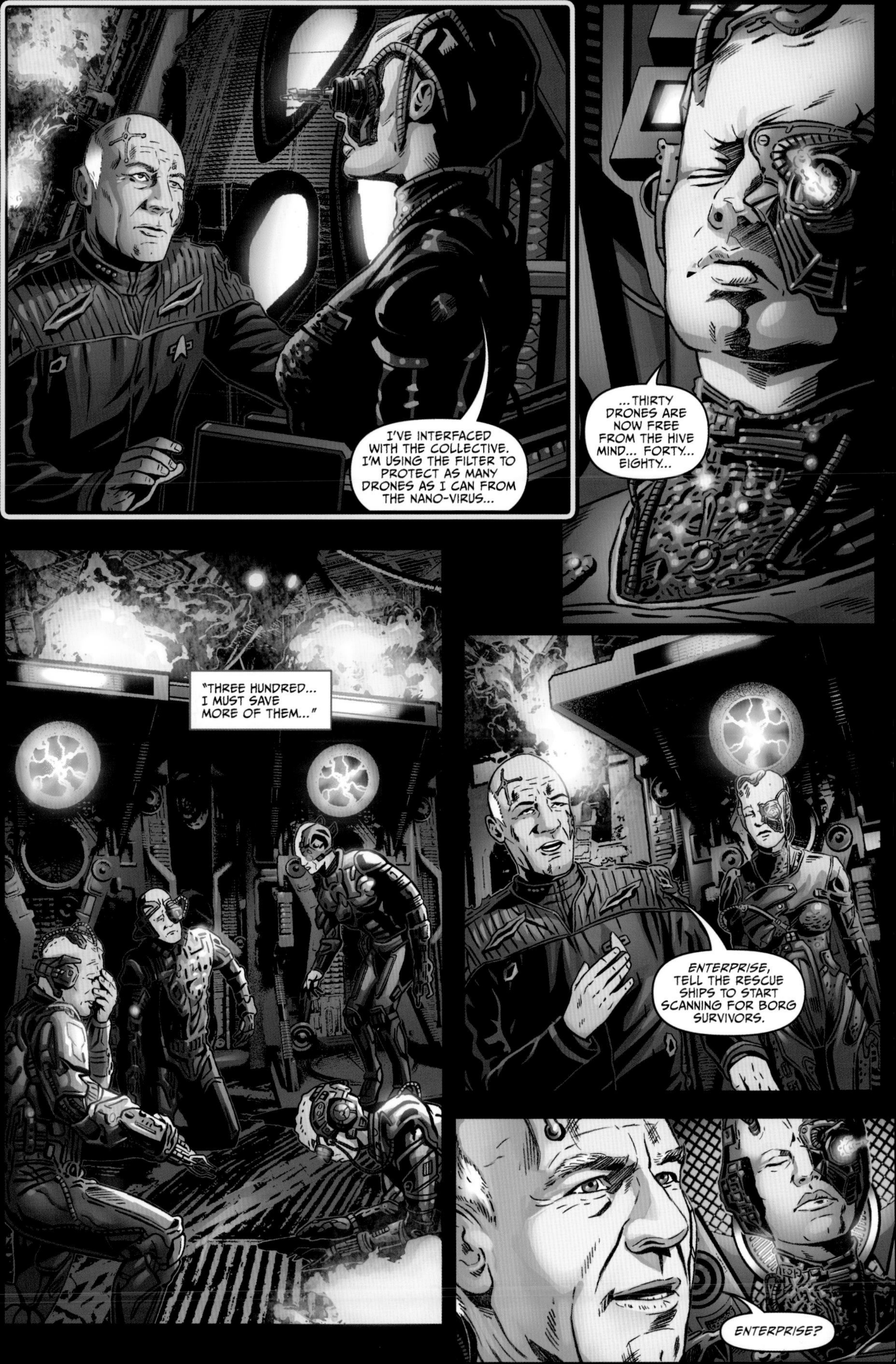
I'VE INTERFACED WITH THE COLLECTIVE. I'M USING THE FILTER TO PROTECT AS MANY DRONES AS I CAN FROM THE NANO-VIRUS...
...THIRTY DRONES ARE NOW FREE FROM THE HIVE MIND... FORTY... EIGHTY...
"THREE HUNDRED... I MUST SAVE MORE OF THEM..."
ENTERPRISE, TELL THE RESCUE SHIPS TO START SCANNING FOR BORG SURVIVORS.
ENTERPRISE?

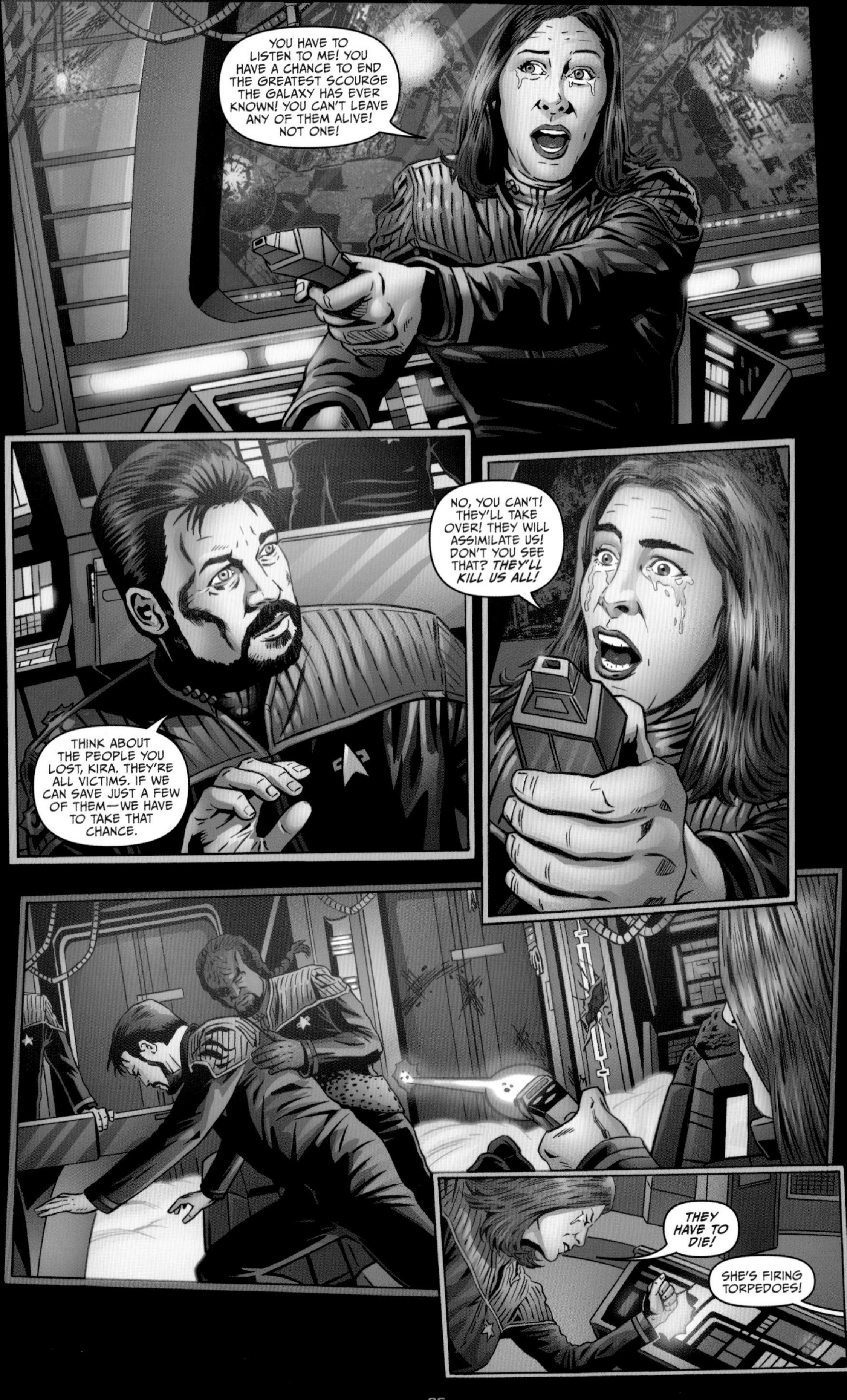
YOU HAVE TO LISTEN TO ME! YOU HAVE A CHANCE TO END THE GREATEST SCOURGE THE GALAXY HAS EVER KNOWN! YOU CAN'T LEAVE ANY OF THEM ALIVE! NOT ONE!
NO, YOU CAN'T! THEY'LL TAKE OVER! THEY WILL ASSIMILATE US! DON'T YOU SEE THAT? THEY'LL KILL US ALL!
THINK ABOUT THE PEOPLE YOU LOST, KIRA. THEY'RE ALL VICTIMS. IF WE CAN SAVE JUST A FEW OF THEM—WE HAVE TO TAKE THAT CHANCE.
THEY HAVE TO DIE!
SHE'S FIRING TORPEDOES!

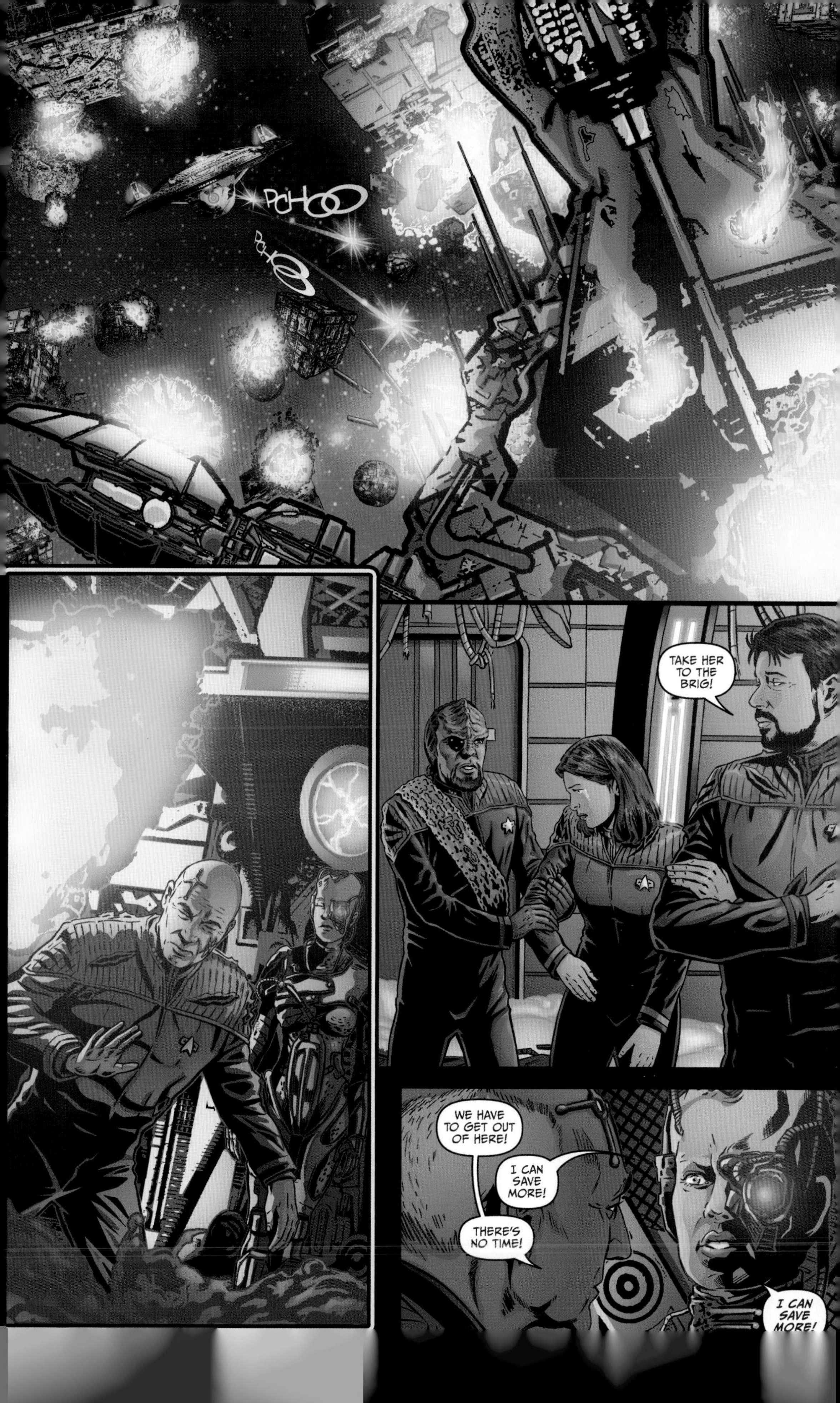
PCHOO
PCHOO
TAKE HER TO THE BRIG!
WE HAVE TO GET OUT OF HERE!
I CAN SAVE MORE!
THERE'S NO TIME!
I CAN SAVE MORE!

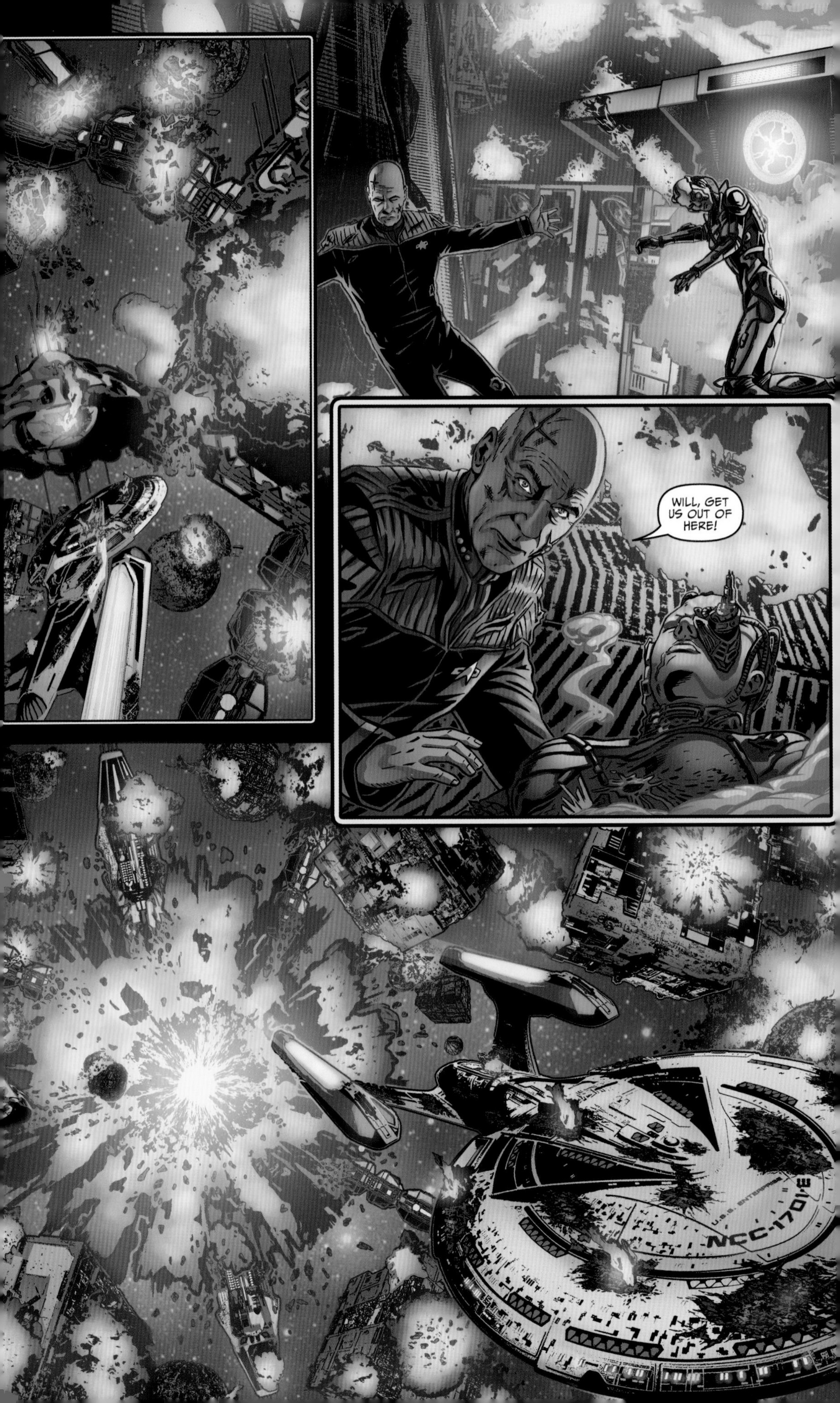
WILL, GET US OUT OF HERE!
NCC-1701-E
U.S.S. ENTERPRISE

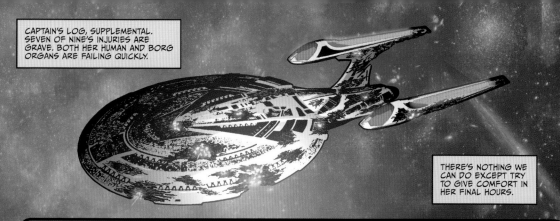

CAPTAIN'S LOG, SUPPLEMENTAL. SEVEN OF NINE'S INJURIES ARE GRAVE. BOTH HER HUMAN AND BORG ORGANS ARE FAILING QUICKLY.

THERE'S NOTHING WE CAN DO EXCEPT TRY TO GIVE COMFORT IN HER FINAL HOURS.

SEVEN...

HOW MANY?

RESCUE EFFORTS ARE STILL UNDERWAY, BUT WE ESTIMATE YOU SAVED THOUSANDS.

I DIDN'T DO ENOUGH.

YOU DID SO MUCH.

I COULD'VE GOTTEN MORE.

THERE ARE THOUSANDS OF PEOPLE ALIVE BECAUSE OF YOU.

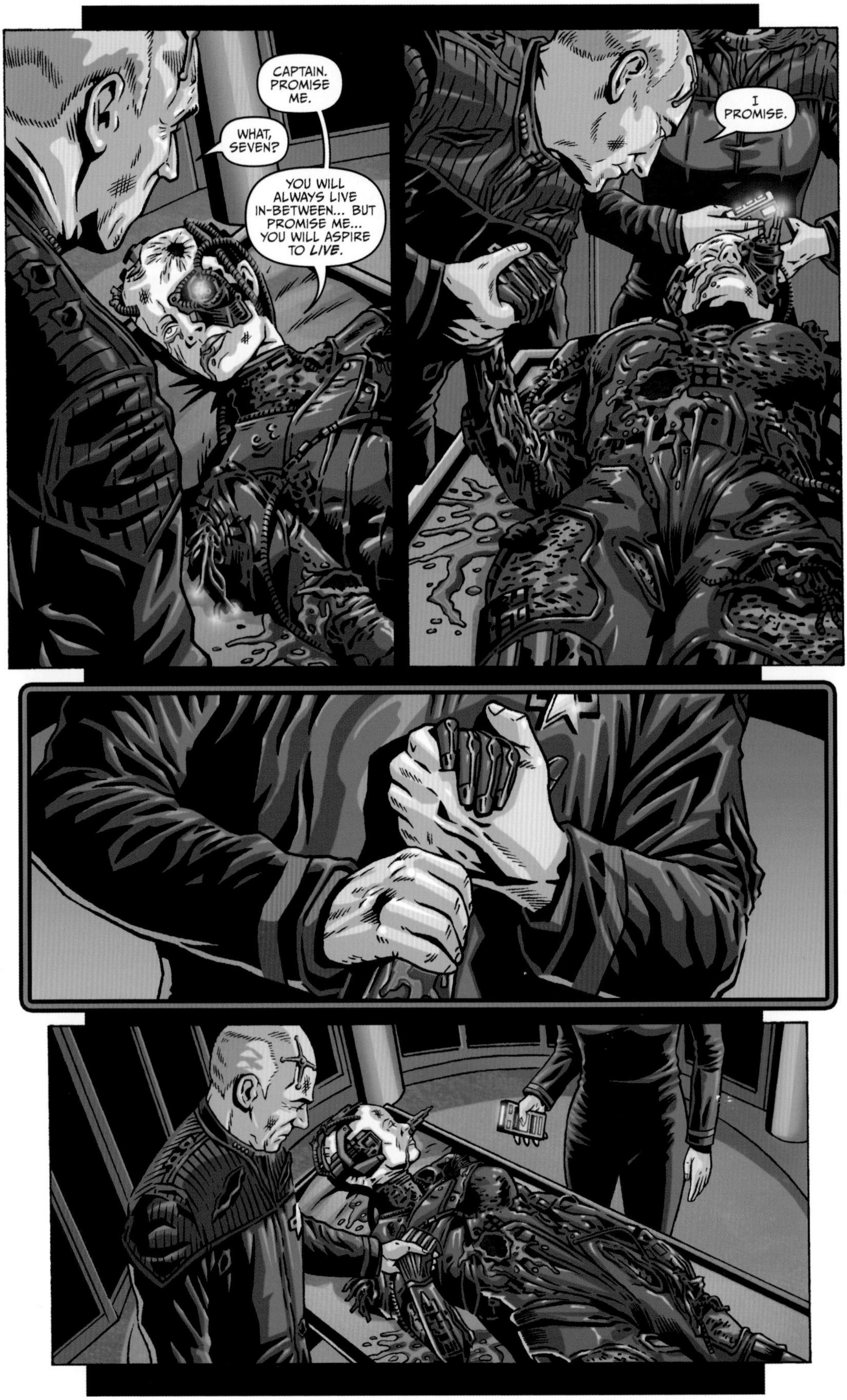
CAPTAIN. PROMISE ME.
WHAT, SEVEN?
YOU WILL ALWAYS LIVE IN-BETWEEN... BUT PROMISE ME... YOU WILL ASPIRE TO *LIVE*.
I PROMISE.

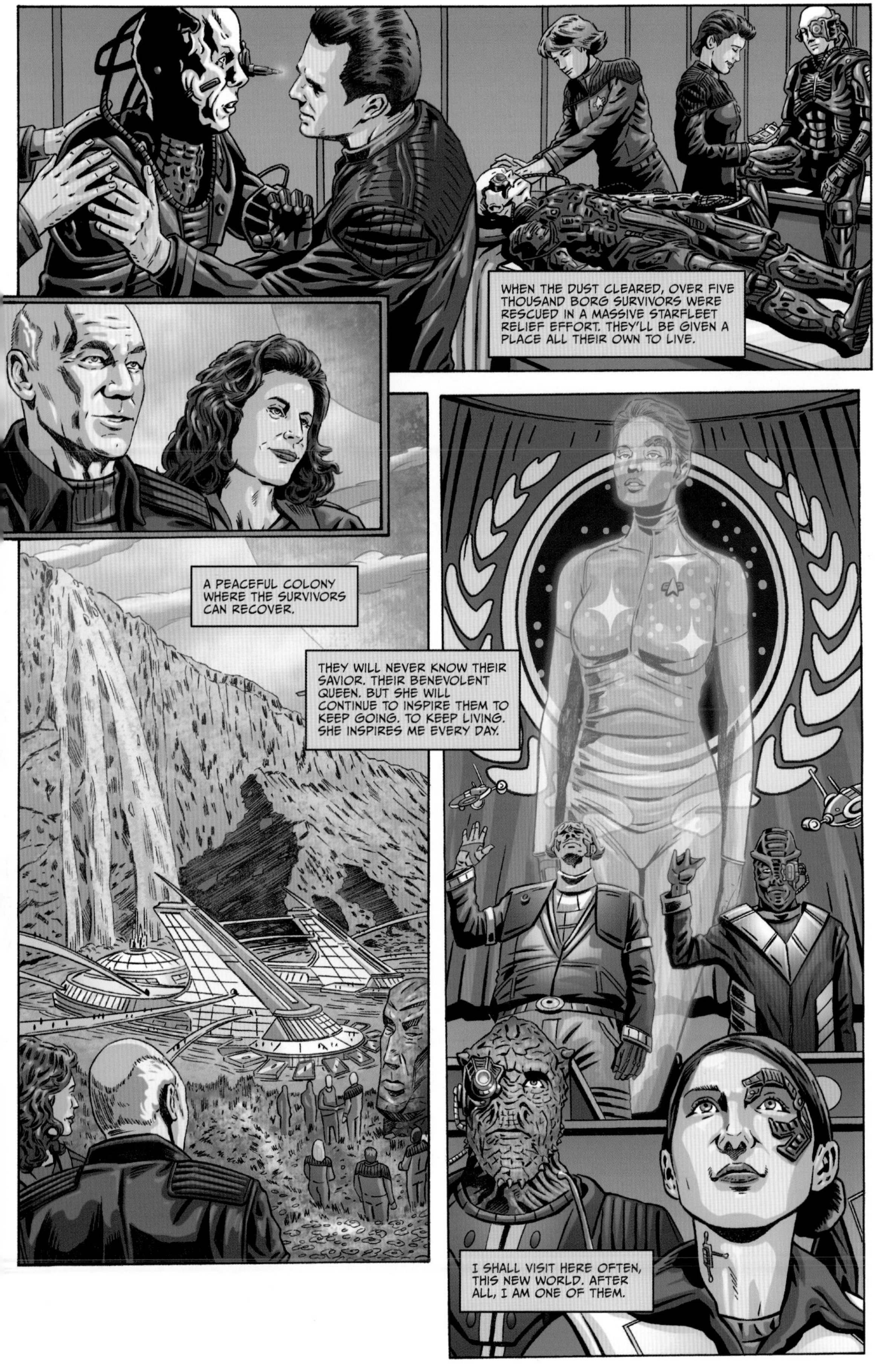
WHEN THE DUST CLEARED, OVER FIVE THOUSAND BORG SURVIVORS WERE RESCUED IN A MASSIVE STARFLEET RELIEF EFFORT. THEY'LL BE GIVEN A PLACE ALL THEIR OWN TO LIVE.
A PEACEFUL COLONY WHERE THE SURVIVORS CAN RECOVER.
THEY WILL NEVER KNOW THEIR SAVIOR. THEIR BENEVOLENT QUEEN. BUT SHE WILL CONTINUE TO INSPIRE THEM TO KEEP GOING. TO KEEP LIVING. SHE INSPIRES ME EVERY DAY.
I SHALL VISIT HERE OFTEN, THIS NEW WORLD. AFTER ALL, I AM ONE OF THEM.

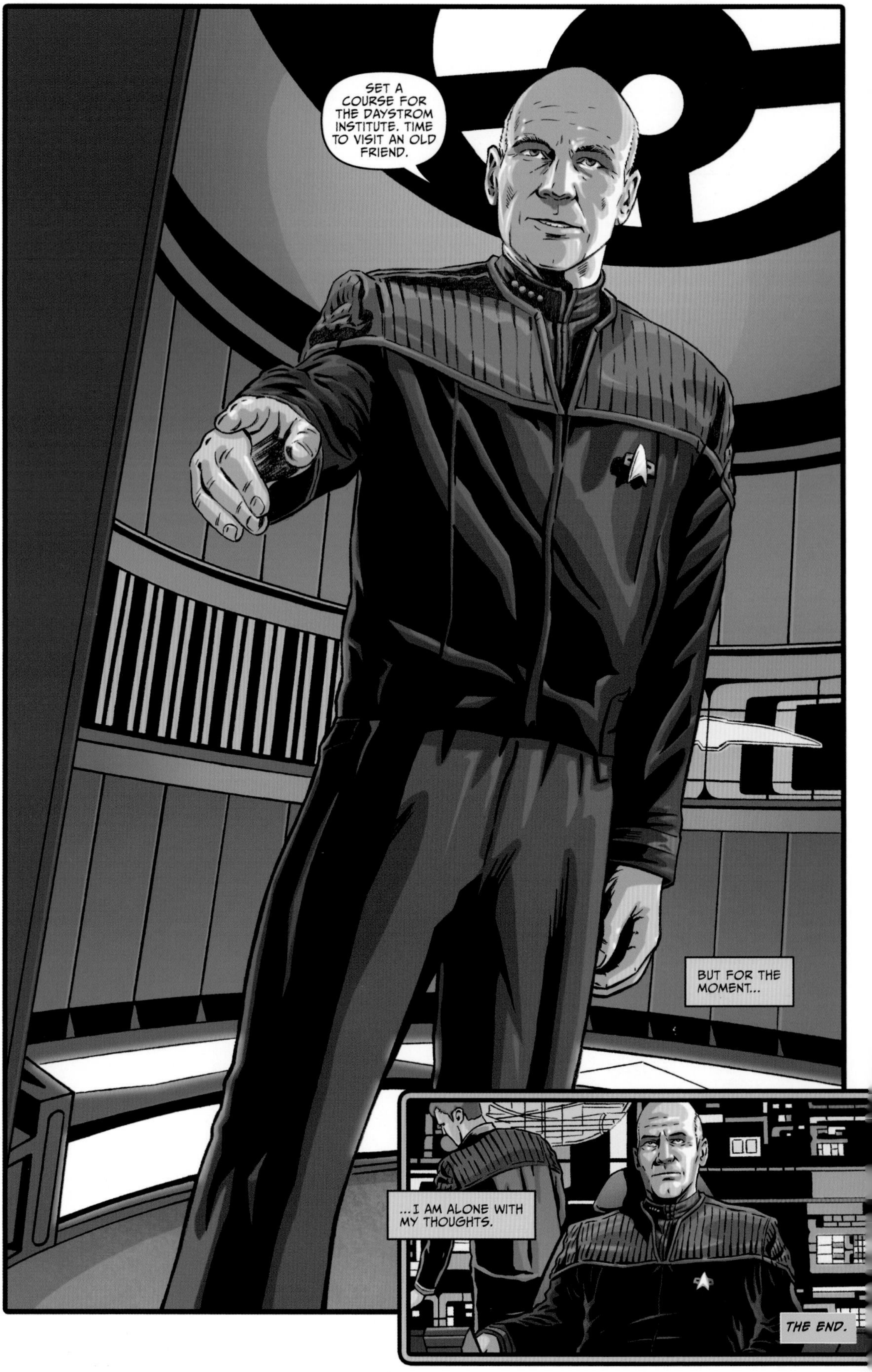
SET A COURSE FOR THE DAYSTROM INSTITUTE. TIME TO VISIT AN OLD FRIEND.
BUT FOR THE MOMENT...
...I AM ALONE WITH MY THOUGHTS.
THE END.

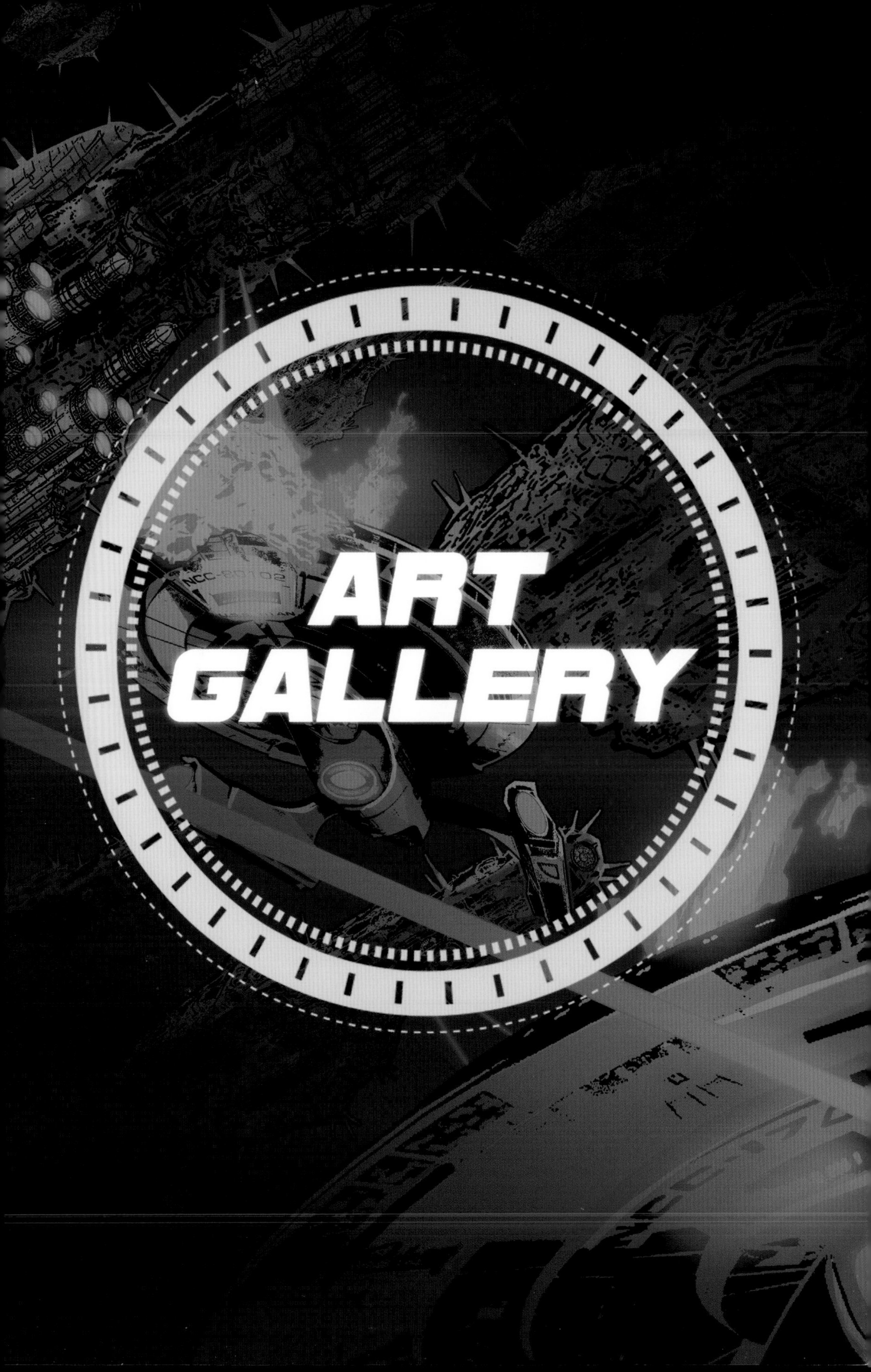
ART
GALLERY

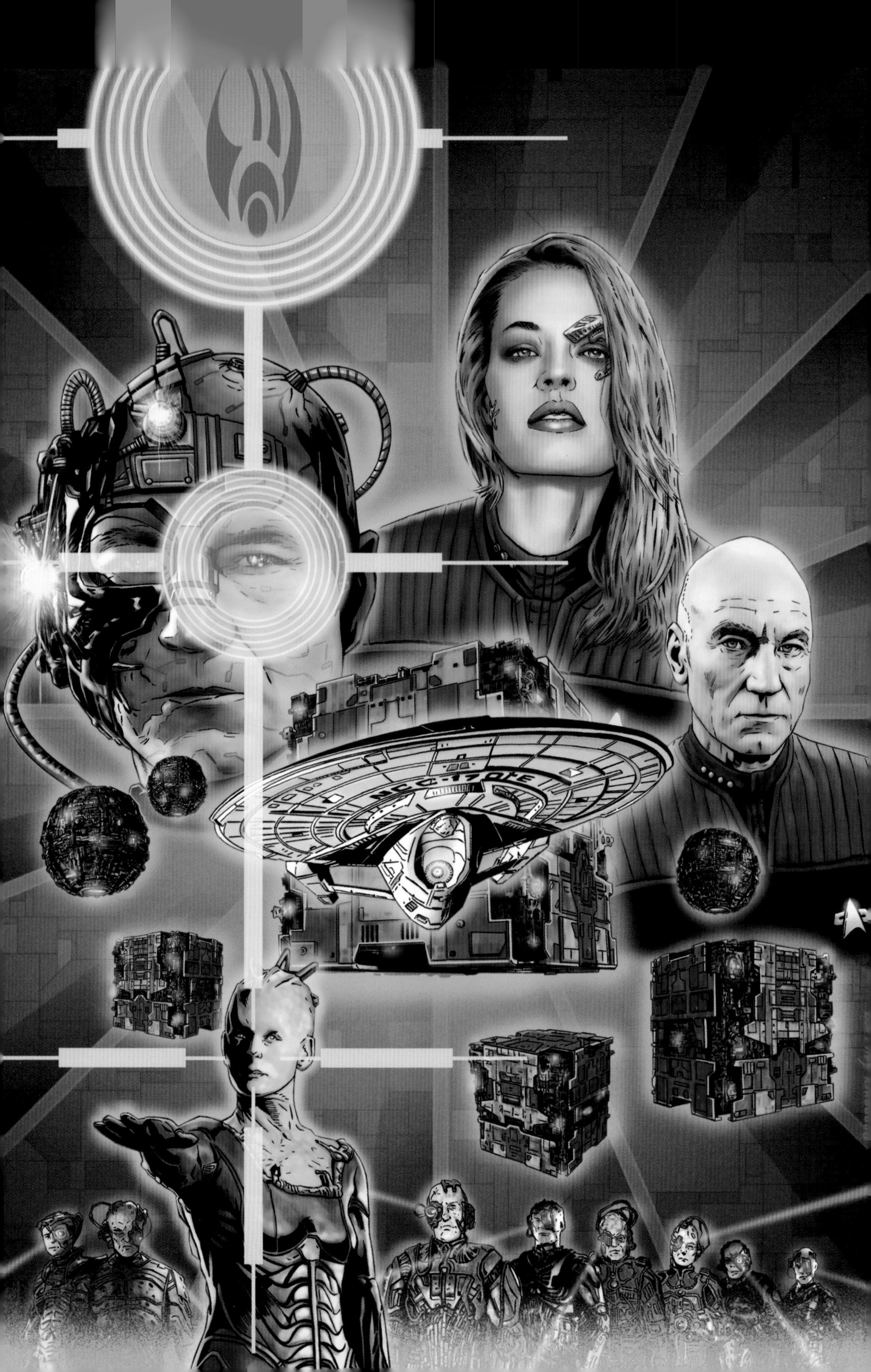
NCC-1701-E

JOE CORRONEY *ART*

Hi-Fi *COLORS*

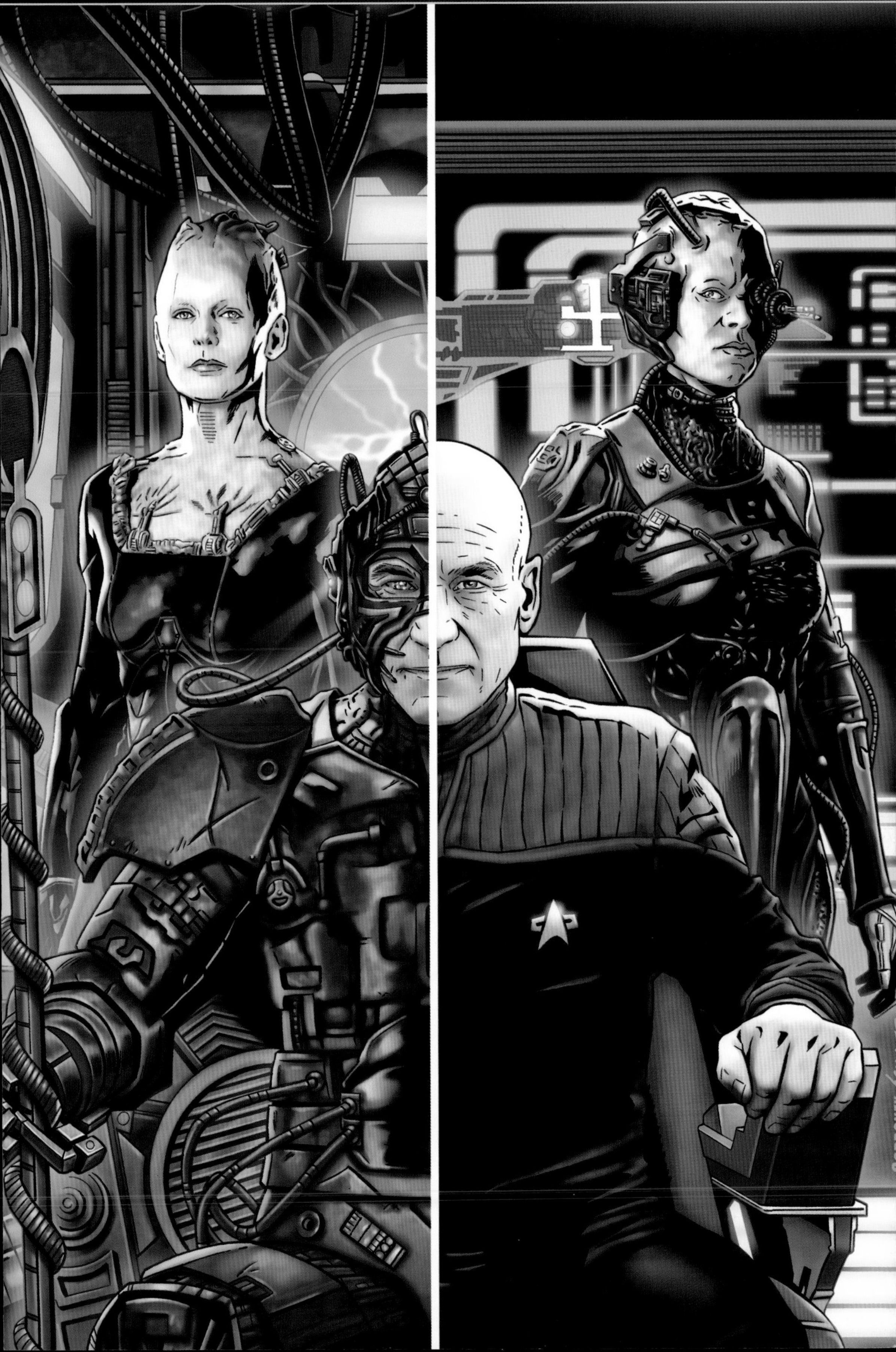

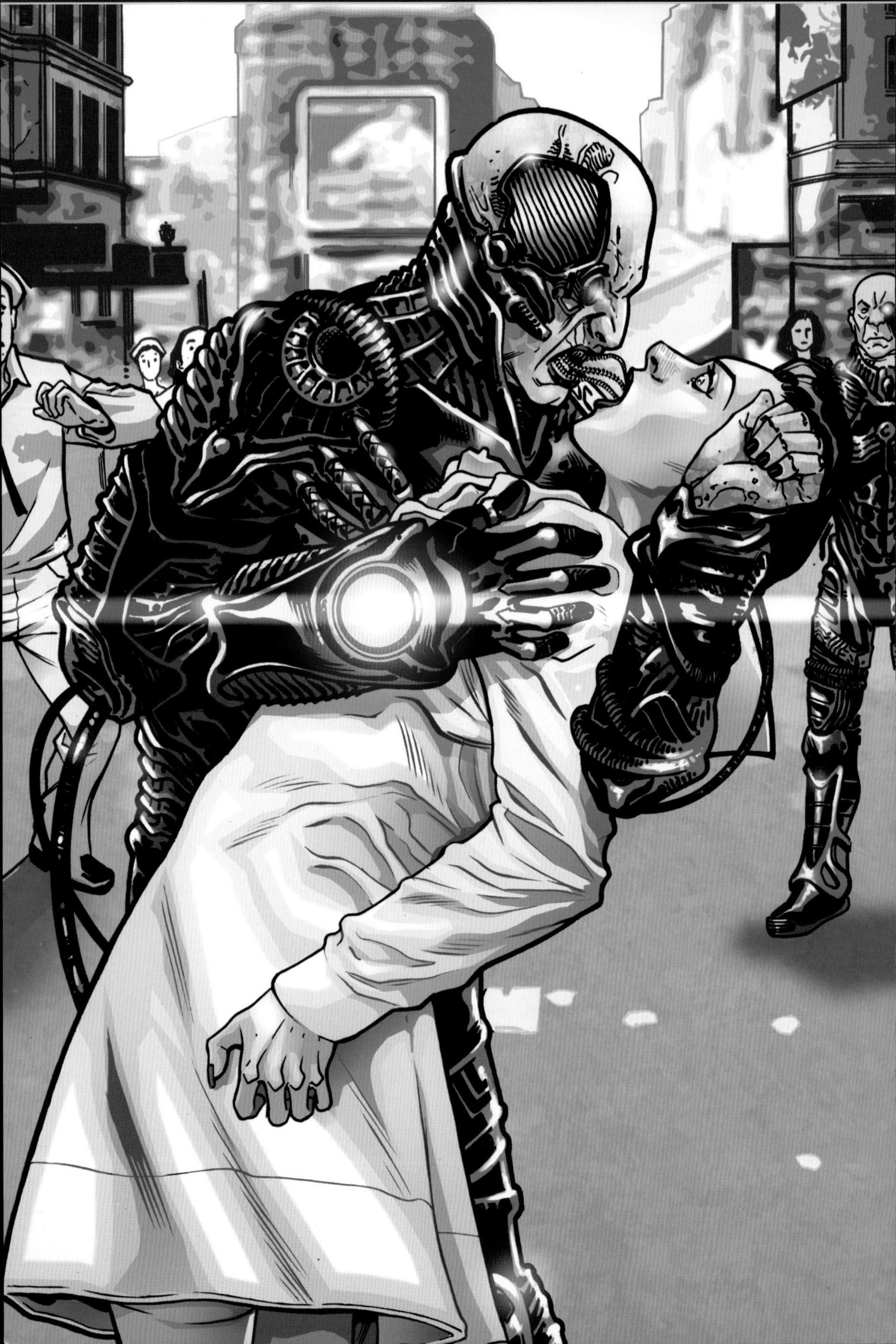

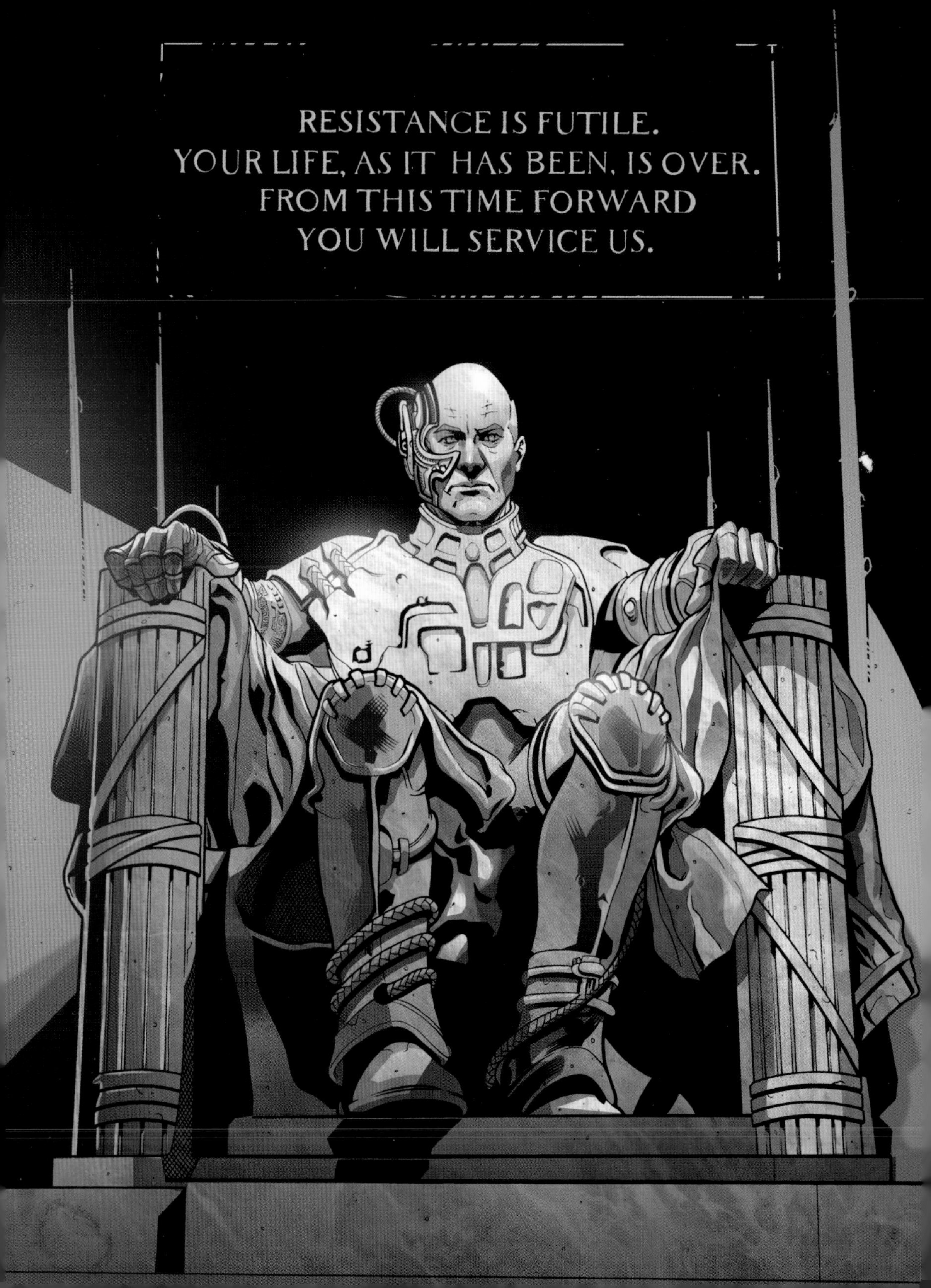
RESISTANCE IS FUTILE.
YOUR LIFE, AS IT HAS BEEN, IS OVER.
FROM THIS TIME FORWARD
YOU WILL SERVICE US.

JOE CORRONEY *ART*

Hi-Fi *COLORS*

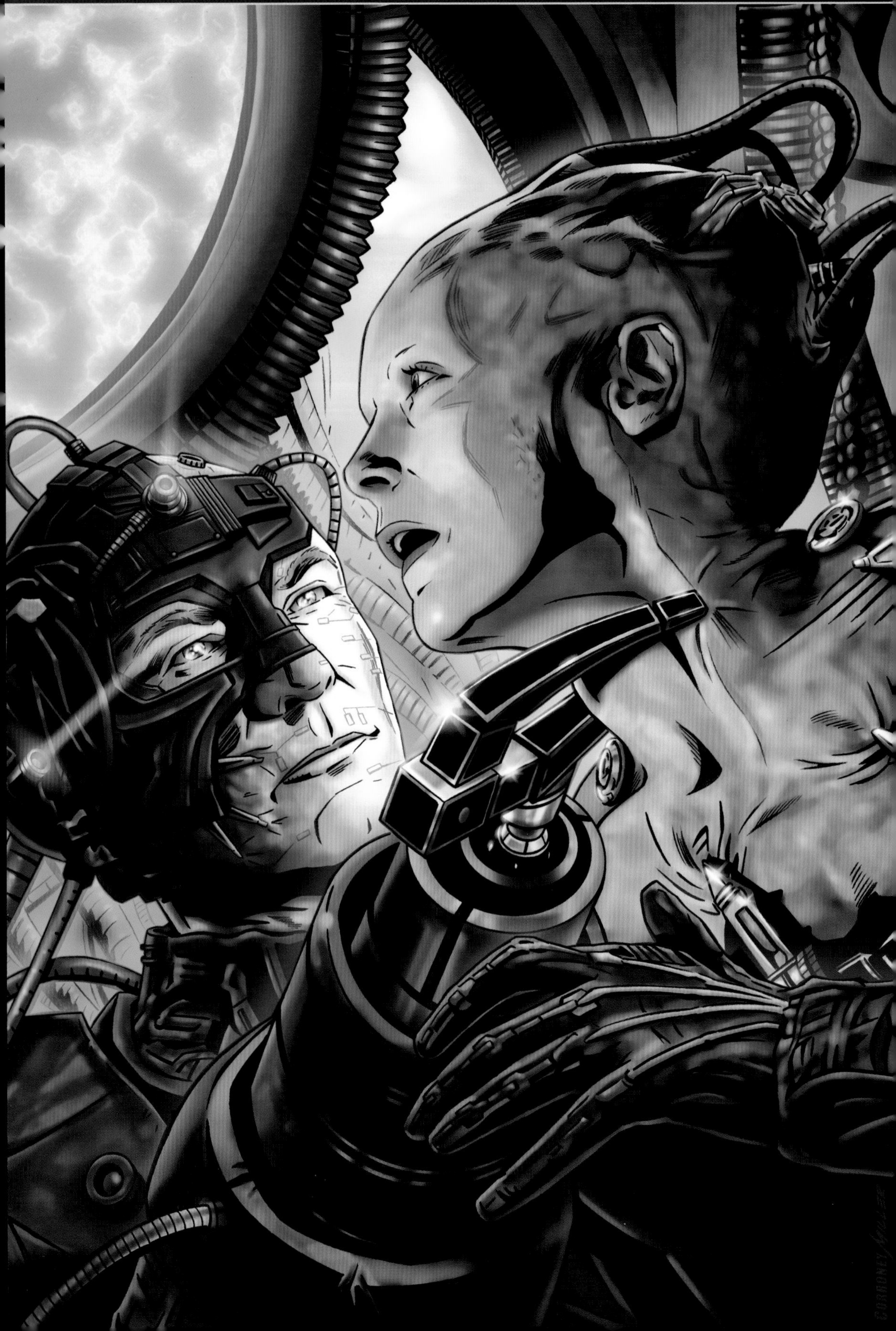

JOE CORRONEY *ART*

Hi-Fi *COLORS*

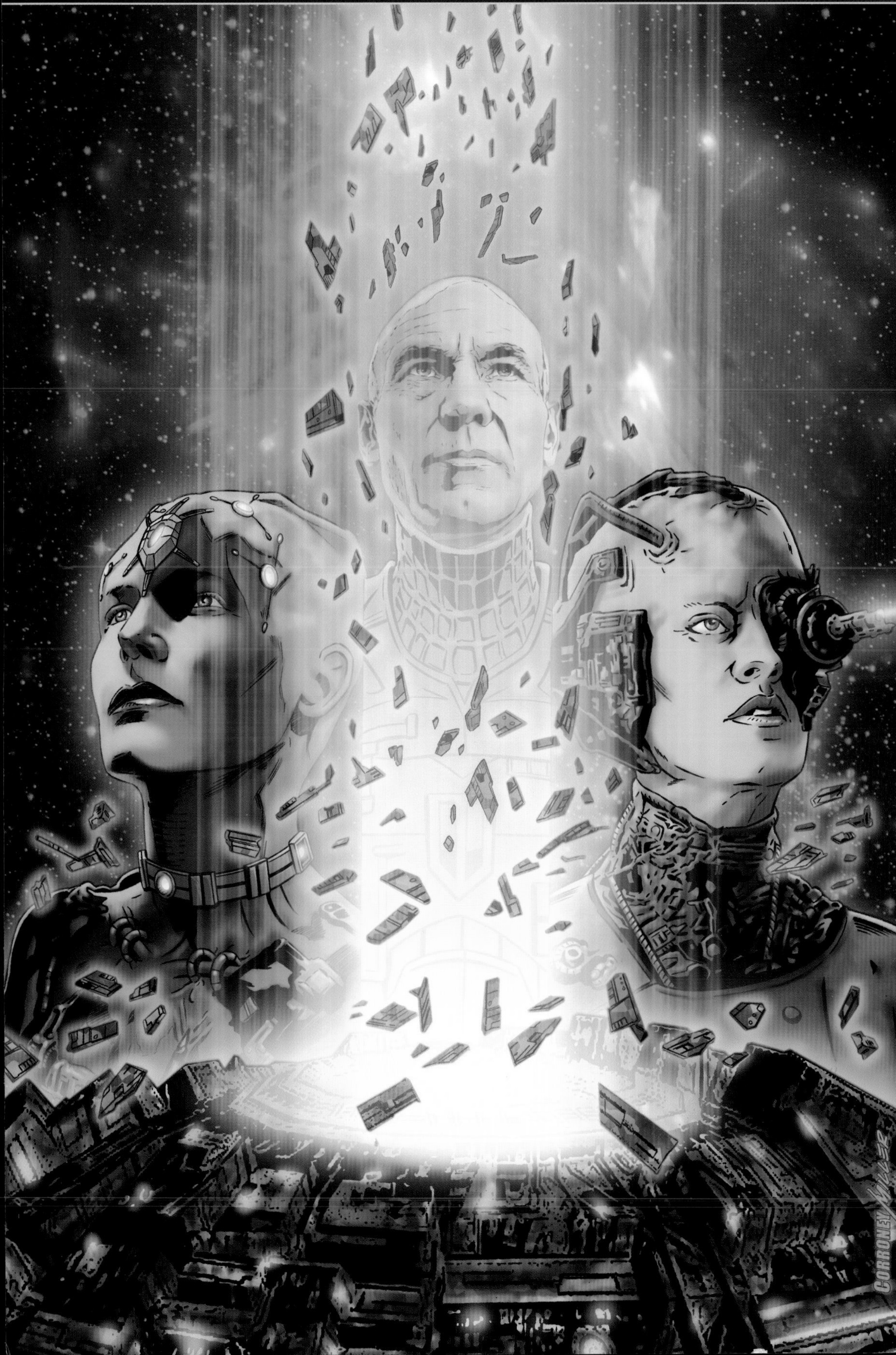
CORRONEY

DAVID MESSINA ART

ILARIA TRAVERSI COLORS

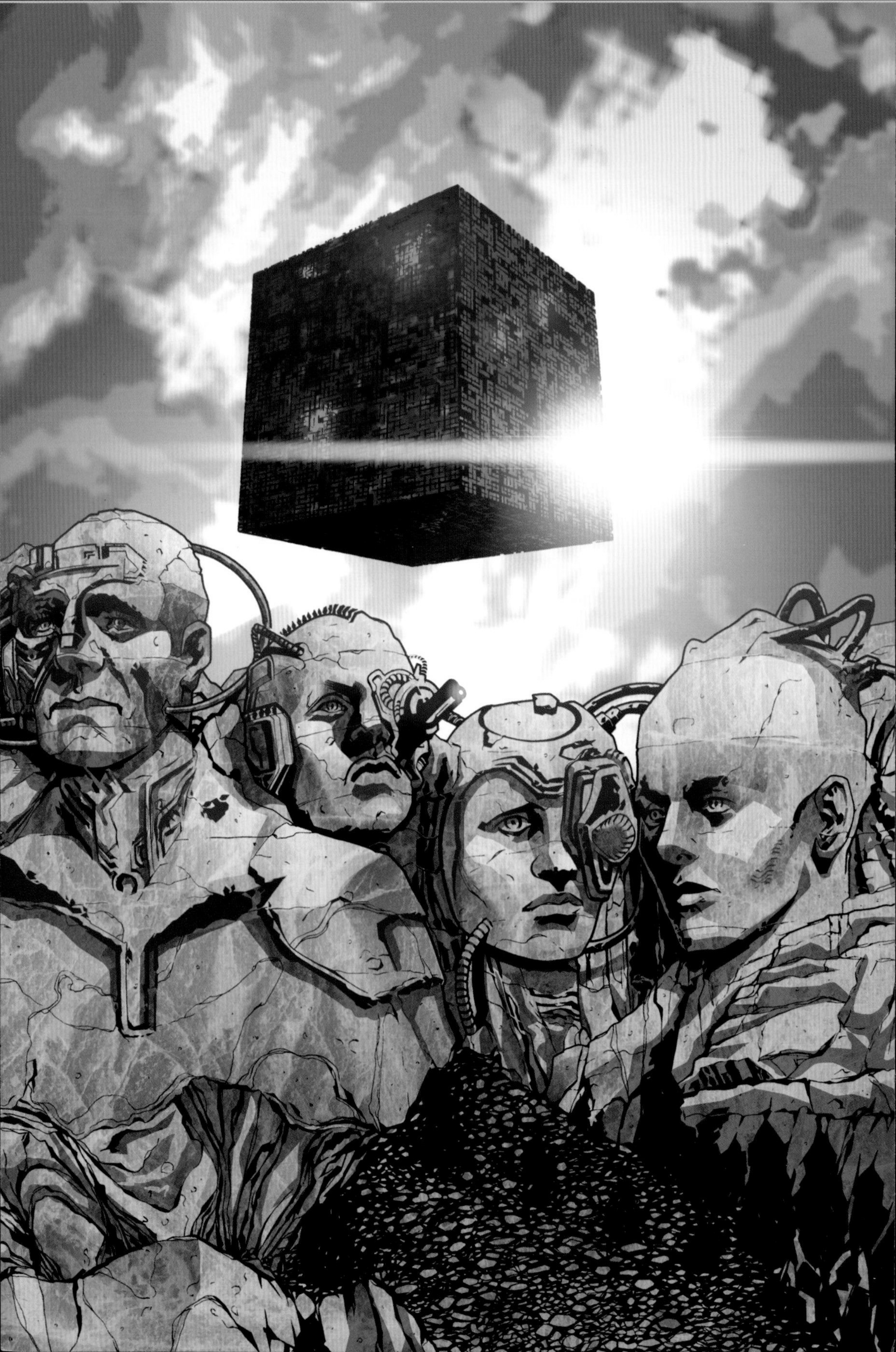

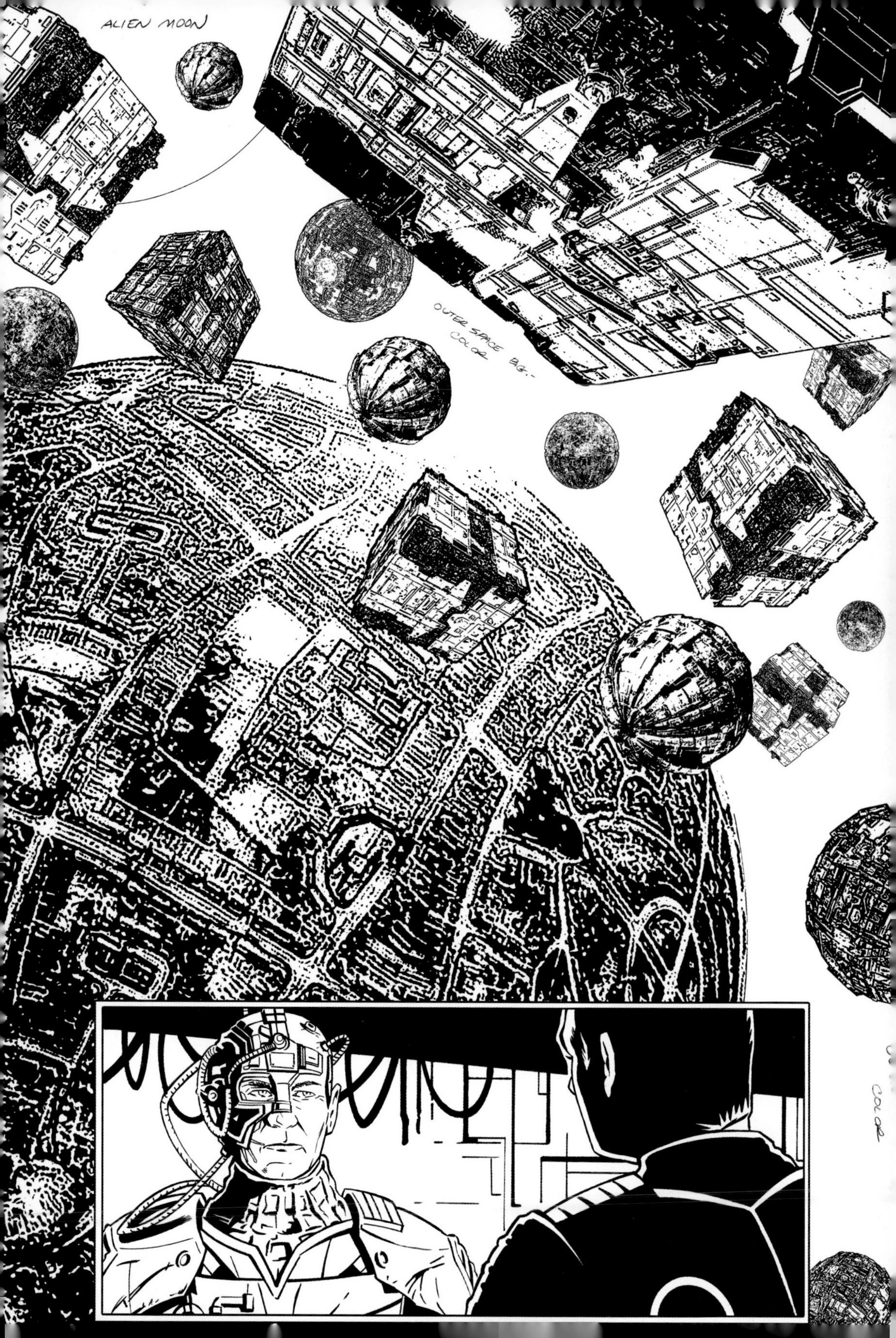
ALIEN MOON
OUTER SPACE BG-
COLOR
COLOR

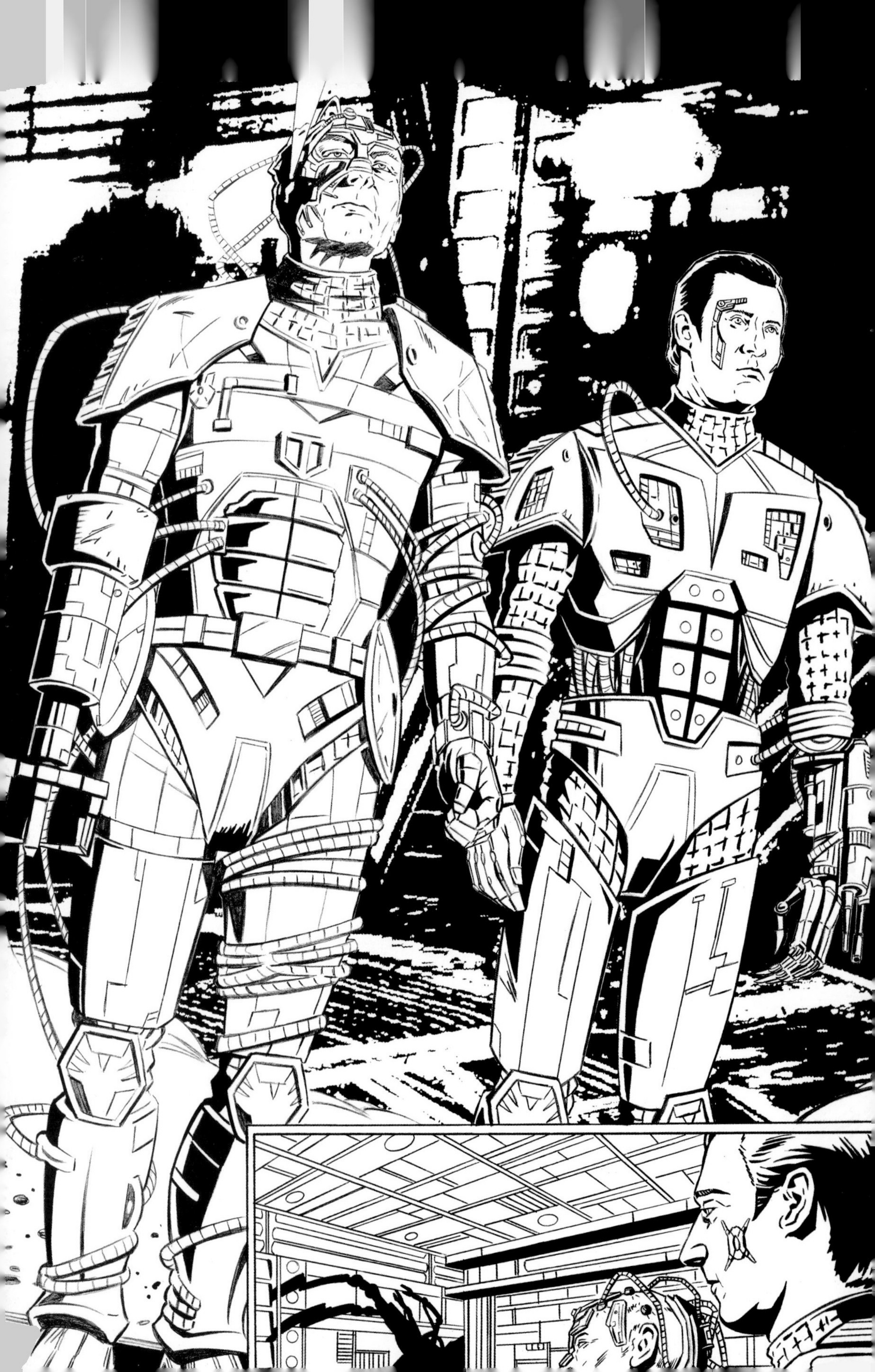

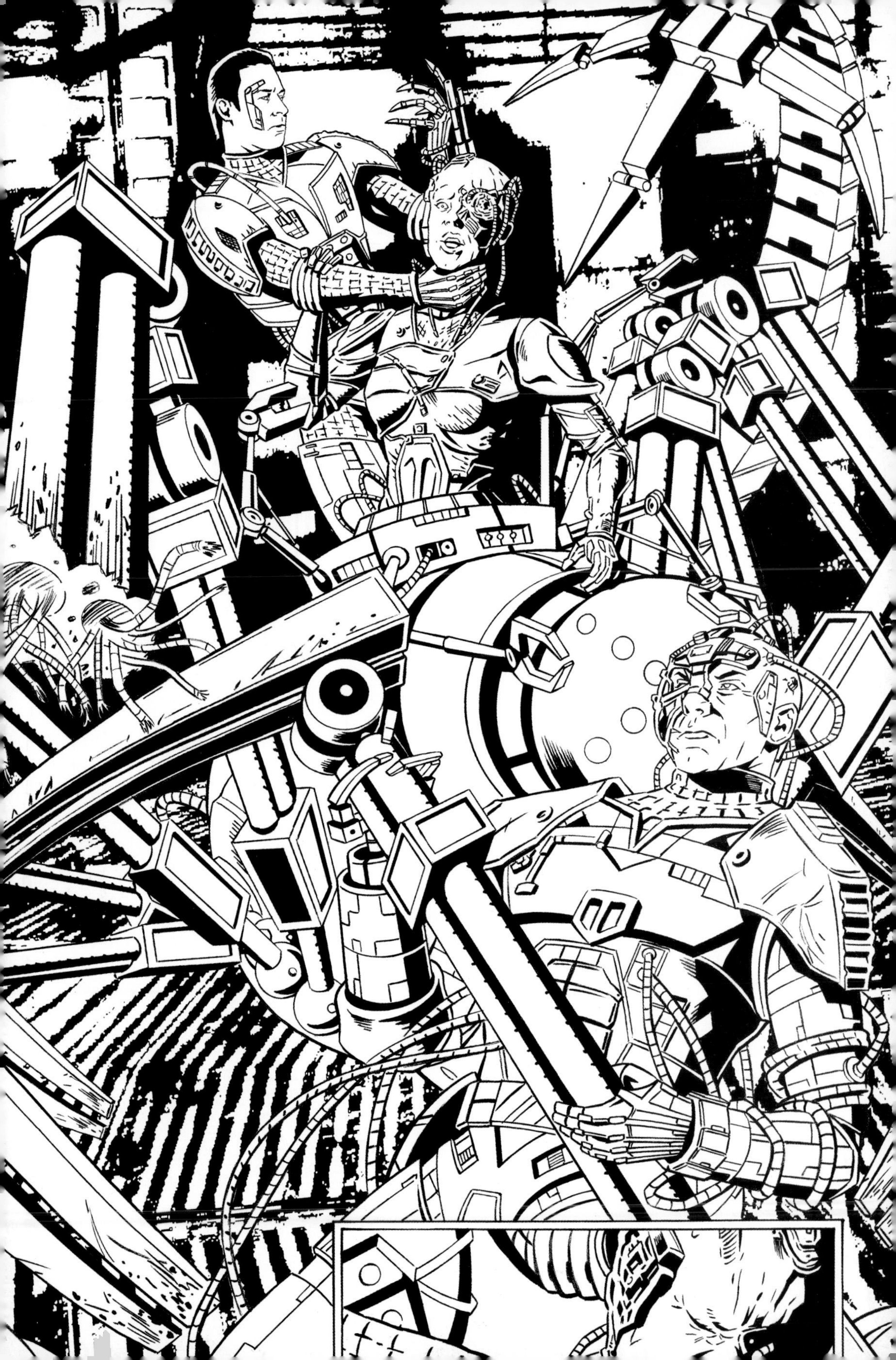

STAR TREK
THE NEXT GENERATION®
HIVE

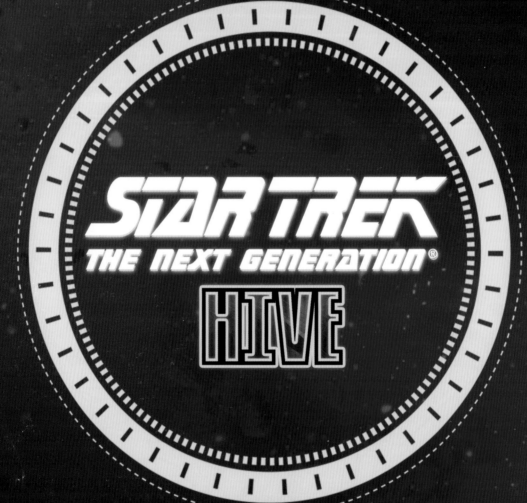